Lynn Galli

Wasted Heart

Outskirts Press, Inc.
Denver, Colorado

Wasted Heart

Outskirts Press
http://www.outskirtspress.com

ISBN-10: 1-59800-959-1
ISBN-13: 978-1-59800-959-0

Printed in the United States of America

Chapter 1

Being a lesbian in Seattle sucks. Let me amend that: being a lesbian in Seattle who's in love with her married best friend sucks. To be fair, I should say: being a lesbian in love with her best friend who's married and doesn't live in Seattle really sucks. *Of course, that's why you moved to Seattle, moron. Now, shut up and deal with the Seattle lesbian scene.*

"Austy!"

Or deal with it after you get off work. "Yeah?" I spun around from staring out my fifth floor office window of the federal courthouse. Another lunch hour shot to hell.

"Crimeny! I've been trying you on the intercom for ten minutes," Short Stack bellowed from my office door. Not that his raised voice and agitated state was unusual office behavior for Kyle Hammer, hence the nickname. Perspiration beads dotted his wide, pale forehead and red splotched his cheeks, but I doubted it had anything to do with his current mood. He had the kind of frame that exerted great amounts of energy just walking, or stomping, rather, around the office and courthouse.

"We're allowed a lunch, you know," I responded calmly. Staying calm was often the only way to get through one of

Short Stack's bellow sessions.

"You're in your office, Austy; that means you're working through lunch. Next time, leave the building."

"It's pouring rain outside, Kyle, and just because I'm here doesn't mean I'm working through lunch."

"I know you've only been here a few months, but this is Seattle; it's always raining outside."

That's right, why the hell did I move here? *Oh yeah, the best friend lives in Virginia, so you moved here to get away from her. Only not all the way, since she's in Seattle a few days every month. God, you're pathetic.*

"What do you need?" I asked as politely as someone who really needed a lunch break could ask.

"New case, international software copyright infringement. There's some corporate espionage thrown in for your enjoyment, too. Chief wants someone who can relate to the whole computer geek thing to deal with it. Since you did so well with the last one, I'm afraid you might catch all these techie claims from now on," he reported in a less than remorseful tone. For five months, he'd been trying me out in every unit of the Criminal Division. Looks like he might have finally decided on Complex Crimes for me.

He raised up the file and flicked his wrist, sailing it perfectly onto the center of my desk. Every time I try that the file opens, all the papers fly out, and someone ends up with a paper cut or poking an eye out.

"Goody," I sighed, my palm landing flat on top of the spinning file. One more to add to my pile of open cases. Assistant United States Attorney, whose stupid idea was that? Crap! It really sucks being in love with your best friend. Married best friend. Married best friend who has a great partner. Married best friend with a great partner who lives in Virginia—most of the time anyway.

The intercom buzzed again officially signally the end of my attempted lunch break. With a grunt, Short Stack swung himself into motion and clomped down the long hallway toward his own office. A superb benefit of being the new hire was that I got the office farthest away from "the action." I'm not sure I'd still be here if I had to listen to Short Stack up close every moment of the day.

I pressed the flashing red button of the insistent intercom. "Yeah?" Eloquent, I know.

"Austy, Elise Bridie here to see you."

"Who?"

"Your one o'clock?"

"No, my one o'clock is Jake Nichols." I clicked on my calendar to double check that I was meeting with Jake at one. So, I'm anal retentive, deal with it.

"She says she's his replacement."

"What?!" I shot out of my seat as if a snake just slithered across my lap. This could kill my case. Jake was scheduled to be on the stand in two days on a huge corporate fraud case, my biggest since becoming an AUSA. How could my FBI agent skip out on me? Not that it was all that surprising. My luck as an assistant commonwealth attorney in Virginia hadn't been much better.

"Are you coming out here to get her, or should I slap a visitor's badge on her and send her in?" The receptionist, Mary, always kept a calm demeanor with the office staff, but she let a little sarcasm slip through with some of us. I'm not sure anyone but I appreciated it.

"Good thinking, especially since Short Stack's already in a mood. Send that unescorted visitor into the office," I joked.

"An unescorted, armed visitor, no less. Two minutes? Or should I tell her to get comfy out here?"

Hell, send her back. I don't care, I thought for a self-destructive moment. If Short Stack doesn't kill me, maybe she'll turn out not to be FBI and take us all out with her weapon. Instead I said aloud, "Two minutes." Always the prudent one, that's me.

An avalanche of pleadings on my desk taunted my obsessive compulsive tendencies to the point of wanting to set fire to my office to avoid looking at the mess. For two weeks I'd let them creep ever closer to my chiseled out workspace. With the announcement of my visitor, I gleefully succumbed to the OCD and shuffled them into an orderly pile in my inbox. I'd probably regret the hasty decision to tidy up without sorting them properly, but company loomed. No time to think about anything other than the fact that the guest chair currently acted like a valet for my still wet overcoat and needed to be freed up for its intended purpose. And nothing short of six months of trials could make the file boxes lining the back wall disappear. A magician would help, but since we didn't keep one on staff at the U.S. Attorney's office, I'd have to continue creating my own illusion that they didn't exist until my courtroom labors fulfilled the hope. It sucks being a lesbian in Seattle who needs to work eighteen hours a day to keep the file boxes from engulfing her.

Swinging my discarded suit jacket on, I headed out to the lobby to escort my unexpected one o'clock. I'd have muttered all the way out there about my bad luck in getting a replacement FBI agent the day before opening statements, but as I found out in my first week here, the U.S. Attorney's office doesn't appreciate nor embrace mutterers. Maybe I had time for a quick online check of one-way ticket prices to Virginia. I could get my ACA job back in Charlottesville where they'd let me mutter all I wanted. Oh, that's right; best friend, in love with, married, great partner—lesbian suckage!

I rounded the corner of the paralegals' maze of cubicles and into the clerks' concourse hidden from view of the lobby by the attorneys' mail boxes. Once the security door swung open, I stepped behind the receptionist's desk. Mary glanced over and raised a two fingered wave as she spoke softly into her headset while staring down at the telephone equivalent of Battleship. All those red lights made it look like most of her ships were sunk.

Two attorneys who annoyed me by constantly quoting *South Park* in staff meetings stood chatting in the lobby. A dazed looking man sat in a comfy chair staring at a rather beautiful, brunette woman directly opposite him. Another woman sat on the couch facing the receptionist, one leg crossed over the other, bouncing like someone kept hitting her patellar tendon. One of the chatterbox attorneys nodded his head in my direction, necessitating a smile on my part. His eyes immediately went back to focusing on the woman sitting across from the dazed man. His cohort made an obvious move of turning to stare at her as well. Perhaps she wasn't wearing any underwear, and they were hoping for a *Basic Instinct* moment. More likely it had to do with the fact that she was as stunning as a movie star, and even without flashing her crotch, most men would be mesmerized. I like women; I should be mesmerized. *Damn!* Married, Virginia-living, best friend.

I walked up to the leg bouncing woman and smiled. "Hi, I'm Austine Nunziata. I guess you're my new computer science expert? What happened to Jake?" The bounce stopped so she could stare blankly at me. Perfect, quick on the uptake; she'll make an outstanding expert witness.

"He had a death in the family and took a short sabbatical to deal with the estate."

Poor Jake. I'd have to remember to send him a condolence card. The news startled me enough that I didn't immediately realize that Bouncy-Leg hadn't opened her mouth. A ventriloquist? That so won't go over well with the jury.

To my right, the object of my colleagues' ogling stood from her seated position. First in my class at Maryland, and I just now realized that Gorgeous is my FBI agent. Let's not even mention third in my law school class at UVA. What was I saying about being quick on the uptake?

I turned with a sheepish smile and said, "Oh, sorry." I figured that would cover both my reaction to the news of Jake's loss and my gaffe at assuming that Impatient Bouncy-Leg was FBI.

"Elise Bridie." Her hand came up to shake mine in greeting.

"Austy Nunziata." I mechanically took her hand. God, it was soft, and snug, and just a wishful guess: skilled.

"You prefer Austy?" She still gripped my hand while her almond shaped, green eyes traveled up from our joined hands to meet mine.

"Either." I reluctantly pulled back from the handshake, baffled by the shock I'd felt at her touch. Not static electricity shock, more like distress laced with embarrassment at assuming the plain, impatient woman in the bad suit had been FBI. Sticking with the theme of uncomfortable remarks, I brought up a mandatory request. "Listen, I know this won't sound trustworthy or even polite, but—"

She didn't wait for me to finish, fishing into her suit jacket for her FBI badge. Gorgeous and a mind reader: dangerous combo. I waited for her to ask to inspect mine, but she probably figured if I came in through the locked office door, knew the receptionist and the attorneys, I must belong here. Satisfied that Elise Bridie was genuine FBI, I gestured back toward the door behind the lobby desk. Elise fell into step beside me as I swiped my ID badge on the security pad to gain entry to the back office.

"Please have a seat. Can I get you some coffee?" I offered when we got to my office, pausing for a response before moving to take my own seat behind the desk.

"No, thank you." Elise looked around the cramped quarters, taking in all the contents before pausing to enjoy the view. "Nice office," she commented.

Had her eyes not flared at the vista, I might have guessed she was being facetious. Yet even at half the size, the panorama of Elliott Bay straight ahead, the Monorail tracks amid downtown to the left with just a glimpse of the Space Needle to the right made it enviable.

"Yes, I'm still getting used to it," I admitted before I realized what I'd disclosed.

Elise twisted her head back from the windowpane and focused intently on me. "Either you're new to the area, or you've been given a promotion?" She tilted her head, and a cascade of sunlit molasses covered her left shoulder. A sly smile that pulled the right side of her mouth farther than the left accompanied the pose after a wordless moment passed. "Of course, I should know better than to draw conclusions based on very little evidence."

My surprise swallowed the sure mirthful huff that would have escaped had we not just met. She'd let me off the hook when she'd nailed me on both counts. Gorgeous, mind reader, and good at her job: triple threat.

To keep from tipping my embarrassment at her accuracy, I refocused our attention. "Well, we should get to work. I don't know how much Jake told you about this case?"

Thankfully, she lifted her head out of that captivating tilt before she replied. "I read through the file and went over his notes. I have a few questions."

"That's why we're here." I opened the witness file folder for reference in case I somehow forgot any of the facts committed to memory in preparation for the trial tomorrow. We did cover me being anal retentive, didn't we?

For over an hour, we walked through the case specifics and what she'd offer as testimony. She was more concise than Jake, more fluent in techie jargon, and definitely more gorgeous. *Get a grip! Best friend, remember? When was the last time you found someone attractive? Let's see; oh yeah, since falling for your best friend. Sensing a pattern here, moron?*

Red digits glared at me from behind her head, indicating that I only had fifteen minutes until the all-staff meeting. "Unfortunately, we're going to have to wrap this up for now. I've got another meeting soon. How are you feeling about your testimony?"

She nodded in acceptance. "Pretty good. Thanks for your patience. This can't be easy on you having to break in a new witness so close to trial."

This time the mirthful huff leapt from my mouth before I could stop it. That mind reading thing of hers was maddening.

"Actually, you've made this very easy."

"That's nice to hear. Jake was right about you."

Curiosity seeped in, but I managed to plug it up before I succumbed. Two things I learned in law school: only answer the questions that are asked, and never ask a question that you aren't certain you want answered. Knowing what people say about me usually doesn't turn out well. At least, not for me.

Her smile started slow and stretched her mouth wide. A crest of upper teeth grazed her bottom lip as she waited for me to say something. When it didn't happen, she added, "Now, I'm thinking he should move to the profiling unit, or he knows you outside of work?"

Not sure where she was going with the question, I didn't respond. Silence: the negotiator's deadliest weapon, or the idiot's best disguise.

"Sorry, that's none of my business. I have to say I've never met anyone who doesn't jump at the chance to hear what others think of her. Especially since it's coming from Jake, so you've got to know it's complimentary. But you didn't bite, not even a flinch. That's remarkable." Her green eyes danced in what I could only assume was delight at meeting such a rare bird as myself. "I'm looking forward to working with you on this and the next case."

"Likewise," I replied before registering what she'd said. "Wait, is there another case already?"

She glanced back at the file boxes on my floor and over to the mass of pleadings in my inbox. "You might not have gotten to it yet. Software copyright infringement in Hong Kong, but we may find it's gone into other countries."

I started to nod before she'd finished. Short Stack's earlier gift. I reached over and grabbed the folder that I'd cleared off my desk for this meeting. "I just got the file today. You're working that investigation?"

"For a while now. I plan to meet with the software company soon. Any interest in joining me? I usually like to show the company that they've got the FBI's attention and the prosecutor's support. We can schedule it for Friday when you're not in court?" She looked both hopeful and understanding, not an easy expression to pull off. And she looked unbelievably attractive. If only I didn't have that love thing for my married best friend who lived 3,000 miles away.

With two mouse clicks, I checked Friday's availability. "Sure, end of day?"

"Which for you means…9:00 p.m.?" She slid into that slow, sexy smile again.

I should be insulted that she thought I worked my Friday nights away. If it weren't pathetically true and she wasn't so damn gorgeous, I might be insulted. "Let's say 4:00? Is it downtown?"

"Redmond."

"Crossing the floating bridge on a Friday afternoon? Maybe we should find out how late the executives stay?" I joked. Even a newbie Seattleite knew to stay away from the bridges on Friday afternoons.

"Already called. She said they'll be there until at least 9:00. They're in the middle of a product launch crunch."

A thought entered my head uninvited, but I shook it off as wishful coincidence. I opened the file folder and asked, "She?"

"One of the company's owners." Elise reached into her tailored suit jacket and pulled out a small notepad, flipping up a few pages. She spoke right when I spotted the name in the file. "Willa Lacey, co-president for Jucundus Interactive."

Oh, come on! What's with my luck today? Willa Lacey, my best friend.

Chapter 2

Jane Metro, that's me, saving the environment, but did it have to smell so badly? Someone on this bus needed a shower, one of those exposures to hazardous waste material scrub downs. I could start driving to work, but then the whole saving the environment wouldn't apply nor would it save my bank book. Monthly parking in Seattle costs almost as much as the lease payment on my car. I could live with being Jane Metro.

The Metro bus screeched to a halt five blocks from my place. I clambered down the stairs after two Seattle Casual gentlemen. They probably worked at some insurance company, or advertising agency, or basically any place in Seattle that didn't have to be in court where a business dress code was still enforced. If only I'd taken a job at a regular law firm instead of the U.S. Attorney's office. I'd spend one Saturday every three months sifting through the latest fashion designed to accommodate the cubicle dweller who suddenly finds himself dropped onto a hiking trail in the middle of normal business hours. Thankfully, he's got all those pockets for his trail mix, first aid kit, and compass to facilitate his way back to the office. Or I could be like these guys and just strip the mannequin of its matching outfit to forgo the hassle of shopping altogether. Either way, business casual started here; the rest of the U.S. owed us one.

I watched where they went before heading in the direction of my loft. Call me paranoid, but eight years in the commonwealth attorney's office in Charlottesville before becoming an AUSA here made me aware of the "things that can happen." I felt fairly safe here, not as safe as I did in Virginia but safe enough.

Virginia. Don't start thinking about that again. Seattle was a great career move, a healthy personal move, and a beautiful place to live. Once you get used to the rain, and the grey, and the dreariness. Locals promised me the summer would be worth the move; yet it was June already, and so far, no sign of summer.

Turning the corner onto my block, I counted the number of people still on the street and calculated my reaction time if someone approached me. Only then did I allow myself to take in the view of Lake Union. Sailboats drifted through the ship canal over to Lake Washington, a pontoon plane took off for destinations unknown, and luxury yachts hosted private parties, many with live music aboard. This was a beautiful spot, and I almost felt comfortable. We can talk about that later.

Lights were dark in Mod Fare as per usual on a Tuesday. The restaurant's owner, Helen, who doubled as my neighbor, kept tourist hours. Friday through Monday she enjoyed being head chef and owner. For the rest of the week, she enjoyed just being. If I had the time or inclination, I could learn a lot from her about living life to its fullest.

Just past the entrance to the restaurant, I keyed into the security door of my building. With a resounding thump, the heavy door closed behind me, and I turned to check my mailbox for the expected bills and junk. I bypassed the elevator and hustled up the staircase to the third floor. This and the staircase in the courthouse served as my only exercise some weeks. One of my Virginia friends, Jessie, a personal trainer who obsessed over all things fitness related would kill me if she knew.

"Hey there," a voice called out from the top of the staircase. I heard familiar whimpering sounds before either the owner of the voice or the dogs came into view.

"Hi, Helen," I responded, shifting my briefcase to my shoulder and sticking out both hands to use as dog blockers. Helen's dog, Cles, a lovable Irish setter and her husband's dog, Cleo, a mix mutt with cattle dog looks, loved getting fur all over my suits and snagging my nylons. My dry cleaning bill suffered the most when I couldn't resist getting in my doggy time with these two. "Hello, Clesy. Com'ere, Cleo." I encouraged both dogs into a manageable love fest.

"One last walkies before bedtime," Helen informed me.

Her friendly eyes radiated worry about her dogs and my black suit. She reigned in the leashes to keep the dogs from total fur devastation of my outfit, and I envied her strength and balance. I'd gotten the impression that she'd not always been the specimen of fitness she was today and savored the new physique more so than someone who'd always been trim. No doubt it was responsible for her being better at living than most people.

We shared the top floor of the building that housed her restaurant. She and her husband, Joe, served as the managers of the building. Four smaller lofts took up the second floor, and Joe spent time dealing with tenant issues when he wasn't building and renting kayaks out of his store next to Helen's restaurant. Technically, Helen's sister owned the building, but they had some agreement that transferred partial ownership to Helen each year. All except for my loft, which I was buying outright.

"It's turned beautiful after the rainy day," I told her, knowing that it wouldn't matter. Helen walked, ran, rowed, biked, swam, hiked, and pretty much anything else rain or shine.

"You just getting home?"

"Yeah, I've got a trial starting tomorrow. If you hear me

talking to myself next door tonight, pay no attention. I'm still tweaking the opening." I gave a final pat to each dog.

"Like I'd hear anything through the extra soundproofing installed when we took over the building. Although if you want a mock jury to try out your opening, just knock on my door." Helen wrangled the dogs past me and started down the stairs.

"Thanks for the offer." I climbed the remaining two steps to our floor.

"Hey, Will called to ask if I'd seen you this week. She's in town and said she couldn't get you on the phone. Guess she thought she'd utilize my proximity."

I wiped the guilty look off my face before turning to say, "That's right, she's here this week. I've been so wrapped up in preparing for this trial I haven't had time to call."

"I told her I hadn't seen you. There might come a time when I want to avoid her and rely on you not to give me up." She laughed easily, very used to dealing with her sister's protectiveness. When she laughed, she sounded like her sister. Her honey blond hair, hazel eyes, button nose, and longer frame differed from her sister as much as a stranger's would. But that laugh, well, it was Willa's. Yes, I live next door to my best friend's sister. Unhealthy, I know.

"Good deal," I responded casually and watched her dogs pull her down the stairs.

Gaining entry to my loft, I dropped my briefcase and slumped against the closed door. Tension drained out of my body. I love being at home, especially this home with its wide open design, strategically placed furniture, and kitchen that would make professional chefs cry with joy. Yet another perk of moving to Seattle: the loft of my dreams rather than my studio apartment back in Virginia. Of course, this wouldn't be possible if it weren't for Willa's generosity, but that was a whole 'nother story.

"Man, that was a long day," I spoke aloud. I talk to myself; get used to it.

My coat slid easily off my arms, and I tossed it onto the

rack by the door then kicked off my heels to pad into the kitchen. My nightly battle with dinner selections was about to begin. The standby salad in a bag with dinner roll always appealed, yet the bag of pretzels and sweet ice tea would probably win out. I'm not a foodie. In fact, if I could hook up to an I.V. that provided enough nutrition to keep me alive, I wouldn't miss a thing about eating.

Three messages waited for me as I passed by the phone. Did I want to listen to them? No. Should I listen to them? Yes. We'll go over me being unsociable at another time.

"Hi, Austy, it's Kami." *Great!* My second Seattle disaster, I mean date, had somehow tracked down my phone number. "I had such a great time last week at dinner, and I was hoping to hear from you. Then I realized that you didn't have my number. I had to ask Ruth for yours when I ran into her last night." *Damn, Ruth!* Wasn't it in the Lesbian Code of Conduct that you don't give out someone's phone number without her consent? Maybe the Code differed from state to state. No one in Virginia would hand out my home phone number. Not even the most obnoxious matchmaker in my group would violate that policy. "I was hoping we could have dinner again?"

"Of course you were," I spoke to the answering machine. Not because I was such a dating delight, but because the date hadn't been one I'd want to repeat in this or any of my next three lifetimes. So, naturally, with my luck, she'd want to go out again.

When we'd met, Kami seemed both sure of herself and a pleasant conversationalist. That opinion might've had to do with my discomfort at being dragged to a bar by my friend Cyrah. I'd never been much of a partier, and I'd left the bar scene back at law school. In Virginia, I'd go with my group of friends to the only gay and lesbian club in town just so I could hang out with them. Here, it seemed the only way to meet other lesbians. Willa introduced me to Ruth who introduced me to Cyrah. I liked Cyrah, loved Willa, and managed not to strike Ruth whenever I ran into her. Now she was handing out my phone number. Yep, sure is great being a lesbian in Seattle.

My date with Kami turned into a dinner instead of the agreed upon coffee because I wasn't yet adept at avoiding Short Stack and his bottomless silo of case assignments. I felt so bad at having to postpone coffee that, when she suggested dinner instead, I had to agree.

At the bar, she'd brought up interesting topics, made amusing observations about other patrons, and supplied inside information about some of the women she knew there. I wasn't wild about the fact that she was sharing all that stuff about her friends, but I figured she'd been a little tipsy and nothing she shared was too personal. When she asked me out, I wanted to decline. Then I remembered how nerve wracking it was to ask someone out, how unhealthy my love life was, and how it wouldn't kill me to get some coffee with her.

When coffee turned into dinner, I grew increasingly nervous. I suck at dating. Most of the time, I feel like I'm possessed by someone else on a date. Someone else who's nothing like me. Where I'm eloquent in court, I'm stilted on a date. Weeks before every date, I take notes on anything interesting I saw or heard to make enough conversation to fill a dinner.

Kami showed up in a definite date outfit, her full figure swathed in shiny silk and some sort of stretchy material that clung to her curves. Her short black hair held finger waves that looked like they'd taken hours to perfect. She had on more makeup than I could stand, but it was supposed to be a date after all. I'd come straight from my office in the same suit I'd worn for fourteen hours already. My own reddish-brown hair, shorter than hers, was styled by the Seattle mist and a swipe of my hand. I sincerely doubted if I had anything left of the light layer of makeup I put on every morning so as not to scare small children. Needless to say, one of us wasn't taking the date seriously.

During dinner, I found that I wouldn't need my "interesting tidbits" notes. Kami did all the talking. Everything from a rundown of her last year's worth of dates to her bitterness about being stuck on the line at her job instead of managing the line. I also got to hear just how much she struggled with her weight which seemed to bother her considerably. I get that a lot, probably because I'm one of those chicks that everyone labels as "tiny" and then promptly hates. I'm short and slender, but I've met people who are shorter and skinnier than me, so back off.

The weight topic shifted through her dislike of her hair and her nose, both of which I thought looked nice, to her role in bed and how it had taken ten years to realize that she was more comfortable as a bottom, but not a pillow princess, mind you. That's when I called for the check. One, I don't like discussing sexual roles under most circumstances. Two, I think adhering to them limits the fun of sex. Three, I don't think you should be admitting that you don't know yourself well enough to understand that you're uncomfortable with your own chosen sexual role. And four, it's definitely not a topic of conversation for a first date. Especially when the only clue I didn't give about the fact that we wouldn't be sleeping together was to have it engraved on her dessert cake. Now that's an idea: cakes for the everyday awkward occasion. See what I'm saying about sucking at dating? I'm thinking up business ideas while she's hinting at bedding me.

We shared an uncomfortable goodbye outside the restaurant with me eluding her attempt at a goodnight kiss and her surprise at my proffered hand. She slid an arm up behind mine to squeeze me into a hug and asked for another date. I told her that I had a big trial coming up, and I'd have to check my schedule. Go ahead, psychoanalyze me. Avoidance issues, right?

Now that she'd tracked me down, I'd have to contemplate utilizing my usual blow off by not calling back or being a grown-up and calling her machine when I knew she'd be at work to tell her that I'm just not in a place to start a relationship right now. That was true, sort of. Kami recited her phone number, and I grudgingly jotted it down on the notepad by the phone. At some point, I'd have to start acting like a grown-up when it came to dating.

The next message began to play just as I finished my purposeful scribble. "So, I heard it rained today." *Funny!* My other best friend, Lauren, left her almost daily message. Got to love cell phone plans that allow for free long distance after 9:00 p.m. The three hour time difference was the only thing that Lauren reluctantly accepted as good about my move out here. She could call for free every day if she wanted. "We enjoyed a tropical eighty-six degrees back here, sister. And no frizzy hair. Doesn't that sound nice? I miss you, I love you, come home! $255 one way ticket. We'll all chip in, or Willa can buy you a plane to use. If you're not getting a ticket right now, at least call me this weekend. Love ya, Young'un." Her signoff brought a smile to my lips. She'd been a third year law student at UVA when I started there, a year earlier than everyone else. I always considered it the luckiest day of my college career when I walked into the law library to check the mentor list and found her name assigned to me. Unlike other school mates, mentors, or advisors, Lauren had an immediate and genuine interest in my success at law school and my assimilation into Charlottesville. And unlike other friends, I took to her instantly because of it and we've been better than best friends ever since.

My recall of that first meeting stopped abruptly when the next message began. "Hey, it's Willa." *Just great!* The phone call Helen mentioned. Helen I can fool with feigned forgetfulness; Willa would be a little more difficult. "I'm in Sea-town for the rest of the week. Let's get together, hon. Dinner, coffee, breakfast, lunch, whatever you've got time for. We're slammed over here trying to get this game done, but I'm going to need a break from the insanity. So call when you can, will ya?" I replayed the message just to hear her voice again. And again, all right, and again, you caught me. I'd hoped to avoid her this trip. All part of my self-prescribed therapy for getting over being in love with my best friend:

1. Don't see her.
2. Don't talk to her.
3. Don't think about her.

Since moving here, I'd violated all three protocols on a regular basis. Although on her last couple of visits, I minimized the number of times I'd seen or spoken to her. It was that third one that I still needed to work on.

Not much I could do about it this time. I'd be seeing her on Friday for work reasons. Not that I really had to go, but I wouldn't let my work suffer because of a self-imposed healing practice. At least I wouldn't call her before I got there. And what was that third one again? Sure, like that's gonna happen.

Chapter 3

"If I understand correctly, Agent Bridie, you're saying that the defendant kept a second set of accounting records on his work computer?" I turned from the jury box to focus on Elise.

Wow, she's beautiful. Like the kind of exquisite splendor that makes you question whether or not it's even legal to be that beautiful. I'm an attorney; I should really look that up. She wore her shoulder length, brunette hair in a French braid, highlighting the sweep of her cheekbones. A jade green blouse wrapped in a fitted charcoal suit complimented her eyes like a design expert picked the next hue down on the spectrum of greens. Everyone in the courtroom was riveted by her testimony. I wouldn't be surprised to find out it had little to do with what she was saying. Why hadn't I thought to request an ultra hot FBI agent for every case I tried?

"That's correct," she spoke confidently. We were only ten minutes into her testimony, and it was burying the defendant. I thought I saw him visibly pale while she spoke of finding his undoctored books.

"Why would someone leave a second set of accounting records on a computer that others can access at work? Especially records that would incriminate him?" The art of jury trials called for the questioning attorney to sound uninformed to allow for the expert witness to hammer home her testimony. Elise's mouth twitched at my thespian-like skills, but so far, no sign of that slow, sexy smile that flared in my office on Tuesday.

"I can only testify as to my experience with these kinds of cases," she responded, saving me from arguing over the certain objection that would have come from the defense. Since taking the stand, she'd been a dream expert witness. I wonder if Marvel would entertain a new comic book with a superhero whose powers included warding off nonsense objections from defense attorneys. Probably not a huge seller, but those of us in the legal profession would be sucked in. "Usually, we find that people keep records on the most convenient computer. They assign a password to the file and think that makes it secure. In this case, the defendant had also deleted the file."

"Objection! Calls for conclusion," the defense attorney called out from his table. He looked good in his $4,000 suit and $500 haircut. I'd come up against him twice before, and each time he hit on me before opening statements. Other female attorneys told me he thought it threw off the opposition to be distracted by his self-assessed grandeur.

Sure to form on Wednesday morning, he walked up to my table and, in a show of shaking my hand, whispered, "You know you want to give me your affection, Austy. Dinner tonight?" I shook his hand and my head at his request then fought the urge to jump in a shower. Smarmy men and, while more rare, women made me want to scrub myself clean.

"Sustained." The judge looked as bothered by the garbage objection as I was but ruled appropriately nonetheless.

I turned to Elise to tidy up her statement, but before I could say anything, she did my work for me. "Excuse me, I assumed it was the defendant who deleted the file on his password protected computer because it incriminated him, but I can't be certain he was the one who deleted the file."

Smart, sharp, and sexy. Everyone on the jury smiled at her

response, taken in by her honesty and wise experience. Four of the male jurors looked like they'd spent the last ten minutes fantasizing about her.

"If it was deleted, how did you get to see what was on it?" Was this question really necessary anymore? People had to be aware by now that deleting a file didn't mean it was wiped from the hard drive. Just in case, though, I asked the stupid question.

"There are a number of places that a deleted file can sit on a hard drive. I won't bore you by naming every location. Someone with a background like mine can find those places and often recreate a file from entered key strokes."

"Is that what you had to do here?"

Elise smiled modestly. Two men in the front row of the jury box edged forward in their seats. Did I mention that she was a dream witness? "No, in this instance, file restoration was much easier. Whoever deleted the file didn't bother to clear out the trash folder where all deleted files sit indefinitely." Some of the jurors shared her smile obviously aware of this oversight, while six heads reared back in surprise at this revelation. Research done; jurors needed me to ask the stupid questions.

"You can read the file in the trash bin?" I maintained my show of computer ignorance.

"Once you restore it to the hard drive by a couple of keystrokes, yes, you can read the file if you have the password. Or if you have a password generator, which is what we used here to get into the files in question."

Now that we'd established someone had tried to get rid of the incriminating file and that the file was intact when examined, I only needed to take her through the file's contents to attach guilt. I had other witnesses and evidence, but Elise could peg him all on her own.

For the next half hour, I confirmed with Elise that the second set of accounting books did indeed show fraud on the part of the defendant. He'd cheated his employees on their pension contributions, his stockholders on the earnings reports, and the IRS on corporate taxes. It was hard to say which of the counts would be the worst punishment for him.

I'd offered a plea bargain for half of the max sentence in order to save the taxpayers the cost of trying this obviously guilty man. They almost never go for it, especially when they've got a hotshot lawyer like Gregory Stokes. Although I wouldn't be surprised if it was Greg's ego that kept him from accepting bargains that would save his clients the embarrassment of being pummeled in court. On only the morning of the second day, his client was sunk, thanks in most part to Elise's testimony.

"Your Honor?" Greg stood up to address the court. It wasn't necessary to stand, but he loved showing off his suits. "I'd like to request a recess to confer with my client and our forensic accountant."

I glanced at the jury to see where I stood with them. While Greg's smoothness might be appealing, he wasn't besting Elise. They were in trouble. If I didn't think this recess would offer up a deal, I'd insist that we get through all of her testimony before a break.

"We'll take a fifteen minute break. Witness is excused for the moment. Bailiff, please escort the jury back to the jury room." The judge stood along with the jury, triggering loud shuffling sounds from the gallery in their effort to stand on the clerk's order of "all rise."

I waited for Elise to step down from the stand and walk past me before turning back to my table. Greg slithered up to me after whispering with his client. "Don't go far, Aust."

That he shortened my name like we were pals annoyed me, but his order made me want to smile. I had him, and he knew it. "I'll be at the end of the hall." I referred to my chosen break room.

When I pushed through the courtroom doors, I found Elise waiting for me. She smiled conspiratorially as if she knew exactly what Greg had said.

"You did well, thank you, Agent Bridie."

"Elise," she corrected. "And now it's my turn to say that you made it very easy for me, Austy."

I pointed toward one of the attorney consultation rooms, and we started down the hallway. A couple of attorneys from my office said hello to me along the way. Only one of them had a trial in session today. The rest were assisting or taking notes on the way certain judges ran their courtrooms. I did the same thing myself when I had a free afternoon. Being a nerd rocks; well, okay, at least it's good for my career.

The door opened inward, and I held onto the knob as Elise brushed closely by. Near enough that I caught a whiff of lavender and citrus as she walked through. It wasn't overpowering like perfume, probably more like a facial cream. *What are you doing noticing her facial cream?*

"You really know how to command a courtroom," Elise complimented after taking a seat at the oak table.

"I had a lot of practice as an ADA." I waved off her comment, knowing it wasn't so much skill as it was practice makes perfect. Walking over to the coffee station, I offered her a beverage.

She nodded at the coffee and gave another mouth twitch that seemed to indicate she knew I'd deflected her compliment. "Not here, though, right?" She accepted my shrug as acknowledgement but didn't let me out of the inquisition. "Somewhere in the South?"

My poker face failed me at her guess. I laughed briefly, knowing I was caught. After I handed her a cup of coffee, I took a seat on the opposite side of the table. "What gave me away? And don't tell me I have an accent, because I know that's not true."

That sexy smile inched across her face again, and suddenly, I became aware of my elevated pulse rate. The room grew stuffier as I shifted to find a more comfy position under her disarming stare.

"No accent, no. It's a combination of things. Like how

polite and accommodating you are. Couple that with how concerned you are with people being comfortable whether it's in your office, your courtroom, or anywhere else you might be." At my frown, she raised her cup of coffee to prove her point.

I scoffed, amused by her assessment. "Well, aren't I transparent?"

"Not really. The law degree from University of Virginia helped a bit."

That was startling. Short Stack required us to display our degrees somewhere in our offices. I hid mine among my law books, clock radio, and ridiculous trinkets that my Virginia friends sent with me. People focused on the trinkets, but no one noticed the degree. No one.

I regained my demeanor and joked, "You cheated. All that stuff about politeness and accommodation; smoke and mirrors."

She tossed her head back and laughed genuinely. *Oh my, what a nice laugh. I could listen to that for a long while.*

A knock sounded at the door, and I snapped back into focus. Gregory Stokes strode inside like he not only owned the place but built every scrap of it with his bare hands. He faltered when he saw that I was sitting with Elise. A momentary crack splintered his brashness as he stared at her. Aha! Even the great Gregory Stokes turns into a quaking pile of insecurity when confronted with a gorgeous woman.

"Can I help you, Greg?" I enjoyed seeing his poise slide away like powered sugar off a donut.

"Huh? Yes, I wanted to discuss the status of our case."

Elise stood and exited without being asked. I looked back at Greg and said, "I'm all ears."

At full throttle, Greg's artificial magnetism sucked in most of the oxygen supply in the room. "We're prepared to accept your plea bargain."

During our first trial against each other, I learned to use pauses effectively to give Greg enough time to stop being in love with the sound of his own voice enough to ponder my reply. This time was no exception. "I believe I told you that offer would expire as soon as the trial started, Greg."

"You're kidding? You know we could take this the length and win."

"Not after Agent Bridie's testimony which is why you're in here now." I had to lock my jaw shut to keep from laughing at his crestfallen look.

"I've advised my client to go the distance, but he wants this over with. What are you prepared to offer now?"

If only I was wired for sound. A couple of attorneys in my office would love to hear Greg admit defeat. "He's looking at guilty on all counts for pension, securities, and tax fraud. All told, a very likely forty year sentence and fines doubling his gains. You had your chance at twenty with parole and repaying the gains. I'll give you twenty-five, no parole, and double the gains."

His mouth dropped open like he'd unhinged his jaw. He settled seventy percent of his cases, I'd found out. Most to the benefit of his clients. Not the outcome he'd be accepting with this case, and his wide open mouth revealed his displeasure. "That's hardly better than max."

"It's a lot better than max, and you know it. My guess is that your boy will want to take the extra fifteen free years that I'm offering to enjoy the money that he's probably siphoned off of the other companies he ran before hitting this mother lode."

I'd been kidding, but Greg's expression told me he thought my guess was probably true. He held out his hand to shake. "I'll convince my client to take it."

I stood and took his hand, glad that I wouldn't have to waste another week on this case. "You've got five minutes till we're due back."

He smirked a confident reply. "It's done. Since you got the better of me on this one, I think you should spring for dinner tonight."

I chuckled at what I presumed was a joke. Greg's light blue eyes flitted from one side of the room to the other with a confounded look. Perhaps no one ever thought he was kidding, or maybe he hadn't been kidding. Just the thought made me again yearn for that cleansing shower. He returned from his isle of confusion and stepped back to open the door for me with a grand show. We found Elise sitting on the bench across the hall.

Greg strode confidently over to her and shook her hand. "I want you on my team next time, Agent Bridie. Shall we discuss this over dinner?"

Elise smiled politely and shook his hand. "Maybe when you stop defending scumbags, Mr. Stokes." She didn't clarify if her conditional acceptance applied to joining his team or going out to dinner with him. I found myself rooting for the former.

Speechless, he turned and walked toward the courtroom ahead of us. I pictured him building a summer home on his growing land mass of bewilderment.

Addressing Elise, I reported, "Looks like we've wrapped this up."

Inside the courtroom, Greg's nod told me our deal was a go. Minutes later with the judge taking his seat, I entered our plea agreement for acceptance. He listened to the terms, granted approval, and thwacked his gavel to signify the conclusion of this case. Music to my ears.

Elise and I went back up to my office where her raincoat and umbrella were stashed. Mary raised her fist for a pound as I went past her reception desk. She often heard courtroom news before the attorneys trying the cases did.

As I was following Elise inside my office, I heard Short Stack's voice. "Austy!"

The heavy pounding of his steps gave him away, but I turned to watch his progress anyway. "Kyle."

"Heard you pleaded out."

"That was two seconds ago. How'd you find out?

"I'm omnipresent, Austy. Think of me as godlike."

I rotated back toward my office and rolled my eyes, forgetting that Elise would catch my exasperation. She gave me her courtroom mouth twitch before Kyle joined us.

He stopped at the doorway, noticing Elise. "I understand your testimony was very convincing, Agent. Nice job."

"Thank you, but Austy walked it over with the jury."

"Well, I wanted good results on this one and couldn't have asked for better. Nice job, both of you." Praise from Short Stack? I shivered with the eerie sound of it. "I'd tell you to take the rest of the day off, but you've got too many cases. Plus wise, you work more hours than I do; so why bother?"

That was a little more like the Kyle I knew. His rhetorical question hung in the air for a moment before he turned and left without another word. Along the way, he shared the news of my "win" with every staff member he passed. I knew he'd been sweating over this one, but I didn't expect him to be gleeful about its conclusion.

"He's happy, and from what Jake's said, he's almost never happy," Elise observed, tilting back in her chair to watch Kyle's retreat down the hall.

"Jake would know better than I."

"Why's that?" Her green eyes shot back to me in amusing inquisition. "Was I right about your tenure here?"

Damn, her investigative skills were honed. "Five months," I relented.

"In this office or Seattle?"

"Both."

"I bet there's a story there." She stared at me knowingly. "Don't worry, I won't ask. Anyway, congratulations on your win today."

"It was a plea, and you're the one who forced their compliance."

Her head nodded but not in agreement. More like she was considering what to say next. "On to the next case for you, I guess. Shall I swing by here at 4:00 tomorrow for our meeting?" When she registered my hesitation, she added, "I'm a big proponent of carpooling, and I'm a safe driver." I had the feeling if we'd been in another setting, she might have winked at me.

With the trial prep, I'd nearly forgotten about the meeting with Willa. Best Friend Willa. Married Best Friend Willa. Married Best Friend that I'm in love with Willa. Damn! I'd almost made it a whole day without thinking about her. Okay, it wasn't quite noon, so a whole half-day without thinking about her.

"That would be great. It'll save me a drive in," I managed, now preoccupied. Here I sat across from a stunning woman who at best was flirting with me, at worst offering friendship, and all I could think of was the unrequited love of my married best friend who lived on the other side of the country.

Maybe I should call Kami for another date to distract me from this destructive and wretched fixation. *Sure, that'll work. Sharp thinking, moron.*

Chapter 4

Bridge traffic sucked almost as much as my love life as a lesbian in Seattle. I was glad I wasn't driving. I'd be riding my clutch all the way across the stop and go parking lot that was the 520 floating bridge. I liked my MINI Cooper S too much to do that to it. Elise's automatic Infinity didn't seem to mind the crawling pace.

Lake Washington, calm and blue on the north side of the bridge, while choppy and misty on the south side, played host to hundreds of Friday afternoon boaters. Sunny and warm nearly all day, proof of the beautiful summers everyone had promised me. If it stayed like this all weekend, I might have to consider not working.

Traffic finally started flowing by the time we'd left the bridge deck. The Infinity found the carpool lane and practically flew for a Friday afternoon. We'd hit Willa's office in no time. Best Friend Willa. Married Best Friend Willa. *Stop it!*

"I've got directions in the glove box." Elise stretched a hand toward my knees while she kept her eyes trained on the road.

"I know where it is," I told her, stopping the progress of her hand to hover over my left knee just short of the glove box. "Take Lake Sammamish and turn left. It's by the courthouse."

Her eyes found mine momentarily, probably tying my mention of the courthouse with my familiarity for where we were headed. “All right.”

She followed my instructions and guided us to a visitor spot in Jucundus Interactive’s parking lot. I stepped out of the car, half excited to see my friend again, half dreading the dull twinge that filled my chest every time I came near her. I smoothed the imaginary wrinkles in my best suit. The one I used for closing arguments. The one that showed great leg and fine taste. Too bad the suit didn’t have the power to make me feel as cocky as it should.

Elise ducked into the backseat to grab her purse and noticed that I hadn’t made a move for my briefcase yet. Lunging further, she plucked my briefcase up and leaned back upright to shut the car door.

“Thank you.” I met her at the trunk and accepted my proffered briefcase.

We rode the elevator up to the lobby in silence. Elise took the time to flip through her case notes while I mutely fought off my imagination full of unmarried best friends, a whole lot of happily ever after, and some unicorns, leprechauns, and flying dragons, too. Time better spent with a therapist, I’m sure.

When we hit the top floor, we stepped out into a full-scale video game where the lobby should have been. A paint effect similar to holographic art coated the walls giving the impression that they were alive. Four game stations clustered into each corner, chirping and calling out for someone to play. Cardboard cutouts of their game characters stood strategically around the lobby as life-size reminders of why the company existed. Only a reception desk and a collection of sofas with matching chairs denoted the actual purpose of the room.

Elise swiftly surveyed the lobby with an intensity that made me think she’d just committed every feature to memory. She walked up to the desk and informed the receptionist whose name escaped me, “Special Agent Bridie and Prosecutor

Nunziata to see Willa Lacey."

I liked that she said my last name perfectly on the first try. No one ever managed that. Everyone assumed it started with "nun" and threw in a hard "i" and "a" somewhere. It really wasn't that difficult: noon-zee-aught-ta. See?

The receptionist, David, yes, David, that was his name, spoke to Elise, "You're the FBI agent on our case, right?"

"Yes, Ms. Lacey should be expecting us."

"Sure, I'll let her know." He spoke next into his headset. "Will? The FBI is here to see you." He grinned and flashed a thumbs up at us. Jocularity flourished at Jucundus. He focused on us again. "She'll be right with you. Please have a seat, or you can play one of our games if you like." His encouragement tempted me, even though I wasn't a fan of computer games.

When Willa appeared in the lobby, my heart actually stopped pumping like a murmur gone terribly wrong. Five seconds elapsed before I felt another heartbeat. Thankfully, Elise wasn't struck by the same affliction and stood to greet Willa. Her stature provided an obstruction long enough for me to regain my composure.

"Hi, I'm Willa Lacey," she introduced herself and took Elise's hand in greeting.

"Hello, Ms. Lacey, I'm Special Agent Elise Bridie." Elise brought up her badge for Willa's inspection. I stood while Willa considered the badge carefully. Elise swept her hand toward me. "And this is—"

"A.J.!" Willa yelped, cutting off Elise. "You're—what are you—woman alive, A.J.?" Her surprise overpowered her normally tactile averse ways, and she grabbed me in a welcome hug that made every worry I'd ever experienced slip away.

"Hey, Will." I pulled back before she felt my heart thundering against her chest.

She flashed her familiar smile, and I felt compelled to jump on a return flight to Virginia so I could see it more often. "This isn't a drop by, is it?"

"No, I'm the prosecutor on the case, Will. Elise asked me to tag along for this meeting."

"I'm so glad. Thank you, Age," Willa relayed happily and lead us back to her office. Once we'd taken over the couch in her office, she asked, "Have you worked together long?"

Elise answered before I could, "Not long enough to know that Austy is called A.J. by her friends." She turned a curious stare toward me.

"What?" Willa exclaimed in surprise, dropping into the chair facing us. "You go by Austy now?" She looked like I'd withheld precious information vital to her existence.

Over the past five months, I'd neglected to mention to anyone from back home that I no longer went by A.J. which my dad had insisted on from birth. He wanted to make certain that his last name, Josephs, was acknowledge when he'd lost what must have been the worst argument of my parent's lives. Because my mother prevailed, she got to give me her last name, while my brothers got my dad's last name. For thirty-two years I'd been A.J. Nunziata or Age to my friends. When I moved to Seattle, I took back my name and liked that it sounded more grown up for my promotion to the U.S. Attorney's office. I was still getting used to it.

"No, well, yes, but don't worry; I don't expect you guys to change what you call me."

Her mouth parted slightly as she took in the information. "You're sure? I can beat the crew into submission for you?" She flashed an uncertain smile like she wished she'd known I wanted to be called Austy all along. See what I mean about her?

Waving a dismissive hand, I shoved aside her concern like it didn't affect me at all. "Shall we discuss your copyright infringement claim?"

Her concerned, brown eyes seared into mine, accepting that I wasn't comfortable discussing my new Seattle self. "Our art director recognized some of her art in a game she picked up on a trip to Hong Kong recently. Nykos," she paused and looked at Elise, "he's my business partner along with Nathaniel, our engineering lead, examined the Hong Kong version and found too many similarities for it not to be a knock off. That's when I contacted the FBI."

"It looks like this isn't a simple case of piracy. Generally, we can't do much about piracy unless copies make it to the U.S." Elise consulted her flip up notebook; evidently all FBI agents were issued one. I dug into my briefcase for a legal pad to look official and take unnecessary notes. Not that I'd need it, I wouldn't forget what we discussed on this particular case.

"Will?" A tall, youthful looking man stuck his freckled face into the office doorway. "Excuse me." He took note of us, smiling politely, yet staring longer than necessary.

"Nate?" Willa drew his attention back.

"Umm, oh yeah, Nykos told me to tell you that we're sticking Jadara into the ninth level of *Carthage* as a nod to our loyal gamers." His eyes returned to Elise, blatantly checking her out. When his gaze moved over to me, I swiveled my reddening face back to look at Willa.

Noticing my discomfort, she stifled a giggle before addressing him. "Tell Kos that I know what he's going to try to do, and I know enough to keep him from doing it."

"Huh?" Nathaniel flicked his eyes back to Willa.

"Tell him he won't get away with using the original prototype of Jadara. She looks too much like an S&M dom. I'll put a stop to it. I don't care if we miss gold."

"Why not, Will? She's smoking hot!" He had enough decorum to wait two seconds before looking at Elise.

"Focus, Nathaniel. Use the approved Jadara or not at all."

"Whatever," he sulked, sneaking one last glimpse at Elise before leaving.

"I apologize for the interruption, but we're close to launching our fifth game."

"I understand," Elise spoke for both of us. She instinctively knew that Willa disappeared for weeks on end when they got close to shipping a new game. "It was *Xerxes' Lament* that was copied, wasn't it?" She waited for Willa's nod. "Great title. Originally published when?"

"About four years ago. I could get you the exact date if you like."

"Eventually, yes, Austy will need that if this goes to trial. I'll make a list of all the information we'll need to carry forward with this case."

"I'm good with lists." Willa grinned and tipped her head at me. She made lists for everything, including which lists she needed to make.

"You've never sent your master code through email to anyone?"

"Never. That's not good software practice."

"Do you have any telecommuters on staff?"

"No, and there's no accessing our mainframe from offsite either."

"Willa?" We all turned to see three men waiting just inside the doorway.

"What's up, guys?"

Two of the men stared fixedly at Elise as the other one slowly pulled his eyes from me to Willa. "Nykos wants you to know that you can't stop him." He raised his eyebrows and smirked when he delivered the message.

Willa laughed that laugh that I missed so much. The laugh that made me move across the country so I'd stop pining for her. *Yeah, that worked out well.*

"Seriously, tell Nykos that I'm in a meeting, one that he's encouraged to join anytime." The men continued to stare at Elise, glanced at me, then back to Elise. Willa snapped her fingers loudly. "Hello? Guys, stop gawking at the beautiful women and get back to work."

A moment passed before I realized that Willa had been referring to both Elise and me, then another moment to register that she'd just called me beautiful. *Whoa!* A dizzying blush started at the base of my neck surely scorching the collar of my shirt. I barely noticed the men make an effort to pull each other away from the doorway.

"I'm so sorry. These engineers don't get much human contact. And well, as you've seen, they can act like adolescents sometimes." Willa spoke to Elise, not because she didn't want to include me, but because she'd noticed my blush and, like always, wanted to spare me any extra embarrassment.

"I can handle adolescents," Elise offered easily. She seemed to be absorbing the Jucundus environment, one that had taken me a while to get used to. "You were saying that you had a stand alone mainframe?"

"That's right, but our web server hosts an online version of each game. That one obviously connects to the Internet."

"Since it was the desktop version that was copied, I'd say that one of your employees sold the master code to the Hong Kong developer and might've even worked on tweaking it enough to pass as a new game."

"Seriously?" Willa frowned, clearly upset by this news. "It wasn't just someone who copied the game design and art?"

"It could be, but there were a few alterations that were natural progressions of the game not slight variations of it."

"Are you a programmer?" Willa looked at her in interest.

Elise shook her head with a modest smile. "Computer sci major and avid gamer at the time. Yours are clever and engaging."

"Thanks, we like them." Willa winked at me. She didn't play computer games; only her close friends knew that about her. The ultimate irony. Well, not as ironic as a man running a tampon company but still pretty ironic.

"How many employees have you fired, Ms. Lacey?"

"It's Willa, and we've had most of our employees from the start. Five years now."

Elise looked at me as if gauging Willa's honesty. "That's admirable. This must be a great place to work."

"Well, my half of it in Charlottesville is. Redmond's more like a zoo." Willa flicked her hand back toward the open door then caught sight of something that compelled her attention.

From the hallway, we couldn't help but hear, "Where are these hotties you're crying about, Nate? Vinnie, Jim, and Mike all claim you're not lying, my friend, so they better be worth walking my ass across this compound." Murmurs in the background before the boisterous voice chimed in again, "Willa? You made me exercise to scope out Will? I've seen Will, for eighteen years…Oh, with Will, fine. They better be hot, dammit."

Willa shook her head and laughed softly at what I now recognized as her business partner's voice. She glanced at us, held up her palms, and said, "I apologize in advance."

"Hate to interrupt, Will, but you will bow down to my programming superiority." Nykos Ander strode through the door and calmly looked us over before saying, "Yes ma'am, definitely hot."

Willa sighed in exasperation and informed us, "I find that if you ignore them, they eventually behave. Kos, you remember A.J., don't you?"

He beamed affably, took my hand, and actually raised it to his mouth for a kiss. "Sure, you're the one that's afraid of your love for me."

"Nykos!" Willa practically screamed at him, but all I could do was laugh. This guy was funny. He always kept her dinner party invitees back home in hysterics.

"What?" he asked innocently. He turned his attention back to me and declared, "You changed your hair. The blond was nice, but the guys are right, the auburn's hot."

Blush number two. When I moved to Seattle, I stopped dying my hair blond. Something I'd started back in college when I came out. I'd never loved it, but I thought a change appropriate at the time. Then it became difficult to change back after everyone got used to the blond. After relocating, I let my hair go back to my natural reddish-brown and added a couple of inches in length, too. Still short enough for easy styling, but long enough that no one did a double take if they saw me entering a ladies room from behind.

"Yes, Nykos, it's very becoming," Willa confirmed dryly, having already gotten used to the change. "Now would you please act like you've been someplace, and say hello to Special Agent Elise Bridie. She's investigating our copyright claim."

"Nice to meet you, Agent Bridie." Nykos behaved himself with just a handshake this time, but his eyes revealed his desire to cat call or, at least, whistle heartily. He plopped into the seat next to Willa and asked Elise to continue.

"I was telling Willa that it must be great working here," Elise went on politely.

"Sure is. Need a job? We've always got room for babelicious employees."

"Enough, Nykos!" Willa spoke forcefully. "You guys moved past joshing a while back; now you're bordering on hostile environment. Don't make me pull out the sexual harassment tapes and bring in Lauren for another lecture."

Nykos threw his fingers up in the form of a cross and reared back at Willa's threat to call our friend Lauren, who was their corporate attorney. "Point taken. What can we do to help with the investigation, Agent?"

"I'd just asked Willa if you'd fired anyone. I'm not sure if I got a complete answer."

"You think this was a former employee?" Nykos asked.

"It's likely."

"We've only had four employees quit, and they all left on great terms. Other than—"

"No!" Willa cut him off. "The guy's a dufus, but he's not stupid. He wouldn't risk jail time to steal code, not when he has the skills to create his own game."

"Skills but no creativity. Without a design doc, the guy's hopeless."

"This was someone who quit?" Elise inquired.

"I fired him," Nykos spoke seriously.

Elise sat back and waited. When neither Nykos nor Willa offered more, she asked, "He was fired for cause?"

"No," Nykos said and glanced at Willa to answer further,

but she'd gone very still.

"Willa?" I persuaded her to speak, anxious to hear this from her. She'd never mentioned having to fire anyone.

"He left for personal reasons," Willa admitted quietly, prompting an incoherent grumble from Nykos.

"Personal differences, personal clashes, personal problems?" Elise insisted. I could tell she was a good investigator, but right now, I wanted her to stop making Willa so uncomfortable.

"He left because he had a problem with my homosexuality," Willa informed her.

I didn't have time to gauge Elise's reaction before Nykos declared, "The guy was a bigoted asshole, Will, and that's a kind assessment."

"I see," Elise stated calmly. "So, is it safe to assume he left under acrimonious conditions?"

Willa laughed outright while Nykos snorted disgust again. Elise's mouth twitch told me she was joking. Yet another adjective to add to the list: funny.

"He wasn't thrilled, no," Willa reported.

"Was this last November, Willa?" I wanted to know how I'd missed helping my friend through what must have been a devastating realization about one of her employees.

"Lot of stuff going on then." She nodded slightly, admitting finally to the tough time she'd had taking her company public. She'd avoided our group of friends for nearly two months. I hated that time for her and really hated that I couldn't help her through it. Of course, that was when I started thinking about moving.

"His name?" Elise had her notepad at the ready.

"Dean Raymond. Last I heard he'd signed on at a web services design house in Bellevue," Nykos provided helpfully. "I can call over to see if he's still employed there?"

"I can do that, thank you." Elise flipped her notebook closed and looked up at them. "Well, I think we've got a great start here. I'll call you with the information we may need as soon as I compile the lists. Thank you for your time today." She stood up to signal the end of the meeting.

I watched Willa breathe a sigh of relief and wanted to hug Elise for allowing her a quick end to her discomfort. She and Willa shook hands before she stepped past me to shake hands with Nykos.

"Breakfast, lunch, or dinner tomorrow?" Willa tried to pin me down. When I didn't immediately respond, she leaned in for a one-armed hug and whispered, "I know what you're doing, and I won't let you. Right now it's your choice. Don't make me pick for you and camp out at my sister's until you come out of your place."

I forced a chuckle. What did she mean? How could she know what I was doing? If she knew I was in love with her, I'd die. Dramatic, I know. "Lunch works. Will you be here or at your house?"

"She lives here now," Nykos supplied and wrapped his arm around me in parting. He was a big bear of a man, and my face pressed into the Seattle Storm emblem on his shirt. I'd never seen him in anything but Storm or Mariners apparel. "I'm invited to lunch, right?"

"Sure," I said, pleading for any diversion I could get.

"No," Willa replied firmly, not even trying to make a joke out of it.

Therapy rule number one: out the door for yet another trip.

Chapter 5

Soft, warm sunlight streamed through my loft windows late Saturday morning. I'd been luxuriating in the sunshine, reading the latest in my favorite author's legal thriller series for hours. Other Seattleites were probably out biking, hiking, sailing, kayaking, or any other exhaustive form of outdoor activity that so consumed the residents of this town. My mornings off, I read or walked along the Burke-Gillman trail until all the bikers, runners, rollerbladers, skateboarders, and people started to get on my nerves. Sometimes it amazes even me that I've managed to stay out of prison with all that irks me.

My one accomplishment this morning included setting up a deposition with a witness for a trial in two weeks, necessitating the cancellation of my lunch with Willa. I was only mildly guilt-ridden about leaving a message on her cell phone. Since she never kept it on, it was the best way to contact her without actually talking to her. I'm all about the therapy.

Someone knocked on my door, interrupting yet another dim-witted move by the protagonist. Why was it necessary to lose one's practically to heighten suspense? Glancing at the door, I guessed it was Joe. Outsiders need to be buzzed into the building; my downstairs neighbors barely recognized me well enough to say hello; and Helen knew I didn't respond to drop bys. For some reason, Joe either didn't know or didn't care. He was forever trying to get me to take one of his kayaks out or borrow his bike or go sailing with them. This town existed for people like Helen and Joe.

The knocking turned insistent, like its creator knew my policy about drop bys and wanted to annoy me into ignoring it. Flipping to the next page in my book, I focused on the plight of my reckless heroine. I'm nothing if not stubborn.

"Age? I know you're in there," Willa called out. "I told you I wouldn't let you get away with avoiding me, sister. I'll stand out here all day."

Great! I looked down at my t-shirt and jeans, knowing they wouldn't add credence to my excuse of needing to go into the office later. She was going to see right through me. Worse yet, I was going to see her.

Without realizing it, I started toward the door. The book became heavy in my hand, and I rushed back to the closest bookcase to stuff it away so she wouldn't know I'd been reading instead of working. On my second approach to the door, I caught my reflection in the bathroom mirror. Panicked, I took stock of my appearance. Hair gelled into chaotic order, check. Base layer of foundation to even out complexion, check. No courtroom eyes-back-to-me blush, lipstick, or eye shadow, but screw it; she's partnered. Pitiful becomes me.

A proffered bag of delicious smells preceded Willa's warm smile through the door. Her brown hair was pulled back at the sides and held by a simple barrette, taming her natural waves. Dark brown eyes perfectly spaced to balance out her squarish jaw and enviable lips took her smile to another level. No one would slap a brand of traditionally beautiful on her, but get to know her and you'd think you were talking to the most enthralling woman alive.

"Hi, Will. What are you doing here? Didn't you get my message?" I took the bag out of her hand then closed and locked the door behind her. The epitome of cool and casual.

She studied my attire, realizing I'd blown her off. If she was hurt, her face didn't show it. Masking emotions was her superpower, something the Virginia crew tested often just for fun.

We stood just inside the door, and I fought the impulse to hug her. I'd hugged her nearly every time I saw her in Virginia until a joking comment by Nykos that he'd never hugged her in their eighteen year friendship made me aware that Willa wasn't a hugger. How could I have not known that? Thus began my realization that I had to break away from her.

She seemed to be waiting for me to hug her. She was a smidge taller than me and no doubt learned that when you're short and slim like we are, you're a hug magnet. An awkward moment passed with me clamping down on my desire to touch her before I remembered my manners. Gesturing with my hand, I invited her farther into my loft.

"The place looks great, Age. You've finished decorating? Very homey. Very you."

"Thanks." I set the bag on my dining room table.

"Helen made us lunch. Don't be surprised if it shows up on next month's specials in her restaurant. She loves to use me as a guinea pig."

She did the same with me. Apparently Joe liked everything, rendering him worthless as a food critic. "You didn't have to do that."

Willa stared me down. "Yes, I did. When's your depo?"

I contemplated lying to up the start time, but what would be the point? She was already here, so therapy practice number one got scrapped again. "At two."

"Good." She checked her watch. "Hope you're hungry."

She'd brought spinach lasagna, a new vegetarian trend with Helen, and freshly baked, wholegrain bread. Both turned out to be delicious, and we enjoyed cheerful mealtime chatter about our work mostly. I only thought about kissing her once. Okay, three times. Then I was wracked with guilt because I love her partner, Quinn. Friend love, like I felt for all of the Virginia crew, except Willa.

After lunch, we settled on the couch where I hoped to continue talking about the antics at her company. That place could double for an insane asylum, but the good kind where lead characters on a soap opera get committed. Luck didn't follow me into the living room, though.

"Do you want to tell me what's going on, Age, or do you want me to guess?"

"What do you mean?" The picture of innocence; yep, that's me.

Willa pursed her lips into the smile that showed a slight dimple on the right side of her face. "I accepted you moving out here. If you'll remember, I was the only one who did." She referred to the fact that the group threatened to handcuff me to Des and Skye's basement pipes to keep me in town. "Of course I knew I'd get to keep seeing you, not as often, but more than they would. During your first few months here, I got in all kinds of quality Age time. These last few trips though, I can't help but feel you're avoiding me."

I opened my mouth to protest, but I really didn't know what to say other than, "No."

Her eyebrows shot up in humorous surprise. "It's just my imagination, is it? You've called once, maybe made it to one lunch invitation, and that's not avoiding me?"

"I'm trying to get a handle on my case load, Will. You're the same way."

"I know. That's one of the reasons we get along so well. I understand, really I do. But I wanted to make sure that I haven't done anything to upset you?"

Upset me? Being understanding, wonderful, caring, oh yeah, and partnered. No, nothing upsetting there. "Of course not, Willa." I meant it, or at least in the way she meant it.

Willa studied my expression for a while, trying to determine if I was being truthful. "Okay, then," she said when she was satisfied that I wasn't placating her. "I don't like to pry, Age, you know that. I also don't like when people think they know me better than I do. But I think this move has been difficult for you, and you're trying to keep from using me as a crutch. Maybe you think that going cold turkey will make you forget the friendship and love you had back in Virginia and force you to make a life here. I respect that effort, but we all miss you, and just because we can't see you any day we want doesn't mean that you have to wean yourself off us."

My mouth went dry as I felt a lump start to form in my throat. This woman continued to amaze me. I turned my face toward the window to shield her from seeing the moisture that formed in my eyes. She was so right and so wrong at the same time. She reminded me of my Virginia clan and that was hard to deal with out here, but really, it was the whole being in love with her that drove me away.

"Age? I'm right, aren't I? You've been trying to make me stop reaching out to you by putting on an act of flaking out on plans and not returning calls. You've even changed your mannerisms." At my look of confusion, she explained, "You're a tactile person, A.J. Or you always were. You hugged or kissed people hello, and you touched people when you spoke to them. I always notice when people are like that because it's so different from me. But you made that comfortable for me, and other than with Quinn, I never thought that would happen."

I shook my head, contemplating how well she knew me. "I stopped because I finally realized that you don't touch people unnecessarily. Took me a while, but I wanted to respect your personal bubble."

"Thank you for recognizing it, but not only was I getting used to it but counting on it." She laughed at the paradox we'd created. "That's not really the point of my being here. I wanted you to know that I won't let you drop our friendship, not for anything. You can blow me off all you want, but I'll keep coming back. I miss you, and you're the only one in the group who'd be able to recognize that I don't really say things like that."

"Yeah, even Jessie tells me she misses me," I joked about

our other friend who wore a tough outer shell.

"Then you get it? I'm not giving you up as a friend. And what really sucks for you is that my company going public put more money in my bank account than I know what to do with. So, if I want to fly everyone from Virginia out to see you every month, I can afford it. If I can't get you on the phone, I can jump on a plane and five hours later be banging on this door. And I know how much you love someone coming by without notice."

She never had a problem making me laugh. When Jucundus went public, I had a momentary fear that she'd turn into a rich bitch and the Willa that I knew would be replaced by a hoarder of useless designer stuff. Yet, other than adding a pool at her house which every one of the friends used, Willa spent very little of the money on herself. For our friends, she'd set Jessie up in a health club of her own with Kayin running the financial side of it; fully funded the college savings of Isabel's daughter; put Lauren into her own law practice; created contracting jobs for Des's construction crew; expanded the popular café in Caroline and Sam's bookstore by taking over the space next door; bought this entire building for her sister to start her dream restaurant and created extra income for Helen and Joe from the renters on the second floor. And for me? She wanted to give me this loft, but I'd only agreed to let her carry the mortgage papers on it while I paid her instead of a bank that would never have given me a loan without a significant down payment.

"I gotcha," I assured her that I knew she'd follow through on her threat. I love my Virginia crew, but I don't want them crashing all over my loft every week just to see them. Houseguests are a nightmare for anal retentives like me.

"Thought you'd see it my way, hon. So, next week when the gang comes into town for Quinn's thing, you'll be all about face time, right?"

Quinn used to play basketball for the Seattle Storm, and next week, her team was inviting back all retired players to celebrate their contributions to their establishment. Willa had arranged for the whole Virginia crew to be in attendance and planned a long weekend of activities for everyone to enjoy here. I'd been looking forward to it.

"Sure thing."

"Good. I've got as many tickets as you want. We've booked three luxury boxes for the game, but I've been instructed to give you no less than two tickets."

"Lauren, right?" I asked about my concerned friend.

"Yep. At least two?"

"Two will be fine. I'll give the other ticket to Cyrah."

"Just tell me if you need more. Like, if you wanted to bring along a certain federal law enforcement officer?"

I coughed in surprise. Elise? Did Willa think we had something going? Is that what we looked like to her yesterday? I joked, "Now you're sounding like Lauren. I've just met Elise, and we work together. Plus, I don't think she's family."

Willa grinned, knowing she'd managed to innocently embarrass me. "Three whole reasons not to bring her. I was merely suggesting you invite your work colleague to what will be a great game and fun with your friends. But, hey, if you had other thoughts about her, that's your business."

I shoved her shoulder gently at her tease. "I'll give the ticket to Cyrah. I wouldn't want to subject anyone else I know to the Virginia clan."

"Whatever you want, but it won't just be the usual crew. Helen and Joe, my friend Zoë and her boyfriend with his two kids, Nykos and his kids, Quinn's friends from when she lived here, a couple other people I know from here and friends of theirs that I probably don't know will be there as well. So, invite whomever you want."

"Thanks, Will, I appreciate it."

"And you're glad I muscled my way in here today?" Her smile made me tremble like a Chihuahua.

"Of course," I managed tremor-free.

She got up from the couch and released a satisfied sigh.

Her smiling brown eyes found mine and stared for a moment before what looked like trepidation flickered through. "Glad enough to hug me goodbye?"

God, I love her! Breath pushed out audibly as I contemplated her unparalleled request. I couldn't manage a verbal reply without professing my undying love for her. My only choice was to lean in and wrap my arms around her back. She felt so good in my arms that I allowed myself a full five seconds just to be.

"Thank you," she spoke softly before pulling away.

I barely noticed her friendly smile and wave as she let herself out. She'd just thanked me for hugging her, like it was a huge hassle. Admit it; she's pretty great, isn't she?

Chapter 6

Soaring through the Seattle skyline on the Monorail, I tingled with excitement for tonight's festivities. Two humorous crank phone calls to my office told me the Virginia crew landed sometime earlier today. For the rest of the afternoon, I'd carried a wide smile and giddy heart rate. I'd really missed them.

Mostly tourists piled off the Monorail when we hit the Seattle Center. Despite the city's hope, the Monorail continued to be a tourist activity rather than a mode of transportation. I traversed the noisy diners in the Center House and made my way over to the Key. I'd be meeting my friend Cyrah at the seats.

Luxury box tickets added to my excitement for the evening, allowing me to sail past the crowd through a private entrance. I heard the kids' voices and laughter before I saw them. Two boys and two girls, somewhere in the pre-to-early-teens, swarmed around Willa. She claimed she wasn't a kid person, but they always loved her.

"Age, thank God!" she exclaimed softly and stood up from one of the stools in the back of the box. Her discomfort with the kids made me chuckle, and I hugged her quickly. "These belong to Nykos and friends of theirs. Kids, say hi to A.J." I listened to their sing-song hello and waved in reply. "Why don't you go check out the food spread in the next box over?" Willa encouraged, and they sprinted from the room in freedom.

"Where's Nykos?"

"Quinn took him and the Virginians down to meet some of the Storm players before the game. I think he honestly believes he's got a chance with Sue Bird." She shook her head in amusement and pointed out the front of the box. Down near the court, we could see Quinn leading them from the locker room over to where the team was stretching on the court.

"He does look a little eager."

"Don't think it'll keep him from hitting on you when he gets up here." She turned back from the view on the court to sweep her eyes over me. "You look nice. I like that suit." Her fingers darted out to touch my jacket but stopped a foot shy of their intended target. My heartbeat sped up in anticipation. As usual, she verbalized instead of touched, "Silk? You always find clothes that I'd want to wear."

"Thanks." I looked longingly at the hand that almost touched me.

"Before I forget, I talked to Agent Bridie earlier this week about the case and mentioned that I had extra tickets to tonight's game." My eyes moved up from her hand to focus on her face. "I encouraged her to join us."

"Oh," was all I could manage. Something that felt like a school of fish dramatically changed direction somewhere inside my stomach. Where did that come from?

"That's what I thought, too." Willa showed me the dimple again. "But she asked if she could bring somebody."

"Oh." I tried to match my earlier nonchalance. So, it didn't matter if Gorgeous Elise played for my team; she was taken. Unavailable women and the idiot who covets them: bestseller potential.

"Hey, Aust. Hi, Will," Cyrah called out when she walked through the door. Ruth and two other women that I'd met at one of the clubs Cyrah'd dragged me to followed her in.

Greetings went around the room, barely audible over the escalation of kids' voices in the box next door.

"I'm thinking we leave those kids in a box of their own," Willa grumbled to me as she left to get them situated before the game began.

Helen and Joe stopped in next with Willa's good friend, Zoë, and her boyfriend, Ken. Inordinately shy Zoë surprised me with a dinner invitation for next week. Willa must have instructed her to get me out more often. My laugh told her I knew what she was doing, but Helen solidified the plans by inviting herself along and threatening to hogtie me if necessary. As outdoorsy as she was, I didn't doubt that she'd know how to use a rodeo rope.

They turned to go inspect the other boxes just as Elise appeared at the door. Joe's head twisted away and he mouthed, "Wow." He looked embarrassed when I caught him, but Zoë's boyfriend didn't bother to cover his near drool. Elise looked down at her ticket and checked the suite number.

Ever the cocky Ruth said, "I don't care if you're in the wrong box, cutie; you can sit with me."

Elise turned her full attention to Ruth. An eternity passed before she let a smile touch her lips. If I knew Ruth, she was sweating under this gaze. Anyone would. As expected Ruth buckled first, laughed like she'd been joking, and looked like she wanted to bolt.

"Hi, Elise." I leaned around the crowd so she could see me.

The full blast of her gaze immobilized me as the simmering smile she'd shown Ruth grew into that slow, sexy number. It was probably her normal smile, but it was still sexy as hell. "Hi, Austy."

"Damn, Aust!" Cyrah whispered to me as Joe mouthed another "wow" in my direction.

It was hard to ignore them but concentrating on Elise wasn't too difficult. She wore jeans seemingly sewn for her fit physique and a cashmere v-neck sweater that clung to her torso in a shade of emerald that matched her eyes. For a long moment I almost forgot that she brought a date and that I was in love with my best friend

"Hi, I'm Helen." Helen pulled Elise's gaze away. "I'm Austy's neighbor slash friend and Willa's sister. This is my husband, Joe."

Elise shook their hands and introduced herself to everyone in the group. Ruth and her friends pulled Cyrah into the hallway when several others from the Seattle lesbian scene arrived. I should really be focusing on them as they were my dating pool for the next decade or more until I decided that I needed to suck at being a lesbian in some other city. Instead, I noticed Elise's "date" step inside the box a minute after all the women had cleared the doorway. Tall, good looking, young, blond, thick eyebrows, did I mention young? He couldn't be more than twenty and that was pushing it. I figured Elise and I were around the same age, but maybe she was a lot younger. He took a position quietly behind her and leaned forward to glimpse the view out the front of the box.

She caught me staring at the boy, or man, or boy-man and smiled. "This is my cousin, Scott. Buster, this is Austy. We know each other from work."

Relief flowed over me like a shower spout opened above my head and released it in liquid form. You know, because he was so young and all. Not because I'd just experienced a fleeting fantasy starring her and me. Well, maybe not so fleeting.

"And this is Helen, Joe, Zoë, and Ken. They all either know or are related to Willa who invited us tonight," she finished. Scott shook everyone's hand with a quiet nod.

"Come on in, sit down." I guided them to the seats at the front of the box. Scott immediately leaned over the edge of the box to scope out the court. "Willa should be back any moment. Can I get you something to drink or eat?" I moved toward the beverages and food set out on the back counter, digging out a selection of everything on two plates.

"Thank you," Elise said for both of them when I served the plates.

“You’re welcome. Please let me know when you’re ready for seconds, or feel free to help yourselves.” I guessed that Scott could pack away thirds and fourths and not be full.

Elise flashed a kind smile. “I’m glad you’re—”

Her statement got cut off by the whoop of hollers from the doorway. The Virginia clan had arrived. “Age!” Had I not immediately felt their love, the surge of bodies might be overwhelming.

“*Amiche mie*!” I blurt in Italian sometimes, thanks to all the time I spent with my Italian grandmother growing up. My friends were used to it, and I suspected, secretly dug it.

Des and Skye got their hands on me first, then Caroline and Sam, and rounding out the couples who tried to hug and kiss me all at once, Kayin and Isabel. Stunning Jessie came at me next, kissed me hello, and gave me a long hug that convinced me once again how good of an act she puts on for the group. She casually dated, casually held friendships, casually tossed aside the compliments on her extraordinary beauty and athletic physique, but I knew there was very little that was casual about this woman. Had known it since we first met at UVA.

That left only Lauren. Tall, slim, beautiful Lauren. She’d been my mentor at first, then my good friend until we skipped past best friends and moved to being more like sisters. Our relationship had the sturdiness that comes with close family, and nothing felt better. Like me, she was an attorney, and also like me, she was single, which lent itself to many outings together. Tears formed in her turquoise blue eyes by the time she stepped close. She bent her 5’11” frame to kiss me and then folded her arms around me tightly.

“Austine,” she whispered, emotion choking her voice. I clung to my oldest and closest friend until both our emotions were in check. I realized I’d been kidding myself about how much I missed this incredible friend.

“Your hair!” Caroline rubbed my head when I pulled out of Lauren’s hug.

“Looking sexy, girl!” this from Kayin, my sister in drastic

hair modifications. Her own short, natural afro replaced a longer weave of straight hair only six months ago.

I scoffed at their attention and introduced them to the only other occupants in the booth. Scott hadn't seemed to notice that others were in the booth, his attention averted to the happenings on court. Elise, however, tried to hide that she'd taken careful note of our hug fest. "Everybody, this is Elise Bridie and her cousin Scott."

As the group introduced themselves, I received pointed stares from Matchmaker Des, Concerned Friend Lauren, and Casual Dating Queen Jessie. Willa and Nykos walked in just as the group finished saying hello to Elise. As host, I didn't expect to see her much, so I allowed myself to yearn while I could.

"Beautiful women who haven't been touched by a man. Heaven!" Nykos joked and received a smack on the chest from Willa. The group took the joke in stride, accustomed to his kidding manner.

"Don't make me banish you next door, Kos." Willa grinned up at him. They had an odd but very close relationship. I'd never really figured it out. "Elise," Willa noticed her finally. "It's wonderful you're here." She introduced herself to Scott and threw a conspiratorial smile at me. I wanted to die. The woman I loved was trying to set me up with a virtual, albeit gorgeous, stranger.

"Where's Quinn?" I asked to get the group thinking about something other than my pathetic, nonexistent love life.

"She's sitting courtside with the rest of her former teammates. They're doing a special presentation during the half. You'll see her later at the party at Helen's restaurant." Willa gave the impression that she enjoyed being the host of this special event, but I knew she wasn't anywhere near as comfortable as she seemed. She turned to Elise and Scott. "You'll be able to make it, I hope?"

Elise smiled politely and replied, "Scott's got other plans, but I'd love to."

"Well, I've got some work to do," Jessie announced with raised eyebrows and made her way into the Seattle Friends of Willa/A.J. lesbian box. With three whole days in a new city, she didn't intend to spend any of those nights alone. *Just what you need. Nothing like sifting through Jessie's leftovers here as well. That is, if you ever get over Willa enough to seriously date someone.*

The lights went down for player introductions, and we all settled into seats. I don't know if I consciously took the one next to Elise, or if the Virginia clan made it so that it was the only open seat. Either way, she was a pleasant surprise. Her comfort with being hit on by a woman and with the lesbian couples gave me hope that she was gay. Although, Helen and Zoë never had any hang-ups either. But, really, what did it matter? Married, Virginia-living, best friend obsession.

After the game, we piled into cars for the after party at Helen's restaurant. I hoped that Helen's place wouldn't turn into a new lesbian hot spot by the end of the evening. Last thing I needed was for all of my future bad dates to witness my comings and goings from home. None of my Seattle friends knew that I lived above the restaurant, and I wanted to keep it that way. The only way to truly prevent drop bys was to make sure no one knew where you lived, which is why I entered the restaurant like everyone else despite wanting to change out of my suit.

"Hey, Age." Quinn came up behind me and twirled me into a hug.

"Quinn, it's so good to see you."

Her athletic frame hadn't lost an ounce of fitness or muscle since she'd retired from basketball. Running around after the UVA women's team as head coach probably had something to do with it. Quinn and Jessie took fitness to another level.

"We miss you so much, girl," she relayed. Her dark blue eyes twinkled from behind the sheen of golden brown hair that swung back into place after she bent back upright from our hug. Like Lauren and Jessie, Quinn was another freakishly tall friend of mine, which had served her well playing ball. "Will and Lauren especially. Did you have to move so far away?"

Not far enough to stamp out my desire for your partner, I should have said. But offered instead, "It's worked out all right."

"So I hear. You're going to prosecute Will's case? She's so relieved about that."

"Stop praising her for moving out here, Quinn," Lauren scolded as she joined us. "I'm trying to get her to come back and go into practice with me. We could have Des custom build an office for you. Full partner, tons of interesting work, and the money's good, too."

"That's quite an offer, L." I couldn't entertain tempting proposals right now because I didn't have the strength to turn them down. "But I'm just getting settled here, and things are good."

"I don't understand why you moved, and I'm mad as hell about it now that I'm seeing you again." I could tell she meant the rebuke lightly, but her eyes shimmered with moisture.

"*Amica, per favore, basta*," I pleaded softly, using Italian because she always takes me more seriously when I resort to Italian. I couldn't take it if she started to cry.

Lauren had the ability to make me shatter every limit of my comfort zone to accommodate her requests. Not that they were so unusual: go home with her to visit her parents who became my surrogate parents, meet her gregarious group of friends who became my friends, go out to a club with her, share personal stuff that I don't usually share with others. If I didn't love her so much, I'd never do any of those things. My move to Seattle hadn't just been hard on me, and it hurt like crazy seeing her this sad. God, why couldn't I be in love with this best friend? This currently single and regally beautiful best friend? Probably because I thought of her as a sister and she's the elevation equivalent of Mt. Rainier. Other than the neck strain, at least I'd still be in Virginia with my comfortable life and good friends.

"Let's give her a break, L," Quinn stepped in, recognizing my weakening resolve. "We can visit any time, and Will's going to convince her to come back on some of her trips out here."

"She better be right, Austine," Lauren threatened, her blazingly red hair swishing over her freckled shoulders as she looked back and forth between Quinn and me.

"I like your friends," Quinn said to change the topic.

"Especially that Elise." Lauren winked at me.

"We actually work together."

"Protesting already," Lauren teased about the way I qualified the relationship. She always accused me of qualifying every relationship I had with women. She was convinced it was the reason I was perpetually single.

I threw my hands up in surrender. When Lauren gets on a why-aren't-you-with-someone kick, it can be hours before we move on to another topic. "I'm going to say hello to my friend Cyrah now. You all keep figuring out my life for me, will you?" They laughed as I made a hasty exit. Instead of heading toward Cyrah, I veered off and went into the kitchen. Nothing like a little alone time to help deal with people who want to run my life.

As expected, the kitchen was empty of people but full of the delicious cuisine that Helen prepared for the buffet. I dragged a stool over so I could sit at a cooking station with my choice of three entrees.

My hands shook a little as I pressed them onto the counter. I'd thought I was prepared for the Virginia onslaught but seeing everyone made me doubt my decision to move here. I couldn't have stayed though. I'd almost forgotten how much seeing Willa with Quinn both hurt and made me love her more. A lot of her appeal was how much she loved Quinn. Twisted, I know.

"Am I interrupting?" Elise asked from the kitchen doorway.

Interrupting, not intruding? Interesting. Barely a distinction, but I loved that she chose the word that meant "coming between" something rather than "walking in on" something. Like it was completely normal for her to think she might be coming between me and my alone time.

"No, no, come in," I offered because it was the polite thing to do but also because none of my friends would have made that same distinction. I stood and gestured to my abandoned seat then circled around the other cooking station for another stool. "You having a good time?"

"Yes, it was nice of Willa to invite me."

"That's Will," I sighed softly and sat diagonally across from her at the edge of the stainless steel counter. Elise noted my sigh with a tilt of her head, no doubt trying to utilize her mind reading skills again. To distract her, I said, "You and your cousin seem close."

"Yeah, he's all of seventeen, and I was a year older when he was born. With the age difference, it's crazy, I realize." She gave a disbelieving shake of her head.

"No, it's not." Certainty spilled out as if I'd knocked over a glass full of it.

Her disbelief now focused on me, but she said with a grateful tone, "You're the only one outside my family who doesn't think so."

"Do you see him often?"

"He used to come up from California for a few weeks each summer, but he's living with me right now." My turn for an interested head tilt. She continued, "Family dynamics and teenage issues, nothing too abnormal. He needed a willing family member who gives him the benefit of the doubt. This past semester went well, so we're taking a look at how the summer goes to see where he'll end up next year."

Awe rolled through me at the thought of taking in a teenage relative. I wouldn't even take in my adult relatives for the night. My hand moved up to act as a shelf for my chin, allowing me to lean forward in amazement. "He's lucky to have you."

"What a nice thing to say, Austy, thank you."

I wanted to know more, but we were interrupted by Willa's voice from just beyond the kitchen door. "Get your antisocial ass back out here, Age. Oh, Elise! I'm sorry. I didn't realize you were in here, too." She'd made it to the doorway but halted when she saw I wasn't alone. Her gaze shifted from Elise to me and held that determined look that always made me want to sit up and be obedient. "Listen, Age, we used the excuse of Quinn's deal to be here, but they all flew across the country for you. Don't hide in here too long. You know you're my saving grace at these social things, hon. So, please, sometime soon?"

Laughing softly, I nodded my head and watched her move back into the restaurant. We both avoided large social gatherings whenever possible but helped each other through the ones that were necessary. Turning back to Elise, I caught her staring quizzically at me.

"She's pretty fantastic," Elise offered tentatively.

"Definitely."

"She introduced me to Quinn which was quite the thrill. I went to a lot more games when Quinn played." She watched me nod enthusiastically; everyone had considered Quinn an exciting player. She added earnestly, "They seem like a great couple."

"Yeah," I agreed instantly and a little too keenly. In the same instant, I realized that I was talking to a skilled investigator who would guess that my reflexive response probably hid something.

Pushing back from her perch into a stand, she gave me a look like she'd known me for years. "Well, that Willa," she paused and placed both hands on the counter, leaning dangerously close to me. "I can see how someone might fall for her." She'd emphasized "someone" like she wasn't talking about Quinn.

Stunned, I didn't react when a hand reached out palm up, three fingers sliding gently under my chin to nudge my now ajar mouth closed. She left her fingers there for a few seconds before turning to leave without another word.

Perfect! Now people you barely know are giving you advice on your love life.

Chapter 7

Almost nothing is better than finding free parking, except maybe sliding into the space easily because you own the tiniest car sold in the United States. MINI-loving, Seattle lesbian on the go.

Breakfast on the waterfront with my friends would start our day together. I approached the restaurant knowing I'd be the first to arrive. Willa and Quinn were driving in from their house in Woodinville, and everyone else was staying at a hotel a few blocks away. I knew they'd be a while. Organizing their collective departure was always a mammoth feat.

When I saw Jessie already sitting at our reserved table, surprise wasn't my only emotion. Even after years of knowing her, Jessie's exotic beauty still struck me. Long, black, curly hair; dark brown, enigmatic eyes; unblemished, olive skin, and artistic features complimented her personal trainer body with its feminine defined muscles. She made men weep openly when she turned them down and lesbians weep silently when she ruthlessly seduced them, moved on, but still gave them hope that she might seduce them again someday. Thankfully, as her friend, I never had to worry about the weeping. Jessie didn't mess with her friends, literally and figuratively.

"Morning, Jess, where's everyone else?" I hugged her hello

and took a seat next to her.

"I told them to show up a little later."

"They actually listened?"

"Well," she started then caught the attention of the eager waiter who brought over a pitcher of orange juice to fill my glass. When he retreated, she continued, "I did tell them I needed time to make a play for you."

Just swallowed orange juice stung my throat as I coughed in surprise. She flashed a brazen smile at my reaction. "You—I—you—what?"

"Hard to believe you're a successful prosecutor, Age. You have such a way with words." Jessie's characteristic sarcasm came out, making me miss her more. She turned a little more solemn and said, "I wanted them to back off to give me time to talk to you."

"Are you in trouble, Jessamine?" Her full name crossed my lips whenever I worried about her, which wasn't often. Jessie had a self-sustaining fortitude, almost nothing affected her. I leaned forward and grabbed her hand.

"That's what I miss most about you. I say that to anyone else in the group, and they're pulling out tape recorders for blackmail purposes later. You go right for the concern, but no worries today."

"Then what did you want to talk to me about?"

She relaxed back against her chair and gave me a long stare. "Your love thing for Willa."

"Oh please!" I objected automatically and released my grip on her.

This wasn't the first time I'd heard this particular teasing accusation. If they couldn't get me to admit whom I was dating, they assumed I had a crush on someone in the group. One week it would be Jessie, the next time Lauren, and more often than not Willa because she was unavailable and never joined in the teasing. Whenever the teasing progressed to obnoxious, it meant they had someone they wanted to set me up with. They'd relentlessly harass me and I'd die of embarrassment, but no one took the teasing seriously.

Exasperated, I continued, "I'm not in love with Willa." Eyes shifty, check. Elevated pulse, check. Pants on fire, check.

"Yes, you are, and it's understandable. We're all a little in love with her." My eyes bulged at her casual and very sure confession. She guffawed, enjoying my reaction. "Truly, and it's funny, really. When you think about it, Quinn's the one with so much appeal: savvy, beautiful, caring, affectionate, former professional athlete even. But it's Willa that we'd all fall for. Her devotion is straight out of the seventeenth century. We all want that from our partners. You've seen the way she looks at Quinn. Please, if anyone ever looked at me that way…I'd change everything. But you know you have to give her up, Age."

My face burned with embarrassment, knowing I was legitimately caught this time. "Does everyone know?"

"No, they're thinking it's the same kind of awe we all feel about her if anything at all. Of course, Willa's clueless. Even when we teased you about it in front of her, she wouldn't put any stock in it. She just figures you're ultra-private like she is and that we like to tease people for no reason, which we do."

I plunked my face into my hands. Some master of illusion I'd been. After last night when Elise seemed to nail me on my feelings, I might as well get Willa's name tattooed on my shoulder. I felt Jessie's hand caress my lowered head but couldn't bring myself to say anything.

"There's good news here, shug. See, I know you'd never come between Quinn and Will. Partly because, as Willa's friend, you wouldn't want that for her, but also because Will's not the Will that you love without Quinn." She moved her hand over my head to squeeze the back of my neck. "I think you're using this love for her as an excuse not to focus on finding a relationship that's right for you."

Lifting my head, I stared at the unfamiliar earnest face of my friend. Heart-to-hearts weren't Jessie's forte. "When did you get like this?"

"I'm always deep on Saturday mornings." Jessie laughed good-naturedly.

Her joke would have been funny if I weren't so embarrassed. I began a confession, "I moved here to—to…"

"I know," Jessie responded wisely. "Not exactly a clean break but a manageable one. Baby steps, but it's time to take a few more. You're fun, kind, sexy smart, and smoldering, babe. Light this whole city up with your charm."

"Gaawwd, Jessa. You're something else."

She tossed a palm up and flashed a cocky smile. "That's true."

My laugh pulled her into a giggle, which was how Quinn and Willa found us moments later. "Morning, Age, Jessie." Quinn studied us curiously.

We stood and hugged them hello. I couldn't meet Willa's eyes, knowing I'd spontaneously combust from embarrassment. Thankfully, the rest of the group filtered in and saved me from bursting into flame. Boisterous greetings went round the table, followed by a fight over who got to sit next to whom. This spectacle, I didn't miss so much. Usually I ended up wishing I could crawl under the table while the group took evil pleasure in extending my mortification. Voices overlapped, and I almost felt sorry for the waiter who was stuck with our table. Almost, but I knew Willa would make sure he'd get the best tip of his life.

"So?" Des's voice rose above all.

Apparently Jessie understood her ambiguous question. She shook her head once and admitted easily, "No go. Struck out."

My blush flared through me as a hush fell over the table. Jessie never had to use words like that. I'm not sure she's ever struck out in her life.

"Rats!" This came from Lauren who never swore. "As weird as it would've been, at least she would have moved back home." In the five months away from them, I'd nearly forgotten that they always talked about me like I'm not at the table.

"What are the plans for today?" Quinn stepped in to save her best friend, Jessie, from certain taunting.

Everyone started talking at once, seemingly moving off the mortifying topic of Jessie's and my coupling. I was trying to concentrate on the proffered suggestions when I felt Willa lean in and speak directly in my ear. "I know Jessie didn't get here early to hit on you. I'm not going to ask what she wanted to talk to you about, but when I was having all that trouble with my company last year, she appeared at my office for a little 'talk.' At the time I blew off everything she said. Took me a couple of weeks before I realized how intuitive and spot on she'd been." As intoxicating as it was to have Willa this close, I tilted back in surprise. She smiled perceptively and finished, "I don't know what she told you this morning, but whatever her advice, take it."

I nodded thoughtfully. Part of my brain wondered what Jessie said to Willa during that difficult period for her. But most of it wondered how I was going to manage taking Jessie's advice. Perhaps Jessie was right about me avoiding a real relationship by convincing myself that I was in love with someone I couldn't have. Why hadn't I thought of that? I was relatively smart; I really should have considered that myself. It sucks when the person everyone in your group considers shallow turns out to be deeper than you.

***

Another Friday evening slowly wasting away. The Seattle lesbian scene awaited me. All I had to do was meet up with Cyrah at her favorite bar or was tomorrow night Girl4Girl? Going out tonight would be overkill if it was. The once per month lesbian event demanded a reserve of energy. Even if it was the right weekend, I doubted if I'd head down to 1st Ave tomorrow night. Last time I went I felt like my forehead flashed a neon sign reading "fresh meat." Cyrah assured me that feeling wore off after a few more visits, but I had little faith in that reassurance.

When I turned onto my street, summer exploded all around me. Every type of outdoor activity took place on the sidewalks and along the lake. Sometime last week, Joe increased his shop's hours to accommodate all the kayakers who wanted to take advantage of the nice warm evenings. Helen's restaurant stayed open two hours later as well. As long as there was light, locals found a way to cram another outdoor recreation into the day.

I resented that they made me feel lazy, but I had work to do. Of course, if my Virginia friends were still here, they'd tell me that I was using work as a noble excuse to avoid living my life. Maybe living in Seattle wasn't such a bad thing.

A kayak floated by on two legs through the door of Joe's shop as I approached my building. One of those handcrafted, wooden beauties that Joe custom made. I expected to see his head appear once the kayak was lifted off his shoulder and onto the rack of its new owner's car, but no familiar Joe. He must have finally heeded Helen's advice and hired someone to help out over the busy summer season.

The new helper and I reached the sidewalk in front of Joe's shop and my building at nearly the same time. I didn't identify his familiarity until he said, "Oh, hi. It's Austy, right?"

My hand went up against the sun's glare so I could see his face clearly. Tall, young, blond, Elise's cousin. "Yes, hi there, Scott. Are you working for Joe?"

"Yep. We got to talking at the game last week. He told me to come by and see if this is something I'd like to do." His eagerness made me want to hug him.

"Looks like it suits you just fine."

"Sure does. Joe rocks. The customers are nice, and Helen always brings over amazing food. This is ideal."

"Well, that's great, Scott. I'm happy for you. Elise must be thrilled."

He beamed with pride. "You bet. We even worked out a deal for a car and everything. That game was the greatest thing to happen to me all year!"

Got to love teenage dramatic flare. "And the basketball was pretty good, too."

He laughed easily. "Guess we'll be seeing a lot of each other this summer."

"Looks like." I nodded in reply and waved when he headed back into the store. A peaceful happiness spread through my body. I'd just met that kid, and I was overjoyed for his good fortune.

The joy pushed me up the stairs two at a time. Maybe a night among available women with Cyrah wouldn't be the worst way to end my Friday night. As I hit the landing on our floor, I noticed Helen's door opening.

"Taking a break, Helen?" I asked when she appeared in the doorway. Joe was always trying to pull her out of the kitchen on busy nights for a breather.

"Little dog walk break," Helen replied as I moved toward my door.

"Hi, Austy." A newly recognizable voice made me abandon the keys I'd just shoved into the deadbolt on my door. I swung around to see Elise emerging from Helen's loft.

"Hello," I said after a stunned moment. My startled state didn't keep me from noticing how tan and fit her arms were in that sleeveless shirt or how her linen trousers fell superbly on her lower half.

"Joe's got her cousin helping him out this summer. He finally listened to me." Helen swiped her forehead theatrically. "Scott's going to save Joe from aging five years like he usually does each summer."

Elise smiled fondly at Helen. "I think Scott's the lucky one in this venture."

"Absolutely not. You know how late Joe would be working tonight if Scott weren't here to help?"

"I'm glad he's working out so far."

"He's a great kid, Elise. I should have thought to have him call you earlier once I knew Joe was going to do inventory tonight. You wouldn't be stuck here otherwise."

Elise glanced at me with a shy smile then turned back to Helen. “That’s okay. We had a nice walk with the dogs, and I can take my book over to sit by the lakeshore.”

“Please come to the restaurant and have some dinner while you wait. Aust, help me persuade her. You haven’t eaten yet, right? Come on, you’ll both love my special tonight.”

If I didn’t know Helen well, I’d think she was trying to set me up. But knowing Helen, this was equal parts guilt for keeping Elise’s cousin past normal work hours and feeding the people that she knew. Still stuck on Elise standing on my landing, I barely noticed Helen staring expectantly at me.

“Um, sure, thanks, that sounds good. Elise?”

“That would be nice. Thank you for the suggestion, Helen.”

“Let me make sure there’s a table cleared for you.” Helen excitedly swept down the stairs.

Elise watched her speedy retreat. When she raised her gaze to meet mine, it felt like she’d just caressed my face with something incredibly soft. I sucked in a shallow breath at the sensation.

“…really, I can occupy myself.”

“I’m sorry?” I shook my head, not hearing what she’d been saying.

She tipped her head, questioning my sudden loss of concentration. “I said if you have other plans, I’m fine to eat by myself. Scott shouldn’t be too long. I’m definitely going to have to revise the timeline on getting him a car.”

“I know better than to pass up one of Helen’s specials,” I asserted with more confidence than I felt.

“Did you want to change out of your suit first? I don’t mind waiting.” Her eyes skimmed slowly over my frame. I thought I saw an approving glint when they moved back up to mine, but I couldn’t be sure.

“No, I’m fine.” I stepped toward her to start us down the stairs, but she held up a stopping hand.

She crossed the short distance and leaned past me so close that I felt her brush my suit jacket. I don’t know what was more remarkable to me: that I didn't move or that I didn't want to move. She smelled of lavender again, and my face nearly touched her well-defined bare shoulder as she completed her stretch. When she tipped back upright, I found myself slightly above eye level with her full lips not entirely conscious that I was desperate for her to kiss me.

"You left your keys in your door." She raised her arm and jingled my keys near her head.

The sound jerked me out of the sudden craving to snatch her face in my hands and devour her mouth. Still bewildered, I felt her hand grasp one of mine and bring it upward where she dropped my keys into the awaiting palm. She used her other hand to wrap my fingers around them and lightly squeeze my fist.

"Thanks," I said a little breathlessly, floored by my feelings of desire.

"You're welcome," came her soft response. Her eyes considered mine briefly before she stepped back. "Shall we?"

She started down the staircase not waiting for my reply. Before tonight, I'd never been the type of person to check someone out as they walked away, but my eyes weren't listening to my brain this time. *My, my, my. She just paralyzed you with a look, and now you're checking her out from behind. Who cares if this is only a casual dinner between work acquaintances? Stop analyzing and enjoy the evening.*

Chapter 8

"You're not done?" Elise looked down at my barely touched meal. We'd been eating and talking for over an hour, about what, I couldn't tell you. Just like my meal, I hardly noticed anything other than the way her lips moved and her eyes glittered. Her hands, definitely skillful I'd decided, floated and gestured often while she spoke. "You weren't hungry, were you?"

My head shook twice on its own and a breath escaped with a smile. "I, I don't, I'm…" I stammer when I'm nervous; get used to it. So far I'd managed not to act like a pod person on this sort of, wannabe date that's not a date because I don't know if she's gay or interested. I waited for her to playfully echo my stammer; everyone always did. However, she seemed happy to wait patiently. After a cleansing breath, I finished, "I don't eat a whole lot."

Her soothing eyes slinked down along my torso and back up. "I imagine not." I braced myself for the likely ribbing about how "little" I am. Not that she had much room to talk, taller by maybe four inches and the very definition of height-weight proportionate. "At least you eat real food. I used to know some women who would eat rice cakes and tissue paper to feel full then smoke to satisfy their oral fixations."

Relieved that she hadn't made fun of my size, I laughed at the off the wall comment. "Sounds like you hung out with a bunch of models." I'd been joking but her raised eyebrows and shy smile told me I got it right. "Oh." I found that was a universal application for all manner of conversational halts.

"How do you do that?" she asked after a long pause. At my look of confusion, she continued, "Control your curiosity like that? I don't know one person who wouldn't question me further about my conversation slip. And we already discussed you not asking me to tell you what Jake said about you."

My turn to smile. "Slip, eh?"

"Yeah, a slip. I never mention—"

Helen materialized out of thin air, startling us. "Am I a culinary genius or what? I must be, because you ate more than you usually do, Austy. These leftovers should take you through the middle of next week, wouldn't you say?" Helen joked before turning to Elise. "About a half hour more for Scott. Would either of you like some wine? We just got in Warren's newest Pinot, Aust." I shook my head at the offer and watched Elise do the same. "Coffee or dessert, perhaps? Although, I shouldn't be rewarding you for not eating all your dinner."

"Coffee would be great for me. Thank you," Elise told her.

"The same, thanks, Helen." I watched her signal for coffee and clear our plates, shaking her head at how much was left of mine.

"Can I ask who Warren is?" Elise inquired after a server came by with our coffee.

"My brother."

Her eyes left mine momentarily moving to the left side of the table. "Josephs? So, that's what the 'J' stands for."

I glanced over to the right and saw that she'd put together Helen's remark and my brother's name from the wine list sitting on the table. She bordered on scary observant.

"Your brother," she started and peered at the wine list again. "Actually, brothers, it looks like, farm or make wine or both?"

"Technically, they're grape growers and own the winery with a fantastic winemaker on staff. My dad sells his grapes to some of the larger wineries."

"Yes, I see." Her finger moved down the wine list to a famous brand maker with the Josephs Cellars label affixed. My brothers' winery went by Josephs Brothers. So they're not exactly marketing geniuses, but they make damn good wine. "No room for sister Austy?"

"Sister A.J. needed to marry Damon next door to be part of the wine business permanently," I relayed in a tone equal parts jest and residual resentment.

"And will I find the surely heartbroken Damon on this list as well?"

Okay, she'd just turned what could have been an awkward comment into a good-natured tease, possibly even flirtation. Maybe I should test it. "I could ask Warren for you if you're really interested?"

Slowly a smile widened her mouth, and my heart beat faster, worried that she'd actually answer in the affirmative. "Warren's older or younger?"

"Younger," I said after a couple of seconds, happy not to have an answer one way or another and to move off the subject of my "intended."

"What aren't you saying?" She leaned forward onto the table.

"Can't you ever turn that off? Or are you always trying to look for something where nothing exists?"

"Nice effort at a deflection." Her hand lifted from the table and sliced downward, pointing at me. "Wait a minute; you're a twin. That's why the hesitation with younger."

"Holy cow, you're like a psychic and a human lie detector. Stop it!" I was only partly joking, freaked out that she picked up on something I'd stopped telling people in college.

She bestowed a throaty laugh that made the men at the next table look over. I hoped that my own response didn't look as goofy as theirs, but that laugh made my skin tingle. "Are you two close?"

"No, no, no. I'm not going to let you practice your detecting skills on me again." I waved off her question. "Especially since you're using this whole discussion to avoid talking about your earlier admitted conversation slip." Her mouth twitched slightly. "So, tell me about hanging out with a bunch of models."

A long moment passed where she was obviously deciding how to respond. "We didn't really hang out so much as work together."

I don't know why I found her statement so shocking. She's certainly gorgeous enough, but nothing else about her said model. Not that I'd met any other models, but it seemed to me that models sought attention, compliments, favors, and any other manner of notice. From what I'd seen, Elise disregarded any consideration people gave her. If she was aware that people found her stunning, she veiled her reaction thoroughly.

"You did modeling work?" Inquirer of the obvious, that's me.

She ducked her head downward as if embarrassed. "It paid for college and grad school; otherwise I wouldn't have done it."

"You did a lot of modeling work if it paid for all that." I found her unease with the subject charming.

"From sixteen to twenty-two." Her eyes moved across my whole face, taking careful note of my reaction.

"Why'd you stop?"

She laughed like I'd said something funny. "You mean, why aren't I still modeling more than a decade later? You sure know how to make someone feel good."

I couldn't stop the blush. I guess that was a pretty stupid question, but she seemed pleased nonetheless. Trying to sound like I knew something about modeling, I pushed on. "Twenty-two seems young to quit."

"It can be, but I only did sportswear jobs where I'd participate in whatever activity matched the clothes or equipment I wore. Most of those jobs cap out at twenty-five. My favorite shoots were for skiwear or equipment because I skied competitively from grade school through college." She shifted her eyes out the window of the restaurant and her breathing became more shallow. "I crashed on one of the jobs. Hundreds of competitive races against the best skiers in the world, and I crash on a modeling shoot." She scoffed and let a hand drop roughly from her chin to her thigh. "They watered down one spot on the course because the ice reflected nicely in the light, but they didn't tell me. I caught an edge and wrapped around a tree. Ended my skiing career, my spot on the Olympic team, and my scholarship at Colorado."

"I didn't mean to make you remember that," I spoke up after digesting her tale. Saying "I'm sorry" didn't seem enough.

"You didn't. Besides, I was the one who brought it up in the first place. It felt good to tell you. I haven't spoken about it in a long time."

"That's quite a lot to deal with at twenty-two."

She smiled ruefully. "Life altering or so my younger self thought. I was too young to realize that it was inevitable. That, actually, it made me focus on a long-term career at precisely the right time in my life."

"I meant, well, I assume you had injuries. That must have been the hardest part. At least, that's what other athletes have told me." I caught a glimpse of amazement cross her face. "It's great, though, that you've got that positive outlook in hindsight."

"Now who's the annoying mind reader?" She showed me a sinister smile, and the look burned itself into my brain. There would be no forgetting that smile.

"Hey, Lis," Scott spoke from miles above the bubble I'd created for just Elise and me.

She did an astonished double-take, evidently caught up in the bubble, too. "Hey, Buster. All done?"

"Yep. Joe's gonna show me how to build a kayak next

week." He was all smiles. It didn't take a psychic to figure out he loved his job and thought the world of Joe.

"Don't let him fiberglass your fingers to the kayak, Scott. He gets pretty liberal with that coating," I joked, and he laughed at the thought.

"Did you eat?" Elise asked.

"Yep, Helen brought over some pork roast for us."

"You thanked her profusely, of course?" Elise pressed in a half serious, half kidding tone.

"Yeah, Lis," he responded in lighthearted exasperation. "You almost ready? I could bring the car around to the front?"

Elise and I laughed at his eagerness to drive her car. She glanced at me with what I hoped was regret, but I was probably projecting. "Sure." She fished her keys out of her purse for Scott.

"Yee-haw!" Scott exaggerated his joy before turning to me. "I'm sure I'll see you soon, Austy."

"See ya, Scott." I watched him practically sprint out of the restaurant in search of Elise's car. "You call him Buster?"

"I've got a grandfather named Scott, an Uncle Scott and every male cousin's middle name is Scott. There are enough Scotts in the family. When he was a kid, he used to run into things all the time and bounce right off them with a huge grin. Reminded me of those great Buster Keaton movies."

"Well, I don't know how good he is at pratfalls, but he is terrific."

"I agree." She smiled proudly and searched out the window. "I'd probably better head out, or he may start doing donuts in the vacant lot next door." She reached into her purse for her wallet.

"Believe me; you'll never win the fight with Helen over paying for a meal that she's invited you to. She considers this like inviting you to dinner at her home."

"You're not kidding?"

"Nope, but she won't let you out of here without a goodbye, though. Come on, let's go find her."

I got up and set my napkin on the table. Elise swung her purse onto her shoulder, and we moved toward the kitchen. True to form, Helen emerged right then, as if she had radar for outgoing friends from her restaurant. We said our thanks and goodbyes, complete with hugs.

A warm breeze swept by as we stepped outside, but I felt a baffling shiver run through me. Maybe I was just too used to a Virginia summer, no matter how warm it might be.

Elise turned to me once we'd cleared the door. "Thanks for enjoying dinner with me."

"An unexpected pleasure," I responded without thinking. "I mean, you know, not you. I, I meant, because I, I didn't...I didn't expect to see you when I got home tonight."

Elise's smile told me she enjoyed my stammering recovery attempt. She let me suffer for a few seconds before leaning in to hug me lightly. Her mellifluous voice filled my ear. "I know what you meant."

Scott screeched the car to a halt in the street, and Elise stiffened in my arms. She stepped back and shook her head, laughing quietly. "Boys. I never really got 'em."

She held up a hand in parting and turned toward the idling car. Music blared onto the street when she opened the door. I would have laughed at the teenage equivalent of a hearing test with all that thumping, but a thumping of my own drowned out his music. Did she just tell me she was gay? Maybe she was referring to how different adolescent boys were to what she went through as a young woman, not necessarily anything to do with men. That was probably it, but my pounding heart clearly wanted it to be the other.

Unrestrained attraction. *Wow!* I'd forgotten what having a crush on a woman felt like. Probably a straight woman and, the way she looks, certainly an unavailable woman. But, still, a woman who wasn't my best friend. I could get used to this feeling.

Chapter 9

Criminals are rarely like what you see in movies or read about in books. They aren't masterminds or geniuses tempted to apply their intelligence for illegal personal gains. For the most part, criminals tend to be idiots, which makes my job easier but sometimes redundant. Let's not even discuss how unlikely it is that they end up looking like George Clooney or Brad Pitt.

Monday, I made an eve of trial offer to the counsel of an accused bank robber to save the taxpayers money and my time on this sure winner. The defendant, after robbing the bank, couldn't get his car to start, so he went back into the bank to call for a tow truck. I kid you not. What's even more idiotic was that his whole defense hinged on what they were calling "mistaken identity." The police apprehended this guy while he was still on the phone in the bank with the cash bags lying at his feet. Not much left to be mistaken there. The only difficult part of the case was the fact that I needed to waste even an hour on it, but sometimes it took the imminent threat of a trial for rationality to take hold.

Tuesday, I managed to have an elusive mail fraud defendant served. Once we'd tracked her down, she'd been in what my process servers were calling hibernation. If she went to work, she never came out of the back office so she couldn't be served. Within ten minutes of my field trip out there, I put the papers in her hand. A lesson learned in my youth taught by my three fly-off-the-handle uncles. Borderline fury mixed with a touch of shrewdness never fails to grab the attention of the person running the joint. It had been a humiliating experience during my adolescence. Yet, as a prosecutor who wants to coax someone out from a back office, I found it both effective and fun, especially since I knew it was an act. I was never really sure with my uncles.

Wednesday, I brought a defendant to tears while taking her deposition. That's always fun. She apparently thought that taking her child across state lines to visit her jailed boyfriend was a smart idea. Even though it wasn't her custody weekend, and she didn't bother to tell the custodial parent. Once there, she decided to remain in the other state to live with the boyfriend's family and refused to acknowledge the custody agreement. She showed up in family court with a set of forged adoption papers to force the new state to accept the jailed boyfriend as the adoptive father. I think she burst into tears because she finally realized just how stupid she was.

This morning, I spent picking off motion after motion on upcoming trials. Overall a productive week. Tonight, I was meeting Cyrah at her favorite bar because I decided I needed a little challenge this week.

Short Stack appeared at my office door without so much as a whimper. Perhaps he wasn't feeling well. "New one for you, Austy." He tapped a finger against the file he held to his chest.

"Is it your goal to burn out every new hire within six months, Kyle?"

"Funny." His expression said otherwise. "You're getting better results than half the veterans around here, and this one's big. Money laundering under RICO. I'm assigning Roger as second chair because he's the only one here who's done a racketeering case."

"If he's got RICO experience, why not have him first

chair?" It wasn't that I wanted to offload my work as much as I didn't like having Short Stack putting someone with twelve years in the office as second chair to someone with five months.

"All the evidence is from computer files and wire transfer orders. Roger could handle it, but you make the jury understand these tech heavy cases so much better."

"As long as you're sure." I sighed and watched the file spin through the air and onto my desk.

"I'm always sure," he declared in parting.

RICO charges, finally, a little challenge sprinkled with enjoyment. Eagerly I opened the file and scanned through the evidence list and witness briefs. When I moved out here, I didn't expect to land a racketeering case in my first year. I'm all about the fun.

"Somebody's having a good day," a now familiar voice pronounced from the doorway.

The smile I'd been wearing from the prospect of the new case widened when I looked up at Elise. That pesky school of fish swam swiftly through my midsection again, causing a little lightheadedness. She was in a skirt today conservatively an inch above the knee but plenty enticing. For instance, I was having a hard time not fantasizing about how soft the skin was at the back of her knee. If my friend Des was here witnessing my perusal of Elise, she'd say something crass like how badly I needed to get laid. Crass, but true.

"Hi," I tried for nonchalant, but I'm guessing she saw right through me. "What are you doing here?"

She tipped her head back toward the hallway and said, "I was going over an investigation on a case that Rachel's taking to trial next week."

"Wasn't Jake on that?" I waved her inside the office to sit in one of my guest chairs. I tried to keep my eyes from staring at her toned calves as she floated into the chair and kicked one leg over the other. Her skirt rode up another couple of inches, and my mouth dried with each revealing hike of material.

Oblivious to my parched state, she responded, "He put in for a transfer to Phoenix to help out the family business now that his father's gone. He wanted to be more available to them."

Jake's dedication helped relieve my dazed reverie. "Amazing how it takes a death to make us realize which things are really important in life."

"You're so right." She sloped into that sexy head tilt again. "Jake asked me to tell you goodbye for him. I think he was a little enchanted with you."

"No." I tossed aside her remark without any consideration. Jake and I had worked seven cases together, and he was never more than affable with me.

Elise studied me for a long moment, not letting up on her sexiness. "Fascinating. You don't believe someone could be enchanted by you?" She was taking great enjoyment from my astonished expression. Before I could react, she stood up to leave. "I didn't really mean that as a question. Good seeing you, Austy."

Sassy, smart, and sexy: the very definition of trouble for me.

***

"Wanna dance, cutie?" I turned around on my stool at the bar to stare into the sunglasses of a tall woman. Sunglasses? One, it was overcast outside, and two, we were inside. Had it not been for the sunglasses, I would have thought her short blond hair, heart shaped face, and surely, collagen injected lips attractive.

"No, thank you," I responded politely.

Sunglasses at Night left without another word. Lesbians know how to take "no" for an answer. For the most part, anyway.

"What was wrong with her?" Cyrah asked from her perch next to me.

I twisted my head toward her with a threatening look. It

annoyed me when friends played pimp and questioned every social move I made. She was hard to stay perturbed with, though, especially with her youthfully innocent face and good nature. Tonight, she wore a leather headband to pull her reddish-black, corkscrew curls off her face and silver eye shadow across her mocha colored lids to highlight her dark brown eyes. No other visible makeup adorned her dark complexion. Decked out in snug black leather, she looked more like she worked on a sci-fi television show. Unfortunately, the extra forty pounds that flattered her fuller frame would probably keep her from getting the starring role.

"Nothing. I don't like to dance, remember?" I answered, knowing Cyrah's selective memory became more and more aggravating as each get-a-date night wore on.

The Rose was in full bloom tonight, all pun intended. Thursday nights were happening; why, I'd never figured out. I found it the best night to join Cyrah because, with work on Fridays, I had a legitimate reason to skip out early. Hence the reason I suck at being a lesbian in Seattle.

Thus far, the evening served only to put me on good terms with Cyrah and the rest of my Seattle lesbian contingent. If I don't make an effort at least once a month to go to one of these clubs, they'd stalk me at my office and the courthouse. They knew that as a tool of persuasion threatening to drop me as a friend wasn't as effective as constantly being in my face.

It probably didn't help my evening's quest much that I couldn't stop picturing Elise's head tilt and sexy smile. I didn't worry about the little details, like not knowing if she was a lesbian, an unattached lesbian, or an unattached and interested lesbian. I focused only on the positives: clever, amusing, beautiful, sweet, and responsible. If the evening here dragged on longer, I'd probably have just enough time to list all the rest of her positives.

"Hey, Cyr, Aust." Ruth came over and kissed Cyrah then raised her palm for a high-five from me. Unless we're on a sports court, I really prefer to forgo the high-five for something more common like a simple hello.

"You alone tonight, Ruth?" Cyrah's eyes glanced about in search of Ruth's usual tag along friends.

"Not for long. Just grabbed a table with Fiona and came over to get some beers." Ruth pushed between us and got a bartender's attention for her drink order. She'd gotten a hair cut and now the black strands barely moved past a buzz cut. When I spotted her earlier, Cyrah told me that she took her hair down to a summer cut once a year. I'd gotten used to the longer style since meeting her in February. She wore a white t-shirt with rolled up sleeves and jeans with rolled up cuffs à la 1950's. How she'd become friends with Willa in the first place always perplexed me. They couldn't be more different, but Willa had this magical way about her that prevented judging people.

"Good get, girl," Cyrah commented on Ruth's date. "You like yourself a girly femme, don't you?"

They shared a smile, assigning labels like they were file clerks in my office. Half the time I sat clueless while they filtered through the spectrum of possible classifications for women in the bar. I was fairly convinced they made up some of the "types" when I admitted that my friends only used the two standards back in Virginia. Apparently in Seattle, you couldn't just be femme or butch. No, there were all sorts of variations, and Ruth and Cyrah loved nothing better than irking me by running the gamut each time. Although, the fact that a lot of the women in the bar didn't exactly dress to kill, or even maim for that matter, probably warranted a special classification. We-live-in-a-town-where-it-rains-280-days-a-year-so-we-might-as-well-dress-for-it femme or butch. Clearly, I'm not as good at labeling as Ruth and Cyrah.

"Speaking of gorgeous femmes," Ruth started, "what's the story with that babe from the Storm game the other week?"

"Huh?" I played dumb, hoping her drinks would arrive soon.

"What was her name, Cyr? You know the one who sat with

that young dude? Silky brunette, emerald eyes, and a face that could allow an artist to retire after only one portrait. Tight body, too. I bet it's even more perfect than her face. Lordy, what fun I could have with that body."

Every muscle I had contracted at her suggestive leer and coarse remark. With each heart palpitation the urge to smack her swelled. Always before, the impulse was fleeting at best, but now I actually wanted to stop her any way I could from talking about Elise that way. I did the only thing I could think of to cut her off without physically assaulting her. I causally introduced, "We work together."

"How do you concentrate?" Cyrah asked in awe. I blew out a single laugh to let her know that I thought she was joking, just not too funny of a joke.

"Is she new to the area? I've never seen her here or at any of the monthlies." Ruth came back from her fantasies long enough to ask a troubling question.

"Really?" I had to work hard at sounding casual this time.

"Nope. Thought she was one of your Virginia lezzies. Ooh, and tell me about that irresistible honey, Jessie. What's her story?"

I let her discuss Jessie's overpowering allure with Cyrah while I considered Ruth's comments about Elise. With her casual observation, she managed to shatter my hope of a normal relationship that didn't include feelings for another unattainable woman. Ruth was in here nearly every night as one of the most popular lesbian spots in the city. She went to all the monthlies, and even some of the gay bars where lesbians were welcome but not exactly encouraged to attend. Logical conclusion: Elise wasn't a high femme, girly femme, dykey femme, andro femme, or any other kinda femme. Screwed, I know.

Chapter 10

Midday on Saturday, I took advantage of another warm, sunny day. Warm by Seattle standards, I should say, at all of seventy-six degrees outside. I envisioned my Virginia crew sweltering out on Caroline's café patio, drinking sweet ice tea and trying to keep from bursting into flame in the over one hundred degree heat. Some things I really didn't miss at all about Charlottesville.

A cool breeze swept off the ship canal as I strolled along the sparse Burke Gilman trail, hearing the shouts of the coxswain on the practicing crew shells, the sailboat horns signaling the University Draw Bridge for passage through to Lake Washington and the splash of smaller craft oars gliding the kayaks and canoes in the canal. Seattle folk loved their water sports.

I thought about driving up to Greenlake and watching some recreation league softball game or perhaps seeing if I could get in on a volleyball game. High ambitions given that a new historical fiction novel waited on my coffee table when I got home. Reading would probably win out, but at least I was outside now. I wonder if Cyrah and Ruth added a new label once they'd met me: booky femme.

Joe's shop was quiet for a Saturday. Only the skeletal metal frames remained where the kayaks would normally hang. The entire stock rented out, probably for the day. A sign posted in the window indicated that the owner was around the corner if customers needed help. To prolong my outdoor exposure, I decided to say hello and followed the directions. It was immediately apparent why the owner was out of his shop. Two forms bent under the hood of a 1965 Mustang Coupe. Short black hair and short blond hair bobbed on the heads of Joe and Scott as they tinkered with the engine of this car. Scott must have reached the end of his timeline on getting a car.

"Nice ride," I shouted, getting their attention.

"Hi, Austy," Scott beamed, straightening up to beckon me over. "Isn't it great? Elise wanted to get something newer, but Joe convinced her that we could work on an older one together. I just picked it up this morning. It got me here and runs pretty well, but it needs a lot of work."

"Starting with a new clutch, which is one thing I'm not very familiar with," Joe admitted despondently. He looked as heartbroken as Scott did about it. Tools at the ready, a '65 -'68 Mustang manual open on the fender, and they stood around like two kids rained out of a championship little league game.

"Well, you're in luck, 'cause working on clutches is the only thing I know how to do with cars," I reported confidently, consumed by a need to erase their gloominess.

"For real?" Scott gawked in amazement.

"To be honest, I only watched my brother put in a new clutch, but I repaired one on a tractor myself. So, we could give it a try, or were you thinking of bringing it to a mechanic?"

"A mechanic's going to be expensive," Joe told me. "We've found a replacement at a scrap yard that's reasonable, but I didn't want to start that work without some help."

"Help's here, fellas."

"All right!" Scott yelped and extended his hand for a high-five. Okay, this was an appropriate high-five moment.

Hours later, Scott and I were the two forms bent over the

engine block working on installing the newly acquired clutch. It took a while for Scott to procure the clutch and for me to study up on all the steps. Things seemed to be going smoothly, even down a mechanic. Joe had to return to the shop an hour ago for the influx of kayak returns as the day ended.

I'd forgotten what manual labor felt like, having left it behind in the vineyards when I went off to college. My hands were greasy and getting rougher by the minute, my back started to ache from the crouch over the engine and perspiration dripped nearly everywhere. Oh yeah, the fruits of manual labor.

"You did more than just watch your brother do this," Scott said after I'd walked through the process of sliding the clutch into place.

"I helped Warren a little with his car, but my other brother, Graham, stranded me in an orchard one morning with a tractor that burned a clutch three rows into my disking of the field. I walked two miles to the nearest farm house to call him. He said if I wanted to get out of the orchard before 9:00 p.m. when he could get away from one of the vineyards, I better learn how to fix the clutch myself."

"Harsh!" Scott decided.

I couldn't help but laugh. "We didn't get along all that well."

"Why didn't you call your other brother or your parents?"

"My parents were out of town, and Warren and I were too young to legally drive, so I was kinda stuck waiting on Graham."

"You drove a tractor before you could drive a car?"

"That's usually the way it works with farmers. All turned out well for you, though, my friend. If Graham had come to my rescue, I wouldn't know what I was doing here." I glanced over my shoulder, taking in the concentration on his face. He wanted to learn as much as help get this clutch installed. "What about you, kid, got any evil brothers?"

He clapped a hand on the fender, laughing heartily. "No,

only evil sisters. Actually, more like meddling. They're all way older. Two are around Elise's age and one's ten years older than me. I'm the last of the cousins by a long stretch. They all hung out together during holidays and summers. Some went to school together, so it's more like they're all one big family of siblings. Then I came along, and Elise is the only one who treats me like the rest of the cousins, not some kid who needs to be told what to do all the time."

"That's a drag."

"Yep. I kinda got fed up with it last fall, and my mom and sisters started to freak when I stopped doing everything they said. Things got worse as my mom dragged the whole family in to 'deal' with me, but one call to Elise and over Christmas break I moved up here." He handed me the right socket wrench without my needing to ask. When he caught my eye, he said, "She's good at fixing things, not cars, but problems."

"Really?" I asked in polite interest, wondering if I should use this kid to find out as much as I possibly could about his nearly irresistible cousin. No, that would be wrong, wouldn't it?

"Yep. We kinda think alike, so she helps me work through things. Best thing is she handles explaining it all to the family so they get off my back."

"Sounds ideal." I shifted back upright and resisted gripping my lower back to stretch backward. I'd be down one t-shirt if I put my hands anywhere near it.

"She's the best, but don't tell her I told you so." He bumped his shoulder against me in jest. Thankfully I was standing against the car's grill, or I might have stumbled from the force of his playful bump. I'm not sure he fully grasped the differences in our statures.

"Your secret's safe with me, kid." I went back to stretching over the engine.

After a long moment, Scott spoke again. "So, can I ask you a question?"

"Sure," I said, hunching down uncomfortably.

"Why don't you have a boyfriend?" I froze for a moment at the unexpected nature of the question. He continued, "I've been working here for a couple of weeks, and no guys come over to pick you up. Maybe I shouldn't have asked. I just wondered why someone like you doesn't have a boyfriend."

Pulling back out from under the hood, I looked up at this earnest kid. He didn't have a whole lot of evidence for his assumption, but for a teenager he was pretty observant. A characteristic that seemed to run in the family. I didn't sense any hidden meaning to his question, so I answered honestly. "I'm gay."

"Oh." Scott used my universal conversation filler to digest my statement. Just as quickly, he turned to the layout of tools, grabbed a different socket, slapped it into my hand, and said with a neutral tone, "Okay."

If only the rest of the country would react so nonplussed about the whole issue. Perhaps his laid-back reaction meant that he knew enough gay people to make it commonplace for him? Maybe a certain captivating cousin? Wouldn't he mention that though? Unless she was seeing someone already. *Stop thinking about this!*

"…doing what you do?"

I'd zoned out, hoping that he'd offer up something about Elise and missed what he asked. "What's that?" I turned back to work on the clutch.

"Your job, do you like it? Is it cool putting criminals away? I bet you're way smart."

"I do like my job. It's nice knowing that I'm doing my part for justice. And I guess I'm smarter than the average bear. What about you? What would you like to do, or is that like a totally adult pressure question?"

He laughed easily again. I was really starting to like this kid. "No, that's okay. I think what Elise used to do is awesome, so I'm thinking about that. But I like driving fast, so maybe an Indy racer."

"A race car driver, huh? Adventurous." I was glad he

wasn't my kid; I'd be far too worried about him circling a race track at 215 mph. "FBI's good too, though. You said what Elise used to do, is she doing something else now?"

"She used to be a field agent. Traveled around a lot because she worked a specialty. Something to do with tracking internet criminals, those sickos that mess with kids. Now, she's an analyst and stays in town mostly. I think she gave up the field work so I could live with her here, but she won't admit it."

Surprise made me fumble with the socket wrench. Elise was so good at computer forensics, I just assumed she'd been investigating those kinds of claims and providing expert testimony since she'd become an agent. This information was definitely worth all the grease on the hands.

I instinctively wanted to put his worry at ease. "Maybe she was ready for a change, and you provided the excuse."

He looked wiser than his years just then and agreed halfheartedly, "Maybe."

"How's it going out here?" Joe called out when he appeared at the start of the vacant lot. "Am I missing all the fun?"

"Leaning a lot, Joe. Austy's saving our butts."

"That's great." Joe peeked over the engine block at our progress. "Didn't you say you had to get home by seven tonight, Scott?"

"Yeah, why?"

"It's six-fifteen now. It doesn't look like the 'Stang is ready to go yet?"

Scott looked panic stricken as he waited for my response. With a growing sense of guilt, I relayed, "We're at least another hour away, Scott, sorry. I didn't know you had a time limit today, or I would have suggested we do this some other time."

"Oh man, maybe Elise can pick me up on her way home from work."

"I'd take you home, but I'm helping out in the restaurant tonight. I can get you to the right bus stop if Elise isn't around, but I don't know if you'll make it home by seven. You got a hot date?" Joe kidded him.

Embarrassed, Scott responded, "No. Just a party I'm going to. A friend's coming by to pick me up. It's a surprise party, so we have to be there on time."

"You better go call Elise or get your friend to come down here to pick you up. Otherwise I'll take you over to the U and get you on the right bus north."

"Why don't I give you a lift home?" I offered. Only part of me thought of the benefit of possibly seeing Elise when I dropped him off. The rest of me felt the full weight of guilt that I didn't tell him a clutch job takes a few hours without the right tools.

"Would you? That's great, Austy, thanks."

"No problem. Why don't you pack up Joe's tools? I'm going to change out of these clothes. Give me ten minutes, and we'll get you home."

He'd already started gathering up all the tools before he shut the hood. I jogged back to the shop and used the workroom sink, digging into the container of special hand cleanser to spread around my nearly solid black hands. The stuff worked like magic. Black rinse turned clear, and my hands looked like always.

Upstairs in the shower, I felt the tingle and heat of excitement at the prospect of seeing Elise. Our meetings had all been casual, nothing I could have prepared for or worried about. Now, something gnawed inside my stomach, and I had to acknowledge that it had nothing to do with the fact that I hadn't eaten since breakfast.

Five minutes in the shower restored my confidence a bit and helped with some of the stiffness from bending over an engine this afternoon. I didn't have time to worry about what I'd wear, so I threw on my favorite khakis and a short sleeve collared shirt. Not exactly "notice me" date attire, but I felt comfortable. And when you're starting to waver from nerves, comfort is key. I finished my usual makeup application and added lipstick and eye shadow to compensate for the fact that my outfit didn't scream "sleep with me."

Scott was just saying goodbye to Joe when I came back downstairs. His t-shirt and jeans were in immaculate order, having been protected by the work overalls that Joe used when spraying fiberglass. The dirty smudges on his face had disappeared, and his hands were grease free. He'd also run wet fingers through his hair to force cooperation. He was a handsome enough kid; maybe I should ask why he didn't have a date tonight.

"Don't let Helen work you too hard tonight, Joe," I teased in parting.

"You guys have fun." Joe waved to us as we started toward the garage.

When Scott and I approached my car, he stopped walking. "Is the MINI yours?"

Boys and cars, I had to laugh. "Yes, have you ridden in one?"

"Nope, always wanted to. These things are cool." He reached out and touched it with reverence.

"Then I guess you've never driven one either?" I gave him a mischievous grin and tossed the keys, hoping his wide-eyed wonder wouldn't make him miss. Only a small part of me worried that he might be a bad driver, but I figured if Elise let him drive, he probably wouldn't kill us.

"No way!" He plucked the keys out of the air and stared at me like I was pulling the best practical joke he'd ever been party to.

Anyone who's ever watched Saturday Night Live in the 90's knows the only answer to that question. "Way," I responded and hustled around to the passenger side. "Make sure you slide that seat back before trying to get in or you might permanently injure yourself." His six foot frame was in jeopardy, or at least his knees were.

"Wicked sick!" he uttered as he slid into the adjusted seat, tweaked the mirrors, put on his belt and started the car. "Sweet."

With that we were on our way. Dropping in on a hopefully available, exceptionally attractive lesbian. Or making a fool of myself over a likely unavailable, insanely gorgeous straight woman. Either way, the unfamiliar blast of exhilaration mixed with apprehension was a welcome change from my usual Saturday evening quiet.

Chapter 11

We pulled off the freeway at 220th and headed down to the Edmonds waterfront. Quaint homes lined both sides of the street as we entered the residential area. Scott turned into the driveway of a craftsman style home painted pale yellow with white shutters. Evergreen plantings, Japanese maples, and river rock covered the front yard. Not a blade of grass in sight, the only house on the block without a cookie cutter lawn.

"It doesn't look like Elise is here, but let me show you the house," Scott offered politely as he turned off the engine.

"That's all right. I just wanted to get you home in time." Disappointment besieged me, but I managed to sound relaxed.

"Thanks for letting me drive. This is a great car." He moved to get out.

I started to follow his lead just as the front door opened and Elise stepped out onto the porch. Her sudden appearance stunned me into temporary paralysis. She had her hair in a ponytail, wore walking shorts that showed far more leg than I'd seen on Thursday and a shirt open to a tantalizing bit of cleavage. I had to close my eyes to gain control of my heartbeat.

"I was getting a little worried, Buster. Sean called to say

he'd be here in five minutes, and you weren't back yet." Elise glanced at the car. "Where's your car?"

I completed my earlier effort of stepping out of the car. Shyly, I waved. "Hi."

Her head jerked toward me, obviously caught off guard. "Hi. Did something happen?"

"We got too late a start on my clutch to finish it. Austy offered to drop me home."

Elise processed everything more quickly than I would have had the situation been reversed. Hell, I'd had about twenty minutes to prepare myself for seeing her, and I could barely open a car door. "And how is it that you stepped out from behind the wheel if Austy was driving you home?" She gave him a teasing smile.

"She offered, Lis. Honest!" He threw his hands up in surrender. "It's way fun to drive." He tossed the keys back to me. "Thanks again, Austy, for everything. You're a good teacher. Can we finish up tomorrow?"

"What's going on?" Elise advanced, waving a finger back and forth between us.

"She worked on the clutch with me today. Taught me a lot. My car's gonna be so tricked out by the time I'm done with it."

"We should have it done in a couple hours max. I'll stop by the shop tomorrow afternoon, and we can get to work."

"Cool, thanks again."

"Wait a minute." Elise held up a palm. "I'm sure Austy's got other things to do with her weekend."

"It was productive and fun, really," I assured her.

Elise looked from Scott to me and back to Scott. "We're going to pin down some rules with getting this car in working order, Buster. Tomorrow night. Here's Sean now." We turned to watch a pickup pull up to the curb. Elise stepped right up to Scott and asked sternly, "Are you drinking tonight?"

"Probably."

"Is he drinking tonight?" She pointed at the kid in the driver's seat. Scott gave a shrug. "Then who's driving home?"

She crooked her finger at Sean to get out of the truck.

"Hey, Elise," he called from his perch on the running board, looking over the truck's cab.

"You're driving my cousin to this party. Are you going to be drinking?"

His hands slammed down on top of the cab. "You told her about the party, dude? Now, we're busted." He blew a stream of air through his shaggy brown bangs in bother.

"Chill out, dude," Scott scoffed cavalierly. "Lying doesn't work with my cousin. Answer her question, or we're never gonna go."

"Hell yeah, I'm drinking; why else go to a party?"

"Then who's driving?" Elise asked.

Sean looked at her like she was nuts. "Me, it's my truck."

"I don't think you understood me, Sean. If you're both drinking, who's driving?"

Her point finally dawned on Sean. "Ugh, yeah. Umm, maybe someone at the party won't drink."

"No, you don't leave it to 'maybe.' Here's what's going to happen. If you both plan on drinking tonight, you're either crashing at the party house, or you're calling me to come get you. Clear?" She looked first at Scott then at Sean. They both nodded their agreement, duly cautioned. "Good, and I know I don't need to say anything about drugs, right?

"Man, Lis! We gotta take off."

"This is the deal, remember? We're having this discussion if you want to go to a party. And we're having it in front of your friend so he understands how serious I am. Got me, Sean? You want to disrespect yourself by using drugs, I won't stop you, but this kid stays clean."

"Yeah, yeah. We don't use anyway." Sean's eyes bulged at her forcefulness.

She stared him down for a moment then flashed a dazzling smile. "All right then, have a great time. I expect a call by one to let me know if you're crashing or if I'm coming to get you."

"Sure thing, Lis." He turned and headed toward the truck.

"See ya tomorrow, Austy. Thanks again for the help."

We watched them climb into the truck as I pieced together remnants of a conversation that centered around my car, Scott's car, our clutch job and how tough, but way cool Elise was. The truck roared to life, more thumping music rang out and off they went.

"To paraphrase Scott, that was the coolest thing ever." I faced Elise.

She turned from the view of the departing truck. "What was?"

"The way you talk to him. I wish my parents had spoken to me like that."

"It's a fine line between sounding like his mother and his older, wiser cousin, that's for sure." Elise grinned slyly.

"I'd say you're doing great with him. He's thinking about becoming a FBI agent, did he tell you?"

"No," Elise replied softly, amazed by the revelation. "I'm sure he'll want to build kayaks for a living by the end of the summer. Or if he keeps taking advantage of you, maybe he'll want to become a prosecutor."

"He's not taking advantage." I brushed a hand through the air. "It's been years since I've worked on a car, and he's great fun."

"We worked out a plan for that car, and it didn't include asking you to put in hours of work." She considered me seriously for a moment. "He should pay you for helping him, but somehow I think you'd take offense to that. So, let me thank you by making you dinner."

"That's not necessary," I replied automatically then kicked myself. My politeness spoils every chance I get.

"It is, but if you've got other plans?"

"I don't, and dinner sounds great. Thank you." I know I sounded rushed, but I was proud of myself nonetheless.

Her eyes widened fleetingly, making me think my response made her just as giddy as her offer made me. "Come on in." Elise spun back toward the house and led the way inside.

When I walked through the front door, my tension relaxed. The same freeing refuge I experienced every time I walked into my loft hit me once she'd closed the door. *How weird.* I didn't have time to analyze the oddity, however, as Elise took me on a grand tour of the first floor's kitchen, living room, dining room, and den. Then she walked us upstairs, pointing out Scott's bedroom, his bathroom and a guest room. She didn't show me her bedroom, which is something I always exclude from a tour as well. Bedrooms are too personally revealing.

"Do you like chicken marsala?" she asked when we headed back downstairs.

"I'm Italian; do you need to ask?" I joked and was rewarded with a grin. "What can I do to help?"

"It wouldn't be a suitable thank you if I let you help." She walked up to the refrigerator and began foraging through to pull out various ingredients for dinner.

I entered the kitchen uninvited and took a position right beside her, pulling a knife from the block and guessing where the cutting board was. She didn't notice where I stood until she swung back from the refrigerator and lightly brushed against me. "Sorry, but I won't accept the thanks unless you let me assist."

Her shoulder still touched mine as she considered me. "Your friends said you were stubborn."

As much as I wanted to stay touching her, I leaned back in surprise. "What? They told you…"

"It took all night before one of them, Des, I think her name was, let slip the stubborn comment. The tall redhead, Lauren, if I remember, smacked her for it. But it was the first thing any of them said that wasn't glowing. They love and admire you quite a bit."

"Yes, I'm blessed with good friends."

"What a wonderful way to put it," she spoke honestly. Handing the mushrooms over to me and my trusty knife, Elise began preparing the chicken breasts on the counter behind me. She glanced over her shoulder at my progress and asked,

"You're not going to ask about what other things your friends told me, are you?"

"I'm sure it was all highly embarrassing and equally inaccurate." I chuckled softly.

"They didn't seem to agree on a lot about you, now that I think about it. You're saying they don't know you very well?" She scanned my non-reaction and asked quietly, "Even Willa?"

Conflicting emotions passed through my body at the sound of Willa's name. It usually triggered a daydream or flood of warmth through my heart. This time, I stayed completely focused on the striking woman before me. Not a difficult task, given that I'd been constantly thinking about her since Thursday, probably even before that. To hear Willa's name come out of her mouth didn't link up.

"Especially Willa," I admitted, eliciting a curious stare. "She and I are a lot alike, which leads to assumptions. Also one of our common traits is not to pry, so we rarely seek verification of the assumptions we're making."

She regarded me with those ever observant green eyes, and I grew tense wishing she'd do something, anything to make this moment pass. I didn't want to talk about Willa with her. Not when she'd taken over most of the room in my head that Willa had occupied for nearly two years.

"About half those mushrooms should do." She indicated to the bag beside me. Turning back to the stove to brown the chicken, she missed the sigh of relief that escaped my mouth.

Soon the enticing aroma of our dinner filled the kitchen. I put together a salad while Elise plated our food. Moving the plates to the table, she reached for dinnerware and napkins and I carried over the salad. We sat at the same time, and I caught her eye. Fire started somewhere in my belly, spreading through my limbs in tantalizing slowness. Could I really be having such severe feelings for a woman I scarcely knew?

Elise pulled a bottle of chardonnay out of the wine rack by the kitchen counter's edge and showed me the label. "I'm afraid I don't have any Josephs wine, but will this do?"

My trusty level-headedness returned at the mention of my family. "Not for me, thank you, but that's a nice wine."

She examined me with an intense scrutiny that stoked the fire burning inside of me. "How is it that the daughter and sister of wine grape farmers doesn't drink?" My head jerked into a double-take. However accurate, her assumption was still surprising. "It's not an assumption," she spoke with the assurance of someone who made a lot of correct deductions. "At least, I don't think it is. There was beer at the game, any type of drink at the party afterward, your brother's wine offered at dinner last week, and, now, you're declining again. Could be four coincidences, but I don't think so."

Not even the Virginia clan picked up on that fact. Of course, I'd done my best to hide it by ordering cokes and telling friends it was rum and coke, or holding glasses of wine or bottles of beer and dumping some down a sink or nearby plant. People tend to get uncomfortable around others who don't drink, and I always wanted to save them the discomfort.

"You're right. I don't usually point it out because people make assumptions why, and it won't matter the real reason even if I was willing to tell them."

"Good enough." She gently let go of the subject, replacing the bottle of wine and rising to fill two water glasses instead.

"It won't bother me if you have some wine, Elise. Really."

She smiled that sinister smile again. "I offered it to test my theory. I don't drink much and never alone. I've seen too many agents lose their objectivity that way. So, dig in."

Cutting a small piece of chicken and adding a sautéed mushroom, I slid the forkful into my mouth. Okay, she could rival Helen as a chef. "This is delicious."

She smiled at the compliment. "Glad you like it. I won't take offense if you don't eat it all. In case your appetite loses out to your ingrained politeness."

She'd nailed me again. As a dinner guest in someone's home I usually forced myself to finish whatever was served to me. I set my fork down and leaned forward over my plate in sincerity. "Thank you." I meant it as gratitude for both her understanding comment and for cooking me dinner.

"No, thank you." She reached out her hand to squeeze mine, and I felt a pleasant jolt through my arm. "This was a nice surprise to have today." Just as suddenly, she pulled her hand away to resume eating.

Mine stayed where it was so as not to break the still clinging sensation of her gently pressing fingers and palm. She didn't seem aware that her touch had spiraled me into a fantasy about what other things I'd like that hand to do to me.

Why couldn't I tell if she was gay? She wasn't exactly staring at me longingly, but then again, neither was I. Still, she had to know about me. Anyone who saw how I greeted the Virginians at the basketball game had to know I was. I'd always been clueless about this sort of thing. Before tonight, it never mattered. Now, it was frustrating as hell.

She started telling me about the process of selecting and finally purchasing Scott's car, and I was grateful for the diversion away from my erotic thoughts. Attacking your dining companion in the middle of dinner probably wouldn't be first on Emily Post's dinner party etiquette list. I had to control these feelings and examine them before I made such a drastic move with someone I worked with, not to mention someone who might not even be gay.

After dinner, she moved us to the living room while I told her about a case I'd tried in Virginia which included a pet psychologist taking the stand and a de facto cult leader who'd forgotten his own cult's purpose. Don't ask. Like always, the story got a jovial laugh.

When her laughter died down, she glanced at me so candidly I stopped breathing. Transfixed by the slight slant of her eyes up from her delicate nose, I knew her mouth was moving, but I didn't hear anything except the thunderous roar of my heartbeat. Her look turned expectant, and I had to respond. "I'm sorry?"

Elise smiled softly, light dancing in her green eyes.

"There's something that's been bothering me for a while now."

"In general, or about me?"

"About you. Something I'd like to know." Uncertainty pierced the sparkle in her eyes.

We sat facing each other on the couch. Her right leg was bent at the knee and pressed into the cushion beside my left thigh. I kept my hands laced together in my lap so I didn't inadvertently reach out and stroke her bare knee up along her thigh. Her face wasn't far from mine having inched closer in keenness during my earlier story. That facial cream titillated my senses again, and I felt a heat rise through my chest and up my neck.

"Okay?" I searched her features to determine what had caused the uncertainly. I lost a little concentration when my gaze hit her mouth but pulled my stare away to refocus on her eyes.

They stayed unreadable on mine for an agonizing minute before drifting downward. I hoped she wouldn't notice the flush at the base of my neck, but they stopped at my lips first. Very softly, she said, "I've been dying to know…"

After a brief pause, she leaned forward and gently pressed her lips against mine. I didn't react for a split second, so astonished. Then her lips moved and mine followed along despite the dizziness swimming through my head and the inferno in my abdomen. I felt her hand grasp one of my own and long fingers from her other hand slid along my jawline. It couldn't have lasted more than twenty seconds, but every nerve in my body sizzled from the pull of her kiss. When her lips stopped kissing me, she kept them pressed against mine and I felt a shiver run through her body. Slowly she pulled back, opening her eyes a few seconds after I'd opened mine.

"Oh yes, they're as soft as I thought they'd be," she whispered through shallow breaths.

Barely recovered, I smiled broadly at her admission. "That's what's been bothering you?"

"Among other things." She blew out a long breath that

mingled with mine.

"I'm glad you decided to investigate."

She slid slowly into that sexy smile, and my heart nearly went on strike from overwork. The fingers of the hand holding mine began to explore my palm, along the back, and between my fingers. I'd been right; it was skilled.

"I am a trained investigator, you know," she spoke in an incredibly seductive voice.

I looked down at her hand caressing mine. It felt like she was making love to my hand. Was it possible to have an orgasm just from having your hand stroked? If I let her continue, I'd probably find out. "Yes, I can see that."

"You want to ask me something?" She drew my eyes up from her hand.

Haziness clouded my thought pattern, making it impossible to figure out what she meant. "I'd like to ask you to kiss me again, but I'm not sure that's what you're getting at?"

With a soft laugh, she leaned in to comply and captured my mouth for another kiss. This one didn't hesitate, demanding and giving all at once. When she pulled away, she said, "I meant that your friends were fishing all night about my sexuality, but I wouldn't play along. If you have doubts, I'll take as long as you need to convince you."

"I should be smart and hold out for more convincing, but you're making it very difficult to concentrate right now." My voice held a little tremor of anticipation.

"Just so long as you're clear on my interest."

My tremor turned into a full blown tremble, and I felt compelled to do something before the shaking caused paralysis. Raising my hand, I cupped her face, letting my fingers rest against her cheekbone and the lobe of her ear. I moved forward and covered her mouth with mine, exploring her full lips until my tongue acted on its own and skimmed the ridge of her upper lip. My action elicited a soft moan, imploring me to press against her while my tongue slipped forward to find hers. She moved her hand from mine up my arm and around my back, encouraging me to fall against her. *God, she can kiss.*

A ringing phone shattered the harmony of our thundering hearts, but the press of her chest against mine made it easy to ignore. How long had it been since I'd kissed someone like this? Never. Nothing compared to her kiss.

"Lis? Are you there?" Scott's voice came over the answering machine.

Elise and I broke apart at the same time, turning toward the sound. I looked back at Elise and nodded my head at the phone.

"Guess, you went out," Scott continued as Elise slowly extricated herself from our embrace. "Anyway, Sean and I—"

"I'm here, Buster." Elise placed the phone to her ear and listened for a bit. "Are you guys all right?...Did they take names?...Good…Sure, he can stay. Tell me where you are."

As much as I wanted to walk over and wrap my arms around her again, I knew what this phone call meant. "Taking names? Did the party get busted up or something?"

"I guess one of the neighbors called the cops. Party's over."

I took a stilling breath and stood from the couch. "Guess it is. It's good that he called you, though. Smart kid."

"Sorry," she started, but I cut her off.

"Don't be. This was the best evening I've had in, well, I don't want to admit how long." I walked toward her, and her hands reached out to touch my shoulders and run down my arms. I settled mine on her waist. "Thank you for dinner, and for…"

"Investigating the softness of your lips?" she guessed with a smile.

"Definitely a nice addition to the evening." I tipped my head up to kiss her goodbye. Too briefly I pulled away and whispered, "Goodnight."

As I walked outside to get into my car, I wondered if being intoxicated by her meant I shouldn't drive home either.

Chapter 12

"Are you really almost finished?" Scott asked down through the engine block.

"Very nearly. Slide that three-eighths under here, please." I dropped my hand down to my side and reached out under the car toward Scott's feet. Things were moving much faster today, and Scott's clutch was a few cranks away from being operational.

"This is so great. I can't wait to drive it again."

His enthusiasm spurred me on. I'd felt something similar all day long while I went through my usual Sunday routine before beginning work on Scott's car. Thoughts kept drifting back to Elise and her kisses last night. Okay, yes, and her skilled hands.

A car drove up and parked beside us on the lot. Dust rushed under the car at me, and I had to turn my head to keep from sneezing. I'd be glad to have this job done. No more working on cars for me.

"Hey, Lis!" Scott called out.

My upraised arms froze on the socket wrench pressed against the clutch. What was she doing here? Equal parts of me wanted to scream in delight and in frustration. I couldn't possibly look worse, and I was so unprepared to see her right now.

"Hiya, Buster. Thought I'd stop by on my way home to see if you were going to need a ride today?"

"Nope, Austy thinks we're almost done."

"That's great news. Hi, Austy."

"Hello." I managed to sound even keeled despite the nerves galloping freely through my system. Wishing I had more to do with this clutch now, I twisted the wrench one final time. Job completed.

"Oh man," Scott interjected. "Looks like Joe's got a rush. I'll be back in a minute, Austy. Lis, can you hand her whatever tools she needs, please?" His tennis shoes swiveled and dashed across the lot toward Joe's shop.

"Are you coming out from under there?" Elise's voice held a playful lilt.

Horrified that she had shown up when I was in this state, I answered honestly, "No."

"Are you trapped?" Her voice rose to a tease.

"No."

"Can't take a break?"

"Stop! You can't just show up like this," I pleaded.

"Like you did last night, you mean?"

"Hey, I was giving Scott a ride home."

"Uh-huh, and that's all I'm checking on. But since you're here, I plan to take advantage of the situation. Please come out from under there."

I sighed, still talking to the engine block. "This isn't fair. Last night you looked all gorgeous and put together, and I won't be making that kind of impression right now."

A hand gripped my ankle and tugged lightly, coaxing me to scoot under the car. Since I was dying to see her and she'd probably stay until I showed my face, I slowly inched out from under the engine block. When I saw her kind eyes and striking smile, I stilled on the ground.

"Hi," she spoke softly, scanning me from head to toe.

Pushing to a stand, I repeated my earlier greeting, "Hello." I swept a hand along my dirty jeans and old t-shirt as if to prove my earlier point of the kind of impression I'd make.

"You're lovely. Really." She smiled widely, "I was beginning to think you never had an imperfect moment. I've only ever seen you in suits and that pristine number last night. This is refreshing."

"Okay, have your fun." I relinquished any feelings of embarrassment.

"Thank you, I will." She moved forward and kissed me lightly. "Mmm, motor oil, good fragrance."

"Watch it. My hands have the power to ruin your outfit."

She stepped back. "I think it might be worth it."

"Hi, Elise," Joe called out from the start of the lot with Scott on his hip. She turned and waved hello. "Did you finish, Aust?"

"Just got done."

"Fire it up, Scott. Let's break in this new clutch," Joe encouraged.

Scott nearly skipped over so eager to give it a try. The car roared to life, and he depressed the clutch, engaging first gear. I let out a long sigh of relief, happy that I'd known what I was doing. Joe stepped around to the passenger side and creaked open the door to take a seat. The car edged forward, and Scott leaned out the window.

"Works great, Austy. Jump in."

"Maybe some other time when I won't get grease all over your interior."

"You sure? Elise? Just a quick spin?"

"You go ahead. I'll help Austy put these tools away."

"Thanks for everything, Austy. Really."

"You're welcome, Scott. Have fun." We waved at the Mustang rolling easily off the lot and onto the street.

"Yes, thank you for helping him, Austy."

"It was my pleasure to help out. Now, stop mentioning it," I joked.

She grinned and threw up her palms. "Okay, but I reserve the right to thank you at a later time." Her expression sent me a tempting promise.

We started collecting the tools and putting them back in Joe's toolbox. Latching it closed, I carried it over to his shop with Elise at my side. She stayed to inspect the kayaks out front while I went to shove the toolbox onto a shelf in the back workroom. At the sink, I started cleaning off my hands then caught sight of my reflection in the tiny mirror above the sink and nearly screamed. My face had spots of motor oil and smudges of dirt and my hair was matted down from perspiration. Appalled, I smeared some magic goop on my hands and applied it to my face before rinsing and sliding my hands through my hair. I used a paper towel to rub over my hair, hoping there was enough left of the styling products to keep it from lying limp.

"Good as new," Elise commented when I walked out from the back room. I blushed at what I figured was a tease. "You're dying to change, though, aren't you? You do live just upstairs. I could give your place the white glove inspection while you change?"

"Um, ah, well," I panicked, as I always do when it comes to my home. I'm never articulate when I panic.

Concern furrowed her brow for a moment before she guessed, "You don't let people into your place, do you? I wondered why you didn't run upstairs to change after the Storm game or before we had our dinner last week."

"It's just, it's not always. I mean, Helen and Joe have been over. Of course, they manage the building."

She grabbed my hands, squeezing them in comfort. "I understand, really. Someday I hope you'll tell me why." As if she could tell I felt bad for having this hang up, she leaned forward and kissed me chastely.

"Lis?" We broke apart immediately to see Scott standing in the doorway to the shop. "What's—are you—when did…?" He wore an uncomprehending expression before he hastily waved a hand and garbled, "Umm, I'll see ya at home, bye."

Watching him sprint out the door and jump into his now

functioning car, I felt a surge of fear spread through me. I turned to Elise who wore an equally shocked look. "You're not out?"

"No, I am." Elise furrowed her brow further.

"But not with Scott?"

"Well, we haven't ever discussed it, but I assumed he knew. I told my mom when I was sixteen, told the gossipy cousin when I was seventeen so she'd tell everyone else in the family. I don't see how he couldn't know."

"He did say that everyone but you treats him like a kid. Maybe they thought he couldn't handle it."

She shook her head in disgust. "Now, that makes me angry. What's to handle, and why withhold information from him? I've never been in a relationship when he's visited before so it never came up. I hope he's not going to freak."

"He won't," I used a certain tone. She gestured to the door to remind me of his speedy retreat. I continued, "No, it's just that I told him I was gay yesterday, and he couldn't have been more ho-hum about it."

She smiled at my description then reached out to rub her hand along my arm. "I definitely want to hear more about that, but he and I have our weekly chat-about-whatever dinner planned for tonight. I think we have one more subject to cover tonight. Can I call you later to tell you about it?"

"Sure."

"Can I have your number to call you?" She smiled playfully.

I laughed and wrote down my number for her. I handed her the card, got a goodbye kiss, and watched her leave.

***

Work sucks when you want to focus on being a lesbian in Seattle. Somehow I didn't think Short Stack would let me take the week off to spend time with Elise. Her boss wasn't cooperating either. We'd spoken on the phone a couple of times, but I hadn't seen her since Sunday. More importantly, I didn't know when I'd have time to see her.

Roger and I were plowing through the file notes on our RICO case, but I kept drifting back to the sweep of Elise's hair when she tucked it behind her ear or the crinkle of the skin around her eyes when she smiled.

"Aust? Hello?" His brown eyes stared at me quizzically. Bushy eyebrows pressed into the point of a V, waiting for a response.

"Sorry, Rog. What were you saying?"

"Looks like we've got more than money laundering on this guy, wouldn't you say?"

I nodded as I glanced at the spreadsheet on my computer screen. Evidence of extortion as well as illegal gambling kept nice and tidy on the worksheet. This screen alone could bring down three people in the organization. Fun at work.

"The FBI is trying to get the accountant to flip on the head cheese. That'll be a nice addition to what we already have here and our experts. Say, have you met Jake's replacement yet?" What looked like a leer skittered across his face. "Agent Bridie, more than half the reason I wanted on this case."

I resisted rolling my eyes, but it was difficult. Roger's married, and Elise and I were dating, well, sort of. As much as four chance meetings, two resulting in kisses, can be labeled dating. What if she didn't think of it that way? We'd spent a short evening making out on her couch and a couple of stolen kisses the next day; does that really make her interested enough for a relationship?

"Aust? Have you met her?" His wide mouth now slid more to one side, coupled with the furrowed brow, obviously wondering if I'd suddenly lost my hearing.

"Yeah, she testified for the Squire case."

"I was a little nervous when they said Jake wasn't coming back, but I've actually worked with her before. She single-handedly brought down a guy who'd been convincing underage teens to meet up with him over the internet. Traced his connection and busted him with an elaborate set up. I watched her interrogation of the guy; she's fierce. It was like she could read the perv's mind. He crumbled, confessed, and agreed to a deal near max. Easiest case I've ever had."

"When was this?" I let my curiosity flare.

"Two years ago. She had a bunch of high profile cases till she took over for Jake. Don't know why, but it means she's around our office more often. And that's not a bad thing."

No, it wasn't. I didn't like that he thought so, too, but that's an insecurity I could live with if it meant I got to see her at work every once in a while.

"Wanna grab some lunch? Von's maybe? We've got a lot more work to do on this case; I could use a break."

A break wasn't really what we needed, but I also didn't want to alienate Roger. He'd been pretty good about being second chair on this case, especially when I explained the process of tracking bank accounts and tracing files. I think it dawned on him that he was out of his specialty on this kind of case.

With a nod, I stood and followed Roger out. At the lobby, I invited Mary, who looked like she desperately needed a break from the ringing phone, and Randall, another attorney I liked, to join us. Roger could be a little intense all on his own. When we hit the ground floor, we piled off the elevator and ran smack into Elise with two other people. But all I saw was Elise.

Her eyes grew large at my appearance and her smile, immediate and private. Oh my, I liked that smile. It assured me I wasn't crazy about the whole possible relationship thing. Roger stole the attention to introduce everyone around, having worked with both of Elise's colleagues in the past. He and Randall started discussing another case with one of the agents, while Mary and the other agent chatted about one of Mary's favorite topics: shoes. Elise crooked her finger in my arm and nonchalantly moved us a few feet away while their attention was diverted.

"I'm glad I ran into you. I was going to call you later." Her eyes shined brightly. "Friday's the holiday for the Fourth, are you working?"

"No." The first three day weekend in Seattle I'd planned to enjoy.

"Good, because I realized we haven't really had an official date yet. So, would you like to go out with me on Thursday night?"

A real date. My heart sped up at the prospect, and I loved that she asked me. "Yes."

She let out a nervous breath as the group was breaking up then graced me with a dazzling smile. "Pick me up at seven?"

"See you then." I returned her smile and watched her step around me to join her group as they got onto an elevator. I would bet money my smile was silly wide, but I didn't care. Seattle lesbian with a date.

Chapter 13

As I stepped out of the MINI parked in Elise's driveway, I could barely feel the warmth of the evening air. Goosebumps spread rapidly up and down my arms covered only by a sheer shirt. The bare skin visible under the deep maroon see-through fabric tipped my nervousness.

Isometrics didn't help in releasing any tension on my way along the slate path, so I resorted to a cleansing breath before knocking on Elise's door. In the few moments it took before I heard any footsteps, I had plenty of time to second guess my choice of black woven pinstripe slacks that gripped my hips and flattered my rear before hanging in a straight line to show about an inch of the heel on my boots. Maybe I should have worn a skirt, but I didn't have a skirt that went as well with the slinky camisole and shirt. Plus, I'm not crazy about skirts.

Unless they're on Elise. She opened the door with a broad smile, elation in her eyes and another outfit designed specifically for her. The silk A-line skirt in white with swirls of black showed off her well toned legs. The delicate spaghetti strap top in hues of green and black drew my eyes to the barely raised mole directly center of her sternum before I took in the rest of her skin along her clavicle and shoulders.

"Wow! You look incredible." The thought tumbled out

audibly before I could form an actual greeting.

Her smile turned into a soft laugh. “Hi. You’re looking great yourself. Ready?” She reached to her left and came back with a leather coat and her purse.

“Sounds like you’ve got something specific planned.” I managed to step back without falling over, suddenly having trouble with my equilibrium.

“I do. Did you bring a jacket with you? I’ve got one you can wear if not.” She hesitated before locking her door.

“Mine’s in the car. Why do we need jackets?” Not that I was protesting. My entire body started shivering the moment her door opened.

“You’ll see.” She turned back from locking her door and surprised me with a close hug. Her arms crossed over my back, hands grasping my sides, pulling me into her. My, she felt good.

“We’re not going hiking or parasailing or something active that’s going to make me wish I’d worn different shoes, are we?” I joked to distract her from seeing how much her hug affected me.

She looked down at my footwear with a grin. “Nice boots. Come on, grab your jacket.”

“We’re not driving? What are we doing? I mean, really?” I wasn’t entirely comfortable being in the dark in any situation, especially dates. Unlocking the driver side door, I pushed the seat forward, and lunged in for my black mid-thigh trench on the back seat.

Elise stood an inch away from me when I resurfaced with the jacket. She replied to my question in an assuring tone, “You’re going to give up responsibility for the comfort of the evening. Leave that to me.”

All of the breath pushed out of my lungs as Elise guessed my worst fear in any social situation. I’ll own being a control freak, but I only apply that to myself. Controlling others is fruitless. She must have picked up on the look of panic that crossed my face, because the next thing I know, I’m pressed up against my car and her lips are caressing mine. How had I managed to endure life for thirty-two years without her kiss?

She ended the kiss with a whisper, “Trust me.”

As if under a spell, I nodded my consent. Only a touch of relief flushed through me with her words. Now my nervousness centered on the fact that she seemed as perfect as any human can be, and I didn’t like to think about how I’d measure up. She stepped back and held her hand out for mine. Automatically, I grasped it like a lifeline and fell into step beside her.

After we’d walked several blocks closer to the waterfront, Elise asked, “I bet you’ve not been on a ferry since moving here, have you?”

“A ferry ride? Perfect.” Knowing our plans eased my nerves a touch.

She took us through the terminal and onto the ferry. Before we’d completed a lap of the passenger deck, the ferry started forward on our way to an unknown destination. Had I been a true Washingtonian I’d probably know where we were headed, but so far, this whole loss of responsibility was working out well.

We stood on the outdoor deck at the front of the ferry and watched the waves crash against the hull as it sliced rapidly through Puget Sound. Elise pointed to the left where porpoises jumped in half circles out of the water and seals poked their heads through the dark blue-green sea. The ferry system should really think about selling sight-seeing tickets instead of just passenger fares. They’d make a killing.

“Can I know where we’re headed?”

“Dinner in Kingston. It’s a cute little peninsula town, but mostly I wanted you to see all this.” She spread her arm toward the vast waterscape and mountainous regions surrounding us.

“I thought Lake Union was a nice view, but this is such a treat. Thank you so much.”

“Have I told you how much I like that you’re polite?”

I scoffed in jest, “Are you mocking me?”

"No. Not many people are these days, and you just thanked me like I'd created this view for you. Hasn't anyone ever told you that your politeness makes her feel special?"

"Not even close," I replied, amazed that she didn't seem to be joking. Most people who've commented on it feel that politeness masks authenticity. My grandmother, who taught me manners, would have taken them over her knee with that observation.

Elise flipped her head to the side to move the hair that had blown into her face. The movement stole my breath. She glanced at me seriously. "Well, you do, and it's a wonderful gift to give."

I bit down on the "thank you" I'd usually say at this point because it seemed redundant given our discussion. She was doing that perfect thing again, and I fought the urge to do something stupid to frustrate or annoy her. That was self-destructive Virginia A.J. not hopeful Seattle Austy. "That's the best compliment anyone has ever given me. Thank you, Elise."

She smiled blissfully, nodded once, and placed a hand over mine on the railing. Once we docked at Kingston, we departed with the rest of the walk-on passengers and walked the length of the Northwest style frontier buildings in town before looping back to the restaurant.

Dinner came and went, but I hardly remembered the taste. She was as easy to talk to as my long-time friends from Virginia. Not one awkward moment all dinner or on the ferry ride and walk back home. Unprecedented triumph, wow!

When we approached her house, the streetlights showed only my car in her driveway. "Is Scott at another party tonight?"

"He went down to Portland to visit one of our other cousins. He wanted to show off his car and hang out with Darren's kids. There's some sort of fireworks deal on Saturday night."

"He's gone for the entire weekend?" My eyebrows shot up.

"Uh-huh, I tried to tell him the fireworks here are pretty

hard to pass up, but like I said, he'll use any excuse to drive and show off that car." She stopped abruptly when I hesitated by the door of my car. I'd been so sure that Scott would be home, I didn't think we'd have the opportunity for more than a dinner date tonight. She tugged on my hand. "Come inside?"

Feeling like I could skip after her, I contained my jubilation because I didn't know what her invitation meant. Desire flashed through me, but she could just be asking me in for coffee. Once inside, she slipped out of her coat and showed off all that tempting skin. My right hand darted up, following my brain's instinct to touch her, but I slammed it back to my hip as she went behind me to help me out of my coat.

"Let me check the messages to make sure he made it okay." She guided us to the kitchen where her answering machine reported in Scott's voice that he'd hit Portland in good time. "Would you like some coffee or tea?" she asked when she'd listened to the other two messages waiting for her. Both relatives, both asking how she was handling dealing with Scott.

Marveling at her calmness, my body fought the tormenting ache at not being able to touch her. I clenched my hands against my sides. "Whatever you're having."

She turned to face me squarely. Two heartbeats passed before she closed the distance between us and crushed her body against mine. Her mouth kissed me fully as her hands roamed my back. It felt like gravity was released in the room and only her hands kept me from floating up in the air. Stepping a leg in between hers, I mashed my pelvis into her hips and felt the length of her body touching mine.

Not knowing how long I could stay upright, I mumbled against her mouth, "Bedroom?"

She tried stepping us back across the living room in our kissing embrace, but a few stumbles forced us apart. Taking my hand, she led us toward the closed door off the living room. Her master bedroom was spacious, comfortable, but most importantly, had a bed. She turned and sat on the edge, drawing me to her as I took her face in my hands to kiss her again.

I pressed closely, and she edged backward as I crawled up over her. I took a moment to enjoy the sight of her stretched out before me. After more than a year's absence from sex, I'd forgotten how much I liked this view. Settling down against her, my mouth began to explore the soft skin on her neck and down along her clavicle. With my right hand, I felt along her hip up to the bare skin of her abdomen. My fingers slipped under her shirt and inched upward. Elise stiffened so suddenly her face jolted, pushing my mouth from hers. I used my elbow to prop myself up and looked down at her now frightened green eyes.

Thinking I'd misread everything, I asked tentatively, "You're not ready?" Moisture formed in her eyes as she looked away for a moment. My body hummed with wanting, but I forced myself to say, "There's no rush."

I began pulling back my hand which rested against the start of her rib cage, but one of hers grasped my wrist to keep it there. She turned her head back to look at me and said, "I want this; believe me. It's just been a long time, and…"

She hesitated so long I had to speak. "For me, too. Tell me what you're worried about."

"My accident," she whispered then glanced at the placement of my hand. "I have scars."

"Do they hurt when they're touched?"

A truncated sob left her mouth, but her eyes told me she was gratefully pleased by my question. When she regained her breath, she replied, "No, but they aren't pretty. No one's ever reacted well. They expect my body to be…to look…like my face."

I pulled my hand away from hers to cradle her face. "I'm sorry that anyone hurt you like that." I kissed the tear that slipped down the side of her temple. "You're very beautiful, and it has only partly to do with how you look."

"Are you inside my head?" she breathed out in relief.

"A little taste of what you've been doing to me for weeks." I brought my knees up around her left thigh then sat back on my haunches. I pulled Elise up with me, kissed her startled face, and yanked us off the bed. "Let me see you. Please."

She nodded her consent. My hands slid up her sides, taking her shirt with them. I found her eyes after the shirt cleared her head and waited for the fear to leave them. When I was sure, I slowly scanned from her eyes down her long neck to that precisely centered mole, taking in the tempting black bra and along her flat stomach. What made her so perfect were the three crescent shaped, dark pink scars near her side where something from that tree must have punched through the skin. Without those scars, she'd be inhuman in her perfection.

"My hip, too," she admitted quietly.

Lifting my gaze, I caught her eyes to convey my certainty. I worked the side zipper of her shirt and let it fall to the ground. She wore those sexy, boy style briefs in black lace, hiding her hip. I pulled her a step toward me, out of her shoes and the pooling of her skirt then took a knee in front of her. My hands drifted up her athletic legs, caressing her full ass before my fingers curled under the band of her underwear and slowly slid them down her legs. I made her step out of them before I brought my eyes up to her left hip. Rough ridges blistered the side of her hip down to the start of her thigh, like she'd been dragged across something coarse. Just below the crest of her hip bone, a jagged, deep purple scar ran down the seam of her pelvis surrounded by white raised specks where the skin held stitches at one time. I wanted to cry for how much pain this must have been for her, but I didn't want to risk that she'd misinterpret my anguish.

My eyes drifted across her firm belly, reveling in the trimmed triangle of brown curls, and over to the other hip that jutted splendidly untarnished. I pressed my lips against the serrated line of purple, feeling her tremble in my arms while kissing up the long, fierce scar and over to the rough skin on her hip.

"You're beautiful, Elise. All of you." I spoke to the scar then stood up to take her in my arms and kiss her mouth. She gave me a blissful smile when I finished the kiss and unhooked her bra. Her breasts, a little more than a handful, brushed taut nipples up against me.

"Thank you." Her breath came a little more rapidly now. "You're turn." She started to undress me, kissing down my neck as she unbuttoned my shirt. I helped to undo my pants and slide them down my legs while her hands brushed my shirt off. The camisole came off in a hurry, and her lips stayed attached to the hollow of my throat as her hands expertly unhooked my bra. Her eyes dropped down to take in my freed breasts, and she knelt to take off my boots before slipping my panties off in agonizing slowness. "So very lovely," she whispered when she stood back up and pressed me back against the bed.

Her warm skin slid against mine as she settled on top of me. Her nipples dragged in a tantalizing dance across my breasts while her lips pulled at my neck. The sensation was so erotic I forgot that I usually like to work first. When her hands began to massage and rub and tweak and caress, I could hardly catch my breath. My senses returned when her mouth relinquished its spot on my neck for a moment, and I used the opportunity to try to roll her over so I could pleasure her.

She resisted my maneuver as only someone trained in criminal detainment could. "Remember the deal?" Her eyes twinkled as she raised her head to stare at me. "You're relinquishing control tonight."

I grew suddenly nervous. My first time with anyone takes a while before I climax. I wanted to prevent any frustration on her part. "Elise? Let me…I'll be faster if I touch you first."

"We're not in a hurry," Elise breathed seductively.

When her thumbs flicked across my nipples, I arched toward her, knowing I'd lost my protest. Her mouth went back to its slow torture of kisses and tickling my neck as her hands grew bolder, cupping and squeezing my breasts. I slid my hands down her smooth, warm back to her ass, gliding my fingers over the curves and between her cheeks. She moaned into my neck but shifted back out of my reach to cover my side. Her mouth moved down my sternum, kissing between my breasts. I felt the wet imprint as it inched across the swell of one breast. Her right hand ran along my side, down past my hip, and behind my knee. Even before her hand moved across my leg and between my thighs, I knew how wet she'd find me. Her tongue began to lick my nipple, alternating between flicking and mouthing the erect bud. She was definitely taking her time, and I thought I'd cry out if she didn't touch me soon. I jutted my pelvis toward her stroking hand, but she continued to tease by raking her fingers along the inside of my thighs. I gasped and clutched her head because I had to do something with my hands, not used to being the center of this much concentrated sexual energy.

Her lips started to move down my body, kissing a pathway of goosebumps over my hips and down my inner thigh. It took forever before her lips found me and her tongue slipped inside my folds. I pressed my shoulders back against the bed, lifting my hips to meet her exploring mouth. With the flat of her tongue, she licked me fully. Intense heat rippled through my body. I gripped the bedspread as her tongue slid up one side of my clit and down the other, ignoring the swollen nub. She released a throaty moan when she penetrated me with her tongue. I bucked upward, swaying with the plunging motion until she withdrew and licked up to my clit, touching directly, lapping and flicking, mouthing the hood and sucking it into her mouth.

My breathing became hurried, matching the rapid fire eruption of my heart palpitations. In response to the rising waves of pleasure, I felt my stomach muscles gradually clench. Her familiarity with my body's needs pushed a loud clanging through my head drowning out all thought. I stopped wondering how she knew what, where, and how to touch so precisely and allowed myself to be mystified by her patience and expertise. My hips began to undulate on their own, and only her approving moans pierced the clamor in my head.

Teeth clenched, eyes closed, and body rigid, I knew climax was moments away when her mouth left me suddenly.

"Look at me, Austy." Her voice startled me. "I want to see your beautiful brown eyes when I make you come."

I opened my eyes at her erotic request and found her face just above mine. She smiled and kissed me, bringing my taste to my lips. I felt her skilled hand cup me, massaging gently. She slid two fingers through my slick, swollen lips, rubbing softly as her mouth left mine to watch my body react. Finally, her fingers began to circle my clit, forcing my hips to writhe in ecstasy.

"Let go. I'm right here," she whispered hoarsely, staring at me. Her other hand pressed against my clenched stomach, rubbing to coax the tension away. "Come for me, Austy."

That familiar swirl of heat and tingles exploded almost on command as I lost focus on her eyes and moaned softly in climax. My body betrayed any decorum, spasming around her still working hand, experiencing the orgasmic quake over and over.

"There you are. Let me hear you." Elise's words scared me, not sure if I could comply. "Come on, Austy, let go."

Her fingers worked my engorged clit over and over, drawing out my orgasm longer than I thought possible. Her ministrations brought me higher, forcing me to release my clenching muscles, resulting in a wild, massive orgasm. It ripped a loud, long groan from deep inside me and my body bowed like a limb in a windstorm, shuddering violently past any hope of control.

"That's it, Austy, exactly what I wanted." She leaned down to kiss my quivering mouth while her hand finally rested against my convulsions. Her eyes stared longingly into mine as she waited for my shaking to subside.

"How—where—how?" I gasped between breaths.

"The better question is how you, being as amazing and beautiful as you are, haven't been made love to properly before?" She smiled understandingly as I finally realized I'd been cheated out of good sex my entire life until now. "I knew you'd be a continuous come, sexy. You're very good for my ego."

Embarrassment touched a part of me, and I battled it by reaching up to take her head in my hands and kiss her in gratitude and wonder. I ran my hands down to her shoulders and rolled her onto her back. Having never been sated first, I didn't know how to deal with my still shaking hands and complete lack of urgency to bring her off right away.

She laughed softly as my eyes scanned her prone form, not knowing what to touch first. I began at her mouth then dragged my lips down her neck. I brought one knee in between hers and pressed the top of my thigh against her, delighting in her wetness. My fingers danced up from her thighs, across both hips and spread out along her rib cage until they found the perfection of her firm breasts. Her nipples grew like spikes against the center of my palms. She moaned seductively, pressing her breasts into my hands and my fingers began to lightly pinch and tweak the sensitive nips. I could do this all night, especially if she kept up her erotic moans. I felt her rib cage rise and fall rapidly and her body began to move against mine covering hers. My mouth had to taste what my fingers found so tempting. Kissing then licking the underside of her right breast brought out another loud moan before I opened my mouth and took in as much of her breast as possible before sucking back out to that hardened nub.

"Yes, so good," she whispered, her breath coming more quickly.

Concentrating on her nipple, I licked, sucked, and grazed my teeth over the firm tip. Elise's hips bucked, soaking the crest of my thigh. I smiled against her breast, not wanting to leave it but needing to taste the other.

"God, your mouth," Elise spoke in a near moan.

Oh yeah, a talker. I liked that so much. I slid my tongue and lips around her breast, then centered on the nipple, nibbling, kissing, and licking when I felt her breathing change.

"Oh my God! I can't believe it!" she raised her voice, pumping out audible moans. "Right there, that's it, yes, yes, Austy!" she shouted as her body convulsed under me, bucking my mouth off her breast. I looked up and watched her head bob against the pillow, a sight that brought out a wicked grin. I never thought I'd find a woman who could orgasm from breast play alone.

"Mmm, didn't think you could do that, did you?" I breathed as she clutched me against her, kissing every part of my face.

"That's never happened to me before." She chuckled softly. "You're amazing."

Leaning over her, I shook my head and teased, "You cut my fun short, sweet thing. I barely got to touch you."

Her eyes widened as she felt my hands drift down her body. She shook her head with a sated look. "I'm good, really."

"Yes, you are." I took her words at their literal meaning and watched her responding smile. "Don't deny me, Elise."

I dipped suddenly, lying between her spread thighs, taking in the beautiful sight of her glistening, full lips. I wanted to get lost in the creases and folds, but I restrained myself, kissing along her pelvis first. I could smell her musk, enticing me to taste her. Tangy and delicious, like nothing I've tasted before. My tongue slipped through her lips, lapping flat along the whole of her. She yelped at my searching tongue. I brought a hand up and rubbed a finger against her opening, sliding in slightly, then farther until it got swallowed whole. I twisted my palm up and crooked the finger inside her, pressing against her G-spot, spongy and rougher than the slick walls.

"There, there, God, Austy, right there." Elise began a series of short moans in between gasping breaths. "You're so good. Don't stop."

I sucked her clit into my mouth, flicking my tongue over the concentration of nerves at the tip, trying to roll with her undulations. My finger stroked her from inside, and my mouth worked her most sensitive nip of skin until her hips lifted off the bed. Elise's body folded in half as she shouted my name in climax. Slick walls grabbed at my invading finger and she throbbed against my tongue and lips. Her body slammed back against the bed while the orgasm rode through her in timed waves. I felt the pulsating nub in my mouth reduce to a quiver and the gripping walls finish with their rhythm before I pulled my finger from her.

I crawled up over her, taking my slick finger and rubbing one nipple while kissing the other. "Mmm, I can't take anymore," Elise rasped, her hands gripping my sides and pulling me up to lie on top of her. "You're the most incredible lover."

I shook my head lightly, discounting the compliment as afterglow. She seized my chin with a skilled hand and forced me to look at her. Before she could repeat her praise, I said, "That's a more accurate description for you, Elise."

She smiled and kissed me with those talented lips. "I believe you meant to say 'thank you for the compliment, Elise,' but I'll let it go."

I ran a hand over the rough skin on her hip, tracing the deformed scar with my fingertips. "I didn't hurt you, did I?"

Elise's eyes glowed brighter at my question. "You'll only hurt me if you don't stay with me tonight."

My heart began to pump harder at the hopefulness in her voice. Was she used to women leaving right after sex? Who would be crazy enough to do that to her? "I'd like that, thank you."

She rewarded me with a brilliant smile, and my heart nearly galloped out of my chest. We crawled under the covers, and she turned out the light. Before my eyes adjusted to the darkness, I felt her kiss me lightly and settle up against me. One of her legs slid over mine, her arm clutched my waist, and her face pressed into the crook of my neck. I gripped the arm draped over my waist, kissed her forehead, and fell into an untroubled sleep.

Chapter 14

Before waking fully, I became aware of a slight soreness in my thighs and abdomen. The dull ache vanished when I opened my eyes to the rewarding vision of Elise sleeping serenely a few inches from my face. Last night had been amazing, definitely worth the raw, underused muscles.

She had her leg bent slightly at the knee and tucked between my thighs. Her right hand was grasping my left while her other hand cupped my neck against the pillow. Sleep had tousled her hair which impossibly made her more beautiful.

Green eyes blinked open slowly, focused, and grew instantly wider. My heart sped up at what looked like surprise crossing her face. In another instant, her eyes crinkled into a peaceful smile as she whispered, "Good morning."

I cocked my head slightly, questioning my read of her momentary expression. "Good morning. Did you sleep all right?"

"You're in my bed; I should be asking you that."

"Incredibly well, thanks for asking."

She breathed out a laugh and moved forward to kiss me. When I felt the press of her lips, I ditched my worries about how many directions my hair must be shooting outward and how repellant my morning breath must be. However, I couldn't ditch the nagging feeling that she'd not expected to see me here, though.

"Elise?" I broke off our kiss. "You seemed, I don't know, surprised when you woke up. You did want me to stay, didn't you?"

Watching her break eye contact, I felt like I'd just gone over an unseen drop on a rollercoaster. My insides levitated while something yanked my body downward, and I fought to keep my eyes open against the dizzy rush. I readied myself to bolt if she had second thoughts.

"I did," she confirmed, raising her eyes back to mine and ending my rollercoaster ride with a jolting halt. My heart rate still pumped swiftly, but at least I hadn't misinterpreted her invitation. Her fingers curled around the back of my neck, pressing gently. She spoke emphatically, "I wanted you to stay. Really. It's just that, well…you're my first morning-after."

Nothing about that statement made sense. I couldn't even manage a coherent question. "Huh?"

She gave a brief laugh before stating, "I've never stayed or invited anyone to stay before. Even before my accident, I always thought the morning was about intimacy. And I've never wanted that, especially after my injuries. Not until you."

"You're blowing my mind right now, Elise." My heart hammered in tune with the buzzing in my head. Everything about her was so unexpected. For a person with control issues, unexpected could do more than twist the insides a bit.

"Freaked?"

I smiled in reassurance to erase the worry that creased her face. She'd given me a precious gift, and for that, I'd just have to learn to love the unexpected. "Not a chance. I'm glad you told me. Now, I can make your first morning-after memorable."

"It already has been." She gave me a giddy smile, and I felt a smile spread across my face to match her giddiness.

I dragged my hand over her hip and dipped down to find her warm, moist center. She sucked in a gasp of air; clearly I wasn't the only one enjoying the unexpected this morning. Her hips tilted flat against the bed, giving me better access.

My fingers started their joyous quest as I promised her, "Really memorable."

***

Spending the weekend with an intelligent, beautiful, practicing lesbian, I couldn't think of a better passage of time. A street fair on Friday, tennis on Saturday afternoon and dinner on the deck of Ray's Café. Dusk descended on us as I drove over Phinney Ridge and turned right on Stone Way instead of heading out to the interstate to go back to Elise's.

"Are you taking us to watch the fireworks at Gas Works Park?" she asked at my change of direction.

"Something like that," I replied casually, not wanting to give away my surprise. A few more turns and, minutes later, I pulled us into my garage.

"Good idea, parking up near Gas Works is nonexistent," Elise commented happily. Over the weekend, I'd found that little things made her very happy. Things like having fresh flowers on the table, finding a restaurant that she hasn't tried yet, or even the sunshine breaking through the clouds. Her all encompassing joy made it frighteningly easy to care deeply about her.

We walked out of the garage, and instead of going toward Gas Works, I turned us toward the front door of my building. Elise stood rooted to the ground as I unlocked the security door. I looked back at her questioning face and smiled reassurance.

"I understand the view is fantastic from my window. At least that's what Helen tells me."

"Are you sure?"

All the trepidation I'd been feeling about this step disappeared with her concerned question. I grabbed her hand and pulled her through the open door and up the stairs. Unlocking the two deadbolts and doorknob lock, I opened the door, feeling Elise hesitate before she stepped inside after me. Stilling relief washed over me when I closed and locked the door. More profound than the usual liberation I felt in being safely at home. That she could be included in my safe haven magnified my sense of relief and my feelings for her.

"Welcome." I gestured to the vast open space, seeing it again for the first time with Elise. No dark unseen spaces, everything laid out for all to see, safe from the outside world. Madness, I know.

"It's amazing, Austy. How do you ever leave?" Elise looked around in wonder at the modern casual furniture, open brick on two walls, and oversized windows looking out onto Lake Union.

"Some days I find it hard," I admitted honestly. One more honest confession this weekend, I should say.

She walked around the open layout, fingering my books, touching some of the furniture and along the brick. I followed her progress, cherishing the fact that I wasn't even remotely uptight about having her here. She stopped at one of the pictures on the shelf near the window. "Is this your grandma?"

"Yes," I said without having to examine it closely. "That's Nonna."

"Nonna? Sounds pretty in Italian. I like that. She's from Italy?" Elise turned back from the photograph with the smile she uses when she's deduced something. Something she did often, and I found it infuriatingly appealing.

"*Sì, è di Bari*," I replied before I realized I'd spoken in Italian. I did that whenever I thought of my grandmother. We had a special bond, speaking only in Italian unless others were around. My brothers never bothered to learn and my mom used to crave English growing up, so she rarely used Italian. "She's from southern Italy, a town called Bari."

"You're fluent? Thanks to her, I bet. And she's responsible for the red in your hair, I see."

"She's responsible for a lot about me," I admitted with a soft smile. "Not my cooking skills, though, dammit."

Elise laughed, having tasted my attempt at breakfast yesterday morning. She turned back to the next picture frame. "You and your brother Warren have the same angular nose and sweep of forehead. At least, I assume this is Warren." She looked back to catch my nod before moving on to another photo. "Your mom has compassionate eyes and a delicate beauty. Not surprising, though. You are her daughter."

I came up behind her as she carefully lifted one photo after another and wrapped my arms around her, resting my chin on her shoulder. "Investigating again?"

"My nature," she said without regret.

"Would you like something to drink?"

She regarded me as I moved into the kitchen. "Coffee, if you're making some. This place is really fantastic. I didn't think they made artist's lofts anymore."

"Lucked out," I responded casually, not ready to tell her that the building had been gutted and turned into lofts at Willa's expense because I'd once mentioned that my dream home was a loft. That would be a conversation for a later time, a much later time. Starting the coffee, I told her, "I'm going to change. I'll toss these in the washer so you've got something to wear tomorrow."

She glanced my way in awe. Another look I'd file in the memory bank. If she kept this up, I'd have to expand my memory's capacity. "We're staying here tonight?"

"Please?"

Her smile provided my answer and eliminated all remaining anxiety. I dashed up the steps to the balcony loft that housed one of the two enclosed areas in the place: my bedroom. Bed made, check. Clothes in their proper places, check. Bathroom clean, check. Who says being anal retentive is a bad thing? I changed out of the borrowed shorts and polo shirt, stripped off the bra I'd been wearing since Thursday night and stepped out of Elise's panties. We were technically a size apart, but I found it highly arousing wearing her underwear. I changed into my best jeans, clingy in all the right places, and a cotton shirt before heading back downstairs.

Elise sat comfortably on the couch and turned to watch my descent with a suggestive grin. “You…look…good.” She drew out each word, stoking the fire that had been burning inside of me all weekend.

“Don’t start or we’ll miss the fireworks.” I was still getting accustomed to her easy use of genuine complements. I ducked into the kitchen, filled two mugs of coffee, and carried them over to her. “Wanna see the rest of the place?”

Taking her through the kitchen to the other enclosed area, I showed her my guest bedroom, bathroom, and the extra room which still didn’t have an official use. Lately I’d been leaning toward an exercise room but only since Jessie poured on the guilt during her visit. We stopped off in the laundry room to start a load with her clothes. Upstairs, we didn’t linger long in the master suite because I was afraid we’d never leave. I’d become a sex maniac practically overnight. Something I’d never had a problem with before meeting her.

Tour completed, we settled back on the couch for the best view out the large windows onto Lake Union. The fireworks probably wouldn’t start for another half hour, so we got comfortable. The line of my leg brushed hers, and she looped a hand over my thigh, pressing her shoulder against mine. Contentment overwhelmed me.

“Do you want to tell me?” Elise asked quietly.

I turned to look at her and knew immediately what she was asking. Panic contracted every muscle into a clenching seizure. A breathing exercise meant to calm my panic started on its own. So much for contentment.

Other than my mom and grandmother, I hadn’t told anyone. What scared me almost as much as telling her was that she’d known there was something to tell about my not easily letting people into my home. We’d only met a month ago, but she seemed to know me better than my long-time friends from Virginia.

“Yes.” My voice sounded hoarse when I finally managed to

speak. I tried clearing my throat, but it only served to increase the dryness. I took a sip of my coffee, and the taste burned down my throat. "I was a freshman at Berkeley."

She waited patiently, but when I continued to clear my throat, she asked, "I thought Maryland?"

"Cal first, then I transferred during my first year. I met a woman there that made me realize the crushes I'd been having on girls since junior high weren't just nothing. We started dating, which apparently ticked off my last attempt at a boyfriend. I thought he was a nice guy, but it never felt right with him. About a month after I broke it off, I started dating Suzanne.

"Brad saw us holding hands together on campus and flipped out, calling us names, getting in my face. When he finished his little rant, I thought that would be the end of it. A week later, Suz had a party at her sorority house and had to clean up afterward so I walked back to my dorm room alone. If I'd been sober, I would have recognized the two guys walking toward me on the path. Two frat brothers of Brad's, but I didn't even give them a second glance. As they passed me, they hooked their arms through mine and without much effort began carrying me back to frat row. I was drunk enough to think it was a joke, until I got inside the house and was thrown into one of the study rooms.

"They pushed me onto a desk and held me there until Brad walked in. He had this scary mean look about him, and suddenly, I wasn't drunk anymore. I'd never known fear like that. He said things that I don't like to think about even now while his buddies kept me pinned down. When he ripped my shirt open, I knew he wasn't simply all talk. I couldn't get away. His friends were strong, and when I struggled, I only managed to hurt myself. I just stopped fighting," I broke off, unable to stop the feelings of powerlessness and shame that assaulted me every time I thought about it. Controlled breathing, controlled environment, controlled actions. Yes, I have control issues; I'll own that. I felt Elise's hand tighten around my inner thigh. Her touch helped me breathe normally again.

I continued because I needed to finish. "Just as he was tearing off my pants, the door opened, and a guy I knew from one of my classes walked in. Brad tried to convince him that we were having fun, but thankfully, Michael was one of those truly decent guys. He was also a junior, so the freshmen frat brothers had to do what he said. They released their grip, and Michael walked me home.

"I stayed in my dorm room for three days. I didn't eat, didn't go to classes, and kept a dinner knife in my hand when I went down to the bathroom. My room was the only place I felt safe, and then I became so afraid that I wouldn't ever leave. It was too easy just to stay in my room, stay paralyzed by fear. When Michael came to check on me, I forced myself to follow him outside. Only now, I had a new awareness for where everyone else was on the street."

Elise had let me talk without interruption. The concern in her eyes made me want to cry, but I welcomed her comforting hug. "Did you report them?"

I shook my head against her neck. "Michael said he'd back me up, but I knew that because I was drunk and they'd say they were drunk that it would be my word against theirs. And Michael might get booted from his frat if he helped me. He told me that two of his brothers worked Brad and his friends over pretty good and were washing them out of the frat. Deep down, I knew I shouldn't find that heartening or enough, but I couldn't put myself through reporting them when it was a slim chance anything would actually happen to them."

"Oh, honey, I hate that this happened to you," she spoke into my ear.

"Other than being more aware, sometimes freezing up when I get scared, and the whole control thing, I hardly think about it. Only when I have a gorgeous woman two steps from my door, and my knee-jerk reaction is to stupidly keep her out."

"Not stupid at all," she said understandingly. "Most people

think of their homes as a sanctuary; you have a legitimate reason. Thank you for telling me."

"Thank you for understanding," I whispered.

She smiled and kissed me tenderly as a burst of color haloed her head. We turned to watch the start of the fireworks show, and I smiled at the symbolism of her kiss bringing on fireworks. We both pressed into the couch, cuddling close as Elise wrapped her arms around my shoulders and pulled me against her chest. I'd never felt more safe in my life.

Chapter 15

Smoke from the barbeque grill misted the summer evening air in Elise's backyard. I approached the house with excitement and trepidation. We'd been officially seeing each other for two weeks, three if you counted the dinner at her place, and tonight I was meeting one of her other cousins and his family. If I wasn't so smitten, I'd normally think this was a little too soon to meet family. But Elise asked me to be here, and so far, I couldn't deny her anything.

"Hey, Aust!" Scott said with a grin when he opened the front door. These last two weeks showed me that Scott was a naturally chipper kid. It took a lot to bring him down.

"Hi there, Scott. Party in full swing?" I asked, stepping inside.

"Yep. Sean and our friend Ced aren't here yet, but Lis and Bri are out back." He turned and walked us down the hallway toward the back of the house.

Elise and I had been treading carefully around Scott. Since he'd never seen his cousin in a relationship before, she didn't want to flaunt the issue. We'd get together for dinner and more at my place a few nights each week, but she didn't like ditching Scott for the whole night. We didn't stay at her house. Not that I had any problem with that. I needed to work up to the idea of making love to his cousin when he was only a floor away. Go ahead, label me a prude.

Last weekend we spent together at her house because Scott stayed over at Sean's. For this weekend, her cousin Brian and his family had been scheduled to stay with her before heading up to Vancouver on a family vacation. When she invited me to join them, I spent the rest of the week trying to smother my anxiety.

"Hope you like kids." Scott rolled his eyes before he headed out through the sliding glass door to join four kids tossing a football around.

Elise looked up and a broad smile sparked her lips as she moved inside to greet me. I felt my pulse pound when I caught her smile, the one that she gave me in public where others might see. She had a few distinct smiles and other than the slow, sexy one and the sinister one, this was my favorite.

"Hi," Elise spoke in a breathy voice, half joy, half relief. I was beginning to crave hearing it, and that scared me a whole lot.

She leaned in to kiss me hello and all apprehension left with the press of her lips. "Hi," I matched her tone after catching my breath. "I brought some wine."

"You didn't have to do that; although, it's not surprising." She looked down at the bottles in my hands. "Josephs Brothers, wonderful."

"Well, it keeps Warren happy. I'm his personal Washington State distribution center." I walked them into the kitchen.

"Come meet Bri and Ginny." She pulled me by the hand out the door. A tall, good-looking man with blond, wavy hair turned with a welcome smile. His wife, a walking Barbie doll, turned with a smile that fell just shy of welcome. "Bri, Ginny, this is my girlfriend, Austy. Aust, my cousin Brian and his wife, Ginny." *Girlfriend? She just called you her girlfriend for the first time. You're a girlfriend!*

"Hi, Brian, Ginny, it's a pleasure to meet you." I shook

their hands. Ginny gave me a limp swan handshake and barely met my eyes.

"It's great to meet you, Austy," Brian told me. "Glad you could make it today."

"I'm happy to be included."

"Kids!" Brian yelled, "Meet Austy. This is our youngest, Hugh, then we've got Dot, Cat, and Chris."

The kids were all blond copies of their dad or mom. Scott and the pictures of his sisters as well as their other cousins were all blondies. I began to wonder if Elise was the only brunette in her family. "Hi there," I called out to them, not wanting to interrupt their game for long.

"You play football?" Chris asked, ready to toss the ball my way.

"Love it," I said, advancing forward but not before I heard a snort from Ginny. I didn't want to think about where that came from.

"All right!" Chris slapped Scott's hand, thrilled that they had another player. Hugh looked all of about eight and Dot not much older, so tossing a ball around couldn't be that fun.

I made sure Elise didn't need my help with the barbeque before joining the kids for a game of catch. They were a fun lot, but Scott was ages ahead of them in maturity even if he was only two years older than Chris.

When they moved on to Frisbee, I went back toward the house to see if I could help Elise in the kitchen. Brian stopped me on the patio. "I can't tell you how great it is to meet you, Austy. I'm glad Elise finally found someone."

"Oh! That's nice of you to say, Brian. I'm obviously glad, too."

"I never really got why she wasn't with someone. I know she's my cousin, but even I can see she's drop dead gorgeous, and yet she never had anyone special."

He clearly meant well, but I didn't feel entirely comfortable hearing this. Elise and I hadn't wasted any time talking about former relationships, and I couldn't care less. Past relationships were just that, in the past. Why dig it all up?

"Has she shown you any of her covers?" he continued.

"Pardon?"

"Her magazine covers? Probably not, if I know Lis." I indicated with a head shake that I hadn't seen any. A feeling of stupidity reeled through me. I never thought to ask, assuming it might be a tender subject for her. "They're amazing. I framed some for her and brought them as a housewarming present. Come take a look." He guided us into the house past Elise working in the kitchen and Ginny taking respite on the couch. With four kids, I couldn't blame her. "Lis, where'd you put the photo spread?" Elise looked up and lost her smile momentarily. "Here it is." Brian reached around the back of the table where a large frame tilted against the wall.

I glanced questioningly at Elise not sure if I was correctly interpreting her sudden look of alarm. Brian hauled up the frame and set it on the table. "I took these two." He touched my arm to get my attention, and I automatically looked down. There were three covers, four inside photos and two others that Brian's finger indicated.

Whoa! A younger Elise on skis in a fashionable outfit looking out over the ridge of a slope that probably required skiers to utter a prayer before attempting. Another showed her at the base of the mountain with skis propped against her shoulder and wind blowing her much longer hair, and one of a helmeted skier with a familiar body in a downhill tuck. Brian's two were of Elise on a podium receiving a gold medal and at the starting gates of a race. The other three were taken in or near the water, including one of Elise in a bikini on a surfboard riding a wave, hair damp and bronzed body drenched. Her body hadn't changed much in more than a decade, but her smiles weren't ones that I recognized.

"You surf?" I asked, finally looking up at Elise. She nodded briefly before busying herself with husking the corn.

Brian answered for her, "Oh yeah, Lis can do just about any outdoor sport. Don't let her take you skiing unless you know what you're doing. You think you'll be able to keep up, but she'll ditch you in a flash. Right, cuz?"

"That happened once, Bri; let it go," Elise ordered with exasperation. She came toward us and took hold of the framed array of photos. "Why don't I put this upstairs in the office? I want to spare the kids."

"They've seen them already, Lis. You know I've got all your magazines. I'm proud of my cousin." He continued to smile even as Elise hoisted the frame and started down the hallway toward the stairs. I went to follow but Scott walked in with two guys his agc.

"Wha'sup, Austy," Sean greeted casually when they fanned out in the living room. This would be our third meeting, and he seemed like a nice enough kid.

"Hi, Sean."

"This here's Cedric."

"Hey," this from a kid who needed a shave badly. Long blond hairs curled around his chin and neck and sporadic whiskers scuffed his upper lip and jawline.

"Hi, I'm Austy." I waved because he didn't offer his hand.

"We're headed out to the garage to look at the 'Stang. Wanna see what Joe and I did yesterday?" Scott asked me.

I still marveled at his lack of the usual embarrassment kids feel with adults around. Three sets of eyes waited for me to say yes, so I gave up my effort to follow Elise.

"We put disc brakes on all four wheels," Scott said proudly when we reached the garage.

"You getting new rims?" Cedric asked.

"Just picked up the first. Gotta wait for my next coupla paychecks for the rest."

"Let's check it out."

"It's in my room. Dude, help me carry back the interiors. Austy, check out the new tranny." Scott ran back inside with Sean on his heel.

I went around to the driver's side and popped the hood. Cedric lifted and propped it up. Joining him at the front, we tipped over the engine block to inspect the transmission.

"How do you know about cars?" Cedric asked.

"Why wouldn't I?" Whenever possible I like to change the male perspective on women's abilities. I knew his question wasn't where I'd learned about cars; it was how a woman knew anything about cars.

"No chicks I know like cars." See?

"Guess you don't know the right chicks."

He wheezed out a laugh that sounded so unreal it had to be fabricated. Kids these days. "Sean says you're a dyke."

I bent back upright and turned to face him. He showed the regular teenage who-you-looking-at face, not the usual malicious sneer that comes with people who use that word as an insult. Still, he needed a little etiquette lesson. "I'm gay or a lesbian. Those are the two words you should use."

"What's wrong with dyke?"

I didn't feel a whole lot of caring in that question. More like provocation. "I prefer gay or lesbian."

"I hear it on TV all the time. From girls, too. Why don't you like being called a dyke?"

"Hey!" Scott yelled from the door. "Don't call her that. What's wrong with you?"

"Chill, dude, I was just asking a question." Cedric stepped forward with hands up in front of him. "Harmless, dude, that's all."

I didn't know the dynamics here, but three teenage boys suddenly seemed too many to be around. "And I was just telling your friend here that I'd prefer he choose a different word." My tone suggested that was the end of the discussion. I gestured back to the car and said, "Transmission looks great, Scott. You're almost done. Only cosmetic changes left. Those rims are awesome."

"Thanks." Scott flicked his eyes at me in embarrassment before turning his glare back to Cedric.

"Well, I'll leave you guys to it. I'm sure the barbeque's almost ready. See you out back in a minute." I walked around them and up through the garage door into the laundry room.

Scott's voice sifted through the closed door. "What the hell, dude? You homophobic or something? She's my friend, and my cousin's gay, too. If you're gonna be hanging out with us, you're gonna show some respect."

Oh yeah, I knew I liked that kid a lot. Elise will be so proud. If I could figure out what was going on with Elise. I went back outside and found her pulling burgers, franks, and chicken off the grill.

"I'll get the corn," I offered, grabbing the other plate.

"Thanks, sweetheart," she said and my heart warmed at her term of endearment. Almost three years since anyone used a pet name with me, and I'd never liked the last one. Baby. Something about that one tweaked my nerves. Elise's earlier odd behavior disappeared with the stashing of the photos. Didn't take a genius to figure out she would rather I hadn't seen them.

"You're welcome. I just had an interesting moment in the garage that I want to tell you about. When do your guests leave?" I asked quietly as we walked the cooked food to her table. Ginny hadn't moved from the couch while Brian took part in a kid pile on in the backyard.

"Tuesday. We're planning to go kayaking tomorrow, though, if you want to join us?"

"I'm helping Cyrah paint her living room. Sorry, I thought you'd be busy all weekend."

"That's okay. The kayaking will be a long day anyway. Tuesday night?"

"Oh yes." Tuesday seemed so far away, but that's life as a Seattle lesbian, I guess.

We called everyone in for the buffet and fanned out into the backyard to eat. Brian kept up a constant chatter and gave me lots of great Elise-as-a-kid stories. Ginny didn't offer much by way of conversation, and Scott was unusually quiet as well. The dynamic he described to me when we'd put in his clutch suffocated us. Brian and Ginny treated him like he was a kid.

They even referred to his sisters as cousins, but they never called Scott the same.

After dinner, Scott suggested a movie that his friends and Chris wanted to see. It wasn't a kid's flick, but Ginny warmed to the idea of a Disney movie with the younger kids as well. Neither appealed to me, but I'd go if they asked.

"Why don't you take them up to Alderwood, Buster?" Elise offered, and I nearly jumped with glee. I should really stop acting like a teenager. Or maybe tomorrow.

"You don't want to see the smash 'em and blow 'em up movie, Lis? Hard to pass up this much fun," Brian coaxed without a grain of honesty. He knew his cousin pretty well. Those would be the last kind of films that appealed to her.

"No thanks, but you enjoy. We'll stay behind and clean up."

"If you're sure?" Ginny asked, more eager than I'd seen her all night.

"Sure, have fun."

"Well, if you're not here when we get back, it really was great getting to know you, Austy," Brian said to me.

"And you as well, Brian, Ginny. Have a great time, kids. Nice meeting you all."

They scooted out the door after much haranguing of coats and sweaters. Not until their cars backed out into the street, did I turn to step into Elise's arms. I didn't want to chance needing to leave those arms if the family came back for something.

"Bri liked you quite a bit." Elise nestled in next to my ear.

"I hope so. He's wonderful. It must have been fun growing up with him."

"Very, the only cousin who'd venture out with me on the slopes."

"I'm not sure Ginny was a fan of mine."

"I don't think it was you personally. I realized today that she's one of those people who loves to say that she's got a lesbian in the family but doesn't like to face the reality of it."

"How are you feeling about that realization?"

"Well, I'm not really a fan of hers, either. For lots of other reasons, so I guess we're even." Her lighthearted tone allowed me to drop my worry.

"God, this feels good," I admitted, pressing closer to her. "I should be thanking you for introducing me to your cousin, but right now, all I can think about is how great it is to finally get my hands on you. This whole evening was torturous."

Elise chuckled and slid her hands up to brush the sides of my breasts. "For me, too."

"Let's get the dishes done so you don't have to worry about that later, and we can return to this for a bit before they come back."

"Do you ever find it scary that we think so much alike?" Elise's eyes twinkled.

I didn't want to admit just how scary I'd found so much about our relationship thus far. All I could manage was a noncommittal nod. We went to work throwing leftovers into the fridge and clearing the dishes into the dishwasher. When the place showed no more signs of a party, we went out to the backyard to recline in the two cushioned Adirondack recliners.

Dusk settled over us and the sound of birds chirped into the open air. Trees provided a mostly private area from the one house which had a view of the backyard. I reached for her hand and slid my fingers over and between hers when I told her about Scott's friend.

"That kid continues to amaze me, you know?" Elise said after my recounting.

"I know," I agreed. Her hand started that erotic massage, and I settled back against the chair, accepting the G-rated intimacy. "Elise? Why didn't you want me to see those pictures?"

"I'm sorry, sweetheart. I didn't mean to react that way, and I would have shown you if you'd asked. It's just that some of those aren't ones I'd choose to show off."

"They're all beautiful."

"I didn't want you to see…" Elise didn't finish her

sentence, leaving me to guess.

"The bikini shots?"

"They were obviously taken before my accident."

"And you thought I'd see your bikini clad body and decide what?" She didn't offer an answer to my question. "That I wished your body looked like that now? I thought we went through this before. You're so very beautiful, Elise. More so now than in those pictures."

"Thank you. You're crazy, but it's very nice of you to say."

"It's not crazy, Elise. Can I tell you something?" I waited for her nod before I continued, "Those pictures, I know they're of you, I mean, I know that's your face, your hair, your body, but not your smile. Or at least, not any of the ones you've shown me."

She flashed me a curious look. "I have different smiles?"

"You modeled for years; you know you do. And I love that my favorites weren't in those pictures. I bet if you showed me all of them, I wouldn't spot them."

"You're the only one who's every noticed that." Elise turned onto her side to glance at me amazed. "What will I have to do to get you to tell me which are your favorites?"

I laughed at her suggestive tone. "Lots and lots of torture."

"See now, that's one of my favorites. So beautiful." Her finger traced the smile on my lips. "Time to utilize my investigative skills, starting with this." She reached down to unbutton my shirt.

"Elise?!" I yelped, grabbing at her hand. "This isn't—you can't—we—"

She giggled at my stunned expression, her hand continuing to expose more of my skin. "My neighbor left for the summer, Austy. No one will see us."

I glanced at the house whose backyard faced us and barely made out in the waning light that all the blinds were closed. No other house had a clear shot of our part of the backyard with those trees in the way. Still, this would be a first for me. We already went over me being a prude, okay?

"We can discuss turning you into an exhibitionist some other time." Elise's seductive voice lulled me into submission.

Through my now open shirt, she pulled my bra down to expose a breast and locked her lips on my nipple. Her hand snaked down to unzip my shorts and push them just over my hips. When she had enough access, she dipped her hand under my panties and her fingers began to circle my slippery clit exactly how she knew I liked it. No preamble, no teasing, no passing GO, just direct clitoral stimulation while her mouth sucked and her tongue flicked my nipple. The open air swirled around my moist nipple whenever she moved her mouth to kiss the fullness of my uncovered breast. The finger pleasuring me ruthlessly attacked, not letting up until the heat built so rapidly I exploded into orgasm in record time.

"Mmm, wow! I was kidding about the exhibitionist thing, but we're definitely going to look into that sometime." Elise smiled that sexy smile, her hand still riding out the pulsations.

Oh yeah, she has you now. You're a goner.

Chapter 16

Work occupied my days for the next week with the added treat of running into Elise in the office every so often. My caseload got a bit lighter with several plea agreements entered, and I no longer cared when Short Stack bellowed at me. Work could be grand when you weren't experiencing lesbian suckage.

"Austy? Agent Bridie on line three for you," Mary spoke through the intercom.

My heart did a little two-step inside my chest. I loved hearing her name, her voice, her laugh. Dopey, I know.

"Hi, Elise," I greeted softly.

"Hey, Austine."

Her tone made me feel sickeningly giddy. The kind of giddy that makes a cynic like me want to smack my own damn self. Thank God, none of my Virginia friends were around to hear this. They teased me ruthlessly enough when I wasn't with anyone. I could only imagine what they'd torture me with if they heard me carrying on like this.

"How's your day?" I asked.

"Good, and I think I'm about to make yours. We just picked up Dean Raymond on the Jucundus case. He'd been in Hong Kong until now, so we'll be able to start building a case against him."

"Way to go, Agent Bridie! That's great news."

"It looks very straightforward, enough to take it to trial right away. Should make your friend happy."

"To have it behind her, yes," I agreed tentatively. I'd almost forgotten about Willa's case and hadn't thought about her in weeks. Nothing like a real relationship to cure a pointless obsession.

"We still on for the weekend?" Elise asked about our first mini trip together.

Wenatchee awaited us with their annual apple festival. Basically, she wanted to show me part of Eastern Washington and turn me into a knowledgeable local. I didn't really care what we did as long as I got to spend the weekend staring at, kissing, and touching Elise.

"All set. I'll swing by tomorrow morning to pick you up unless Scott's out tonight?" I tried to harness the hope in my tone.

"Sorry, no. But he knows we're going away for the weekend, so I'm going to talk to him about new sleeping arraignments when we get back. I think he'd be more surprised if you didn't stay over starting next week."

"If you're sure."

"He adores you and has a great time hanging out with us. I don't see any resentment at all, and the kid's old enough to realize what's going on between us." Elise spoke definitively, and I couldn't help but hope that she implied something deeper and lasting about our relationship.

"Okay then, tomorrow at 9:00?" I heard her assent and finished more bravely than I'd been with her thus far, "I'll miss you tonight."

She let out an audible breath and signed off, "I'll miss you, too."

Five minutes after replacing the receiver, Roger popped his balding head through my open doorway. A confident sparkle lit his eyes as he announced, "I just heard the FBI got a warrant for Louie Evenzolo."

Since Elise had shared the news with me last night at dinner, I had to act surprised. "Good, so we're a go against the top guy on a RICO charge. I'm actually excited, Roger. What about you?"

"Hell yes. This is the biggest fish we've ever landed. I'm afraid the Big Guy's going to want this one for himself." He spoke of the U.S. Attorney.

"Not much we can do if that happens." I masked my disappointment at the prospect. I really wanted to try this case.

"I don't think it will. He's pretty Stone Age when it comes to tech stuff. Unless he wants to miss introducing crucial evidence, he's got to leave it to us."

"Don't let him hear you say that, Roger. I'd hate to lose you as a colleague."

"Funny, Austy. We should schedule some time on Monday to start plowing through what we've got on Evenzolo."

I checked my calendar. "About 2:00? I should be finished with closing arguments on Santiago by then."

"Works for me." Roger waved as he backed out the doorway.

The rest of the afternoon passed by quickly. Writing and rehearsing my closing for Santiago took most of the day since I wouldn't have time for it over the weekend. No working this weekend. It was so nice to have a life to leave work for. I thought about calling Cyrah to get together tonight as I'd been absent from her usual haunts for weeks. She got me to admit to seeing someone during our last phone call. It was the only way to get her to back off about getting out into the Seattle lesbian scene. I don't know how long of a reprieve I'd be given until she wanted to meet my "someone," but I probably shouldn't wrestle the tiger by calling her to go out this evening.

After work, I rode the surprisingly odor free bus through the darkening eve on my way home. Habit kept me breathing through my mouth until I stepped off at my stop, though. Tonight, I went to my left so I could walk past the sail making shop before winding down to my street. Not the fastest route, but I wasn't in a hurry to get home.

I peeked into the storefront window to check on the progress of the latest massive sail before continuing the last two blocks of my journey. At the only crosswalk, I waited for the light to change even though the street was nearly deserted. I do try to uphold the law whenever possible.

A van approached and moved into the closest lane to take the right turn but stopped directly in front of me as the light hit red. My seemingly constant giddiness kept me from getting annoyed that I now had to walk around the front of the van to get across the street. Before I even took a step, the side door of the van flew open with an echoing whoosh. Two men in ski masks jumped out and grabbed me, shoving me into the van. The door closed before a yell escaped my mouth. The sudden snatch and grab supplanted my initial fear with incredulity.

Four strong hands roughly slammed me into a chair inside the otherwise vacant van. I felt the wind blow out of my lungs from the impact and, for the next minute, struggled to replace the air with short wisps. The panic of suffocating overpowered the panic I felt at being held against my will. A pinning force locked my wrists in place on the chair's handles. My focus returned from the concentrated breathing to the grating sound of duct tape being unraveled to secure my legs. On instinct I kicked out, landing a blow on one of the men. A nearly silent curse slipped from his lips before he straightened up and backhanded me across the face. A slashing sting blossomed on my cheek, and the resulting curse wasn't silent.

The pain centered me and helped in assessing my situation. Yelling wouldn't do any good; the street had been deserted. Not only that, it would tip my growing fear. I screwed up every bit of my courage and asked forcefully, "What do you want?"

His hand moved so quickly I didn't see it, but I tasted the blood from my lip after this strike. Duct tape trapped my mouth shut soon after. My face throbbed where he'd struck me, twice now. A faint ringing tampered with the hearing in my right ear. I tried to focus on the pain to keep from letting the terror envelop me.

The van screeched to a stop, and the driver moved menacingly into the back. My learned response to fear was kicking in, numbing my senses. Self-defense courses readied me for another situation like this, but these men had been so quick that I don't think I could have done anything to prevent my being here. Still, nothing could stop the feeling of helplessness that now consumed me into inactivity.

"Austine Josephs Nunziata," the driver spoke gruffly, trying to mask his voice. "See, we know all about you, girly. Your grandmother's name was Anita Nunziata, your mother is Rita Nunziata. Do you get me?"

Those names triggered a welling of frightened tears. I tried to speak, but only muffled moans came out through the strip of tape.

"She gets it," the driver told the others confidently.

"Stupid for a smart bitch, ain't she?"

I twisted to look at the hitter and received another backhand against my cheek. Nothing numbing about the sting this time, and I cried out in response. With the tape over my mouth, I choked on the effort and had to consciously think to breathe through my nose.

"You made our boss real mad, and we don't like so much when Louie's mad. You hear what I'm saying? Here's how you're gonna change that. Drop the charges against Even Louie, or we start getting personal."

Louie Evenzolo? My RICO case. Knowing why they were holding me here didn't help to ease the fear or hurt.

The goon on my left took up the demands. "Keep the bean counter to blame, but drop on Louie or we come back for another chat. That one won't be as nice for you."

His two mates laughed heartily at his threat. My clenched body shivered against the hard back of the chair. Their promise didn't provide much comfort.

"Maybe she needs more convincing?" the one who'd been

silent rasped.

"Can do. The way I see it, bitch, you're easy to get to. See how you're visiting with us right now? You may change your routine more than others, but nobody's untouchable. It's why you're in the mobile Ritz here."

Another round of laughter from the boys. The faces of the people I cared about started to swim before my eyes. I felt my nasal passages begin to swell with the throbbing agony in my head. Calling on my panic breathing exercises, I managed to coax a flow of air into my lungs.

"I hear that you're the only one in that office that can make this stick with Even Louie. Right?" Nearly black eyes peered through the ski mask, looking for an answer. "I asked you a question, bitch!" When he hit me this time, I rocked back against the chair, absorbing the blow. He took the same hand and squeezed my neck enough to hurt but not strangle me. "You the only bitch can read those bean counter's files, ain'tcha?"

Not sure how to respond, I kept my head still. If I admitted to being the only one, they might kill me. If I told them others in the office had similar tech skills, I might be putting someone else in harm's way.

"No? You telling us someone else can work this case? That ain't what we heard. We heard your office used to settle on cases like this because they didn't have nobody to try 'em. That means you're our only problem."

The driver moved back up front and started the van. A sharp swerve turned us around on the road. The two left back with me hung on to the sides of the van, while my chair tipped perilously and slammed back upright.

"Consider this your only warning. We can find you, your family, and that pretty dyke slut you're…hell, whatever it is you dyke sluts do together. She got herself a kid, too."

My eyes grew wide at his threats. Not once had I noticed someone following me, and that was the kind of thing I always notice.

The van slowed to a crawl. The two men who'd snatched me off the street both leaned down to stick their faces right up to mine. I could feel their breath against my face.

"Drop the charges on Louie, or we have a little more fun together next time," the fiercest of the trio hoarsely voiced.

He produced a knife and I slammed back against the chair, trying to put more distance between us. He cut my legs and arms free, opened the door, and they shoved me out onto the pavement. An ankle twisted when I hit the ground, and I rolled brutally for several turns until my newly scraped palms and knees righted me. My head knocked against the ground on three of the spins, creating a pain that felt like someone tore my brain in half.

"Jesus! Austy!" I recognized Joe's voice calling out from somewhere.

I looked toward the sound and barely registered the door to his shop. They'd dropped me in front of my building. I would have considered it convenient, but I knew it was their way of showing me they knew where I lived and could get to me any time.

Message received.

Chapter 17

"Were you hit by a car?" Joe appeared at my side. He lightly touched my back while I struggled to swing my head up to look at him from my position on my hands and knees. "Don't try to move. Let me call an ambulance."

I tried to speak, but the duct tape still fastened my mouth closed. Tilting my head to the ground, I pulled the tape off my mouth. "No," I managed, feeling only scrapes and bruises from my landing on the pavement. A three hour wait in an emergency room for some bandages wasn't going to advance my wellbeing.

"If you got hit by a car, you need to get to a hospital."

"It wasn't a car. I need to call my office." I labored to stand.

"I think you might have a head injury. Let me take you to a doctor." Joe placed his hands under my arms and pulled me into a standing position.

Severe pain shot from my heel and into my lower leg when I tested my ankle. Sprained for sure. Joe felt me stumble and slipped an arm around my waist to help me limp into the building. "I just need to get upstairs, Joe, please."

"Tell me what happened." Concern marked his tone.

We limped into the elevator as I gave an edited version of what got me into this state. When the doors slid open on the third floor, we caught Helen starting her descent on the staircase.

"What happened? You're bleeding. Are you okay?" She stepped toward us and guided her arm around my other side, slowing our progress to my door.

"She was abducted," Joe reported. "Then they threw her out of a van."

"Good God!" Helen raised her voice. "We have to call the police."

"I'm going to call my office; they'll know what to do." I tried to sound reassuring but failed pathetically.

Joe fished my keys out of my coat pocket and let us into my loft. Helen went into the bathroom for bandages while Joe watched me call my office. Roger hadn't left yet, and I gave him a brief rundown of the threats. He wanted to come over, but I talked him out of it by letting him call the police.

Helen tended to the wounds on my palms and the cuts on my face. Whatever she was using stung nearly as bad as the scrapes themselves. She hurried over to her loft to retrieve a wrap for my ankle and came back moments before the police arrived.

Two plainclothes detectives and a uniformed officer waited in the open doorway until Joe waved them in. The throbbing pain in my head and body intensified as they waltzed freely into my safe haven. I studied their detective shields and asked them to sit while the officer returned to "guard" the door.

"Guys," I addressed Helen and Joe. "Some of this may be privileged information to my case. I hate to ask, but would you mind excusing us for now?"

They looked at me with reluctance but left with my thanks and their promise to keep their front door open. Detective O'Neil, a burly barrel of a man, began asking questions and taking notes. Neither he nor the wiry Detective Black seemed fazed by my reddened cheek, bleeding lip, the ice pack on my ankle, or the cuts on my palms. They didn't offer sympathy, which I liked, but they both perked up when I mentioned Louie Evenzolo's name.

"Even Louie? He's like a specter; no one gets to him."

"The FBI just arrested him. I've got an arraignment with him on Monday."

An insistent knocking on my front door drew our attention just as the detectives started hemming and hawing about the "fibbies" and it being a federal case. O'Neil looked at me to ask if he should get the door. My preference would have us ignore it, but the men in my living room might think that odd.

O'Neil went to the door and stepped out into the hallway. I made out several people talking at once, but the door hid them from view. It was getting tougher to focus on direct conversation; I didn't have any hope of following voices in the background. Besides, my attention turned to the roughness of my sofa and the excessiveness of the blazing lights in my loft. Sunglasses indoors suddenly didn't seem like such an outrageous idea anymore.

"Austy?" The one voice I could recognize through any crowd brought my head around in the direction of the front door. Elise stood out on the landing with her colleague George. Seeing her right now when I was barely holding it together, I felt my resolve diminish. My eyes filled with tears and a sobbing breath choked out. She looked at the others and said, "A minute, please?" Like most men faced with teary women, they gratefully bolted from the loft.

When the door closed, she rushed forward and collapsed on the couch to take me into her strong arms. She held me for a long time then carefully brought my face into her hands and kissed around the cuts. "Are you okay?"

"Scared." And relieved to admit it.

"Me, too. Petrified, actually. My AD called on my way home after Roger got a hold of him. I'm sure he told me what happened, but all I heard was your name and I broke every traffic law getting here."

"Thank you," I whispered quietly. The stabbing hurt in my head reduced to a dull throb with the feel of her hands gently turning my palms and lifting my ankle for inspection.

"I'm so sorry this happened, sweetheart. It's impossible to focus right now. I just want to hold you and keep you safe all night."

"I'd like that, too." Relief began to chip away at my fear. Remembering that we weren't entirely alone, I said, "But we're professionals, and those guys won't stay out there all night. Maybe we should bring them—wait! They know about us and that you have Scott. They threatened you both."

Elise sat back against the couch and took in the information. Calmly, she said, "It's just a scare tactic, Austy. Did they mention your family, too?" I nodded in reply. "These guys are wannabes, that's all. They aren't connected; California's off their radar."

"They didn't seem like wannabes, Elise, and I couldn't take it if something happened to you or Scott."

She pulled me close again and said reassuringly, "I'm the armed one, remember? Nothing's going to happen to us."

I wished I could be as sure as she was. Benefits of a career in law enforcement, I guess. "I didn't tell the detectives yet. Should I?"

We hadn't really discussed keeping our relationship private but discretion seemed the right course considering we worked certain cases together. I knew my office wouldn't have a problem, thanks to some unsolicited information given to me by another lesbian at the courthouse. I wasn't as sure with the FBI, though. I got the impression the FBI didn't believe its employees had a personal life. If they did, the FBI certainly didn't want to hear about it.

Elise pulled back and looked thoughtful for a moment. "George is probably breaking the news to them that this is our investigation now. I'll fill George in on having threats issued to your family and friends."

"Okay." It was so easy to let her think for me right now.

"Honey, you're still shaking." My eyes welled again at her concern. Even cradled in her arms, I couldn't get warm enough. "Trust that I'm going to keep you safe until we find these guys and Louie Evenzolo is behind bars."

Her words erased a lot of the fright that still squeezed at my heart. I tried to nod, but the stabbing twinge returned. I weakly muttered, "Thank you."

"Can George come inside, or should I see if Helen will let us use her place?"

"The detectives were already in here, so he might as well come in." I repositioned myself on the couch, my ankle propped up on the coffee table with a slightly warm ice pack draped over it. Elise's fingers wiped my face where she'd kissed me and dabbed at my tears. Her arms went around me one last time before she got up from the couch and let George inside.

Over the next half hour, I gave a surprisingly calm narration of my encounter with Louie Evenzolo's men. Little details floated into my mind like the make and model of the van, their eye colors, builds, and skin tone. I deduced where we'd probably pulled off the road for their three-on-one blitz. George was a font of information about Louie's organization. Until the accountant flipped and Elise traced his bank transfers, he'd been toiling away for three years trying to get this guy. He confirmed what Elise said about Louie being small time, but for some reason, that wasn't much solace.

As my tale wound down, we heard a commotion outside my door. Knocking then shouting. "…friend, that's who!"

George hustled to open the door and was nearly knocked over by Willa pushing past the officer stationed at the door. Petite Willa almost made it by his grasping arm, before Elise waved him off. My surprise at seeing her bolted me into a teetering stand, favoring my hurt ankle.

"A.J.! Are you all right?" She rushed into the living room and embraced me. Desperation deepened her hug, and I responded in kind, happy for the familiarity.

"Now I am," I spoke into her hair, comforted by her customary scent.

"Helen called all over trying to find me. Quinn got to Nykos who knew where I was. I wish I'd been here sooner, hon. Helen told me you were attacked, something to do with one of the criminal cases?" She wasn't letting go, and I didn't care one bit that my body ached or that blood swelled painfully in my ankle.

"Yes."

She pulled her torso back from our hug to study me. "Oh no, look what they've done to your beautiful face." Her fingers lightly traced across my cheek, and I felt my face flush at her careful examination and compliment.

"Willa," was all I could handle saying.

"That's it! You're done here. You're coming back home." Willa's firm tone bordered on anger. "This wouldn't happen to you in Charlottesville. You can have any job you want. I'll hire you for in-house counsel, or Lauren wants you to share her firm, or whatever you want."

Charlottesville sounded great right now. Willa felt great right now. Friends are the best. "Willa." The protest sounded weak even to me.

"Think about it? The group is going berserk. Concerned beyond belief and pissed at me because they think I'm responsible for everything in this city." She'd gone a little rigid, and I remembered that she often dealt with fear by getting angry. "I can't believe this happened to you. I'll never forgive myself for encouraging you to make this move."

Amazed at her caring words, I raised my hands up to her face and forced her to look me in the eye. "Willa, please stop. I moved here for my career."

"Look what it's done to you." Willa's hands gripped the backsides of mine to display my palms.

"I'm fine."

She stared at me with a mix of concern, love, anger, and fear. "You're going to have to come up with something more convincing. Lauren's on a plane tomorrow, Jessie at the end of the week, then Caroline and Sam, and they'll keep cycling through. They don't trust me to be influential enough. For now, we've got to figure out security for you. When is this case resolved?"

My head swam with the prospect of my Virginia friends coming here to get me to move back. "Weeks before the trial even starts."

"Fine, we'll get personal security until you put him away."

"No, Will," I declined automatically.

"Not an option. Either you agree, or I hire them and they follow you around. I don't care if that pisses you off; we've got to keep you safe. Unless you'll consider moving back home until your trial starts? You can stay with me and Quinn."

"No." Friends here, okay; moving back, no; staying with Willa, definitely not. My brain could only comprehend condensed phrases right now.

"Fine, I'm sure there have to be security firms out here that specialize in personal security. Or maybe we can get off duty officers?" Her eyes moved to George and then behind me. "Elise? I'm sorry, I didn't even see you. Are you involved in this case?" Willa's tone moved into hopeful as she finally dropped her arms from her lose hold of me and walked over to shake Elise's hand.

Elise stood as still as a sentry. Her face had gone a little ashen, and she showed no animation when she took Willa's hand in greeting. She didn't look at me when Willa came back over and helped me take a seat on the couch. The look on Elise's face worried me. I'd never seen that expression before, or lack of expression, really.

"George and I are both assigned to the case, yes." Her tone was more dead than flat.

"That's good, isn't it, Age? Can you recommend a security company, or perhaps some of your colleagues for her security?"

George spoke up immediately, "I can arrange for that."

Realization dawned slowly on the inconvenience this would become, but I knew it was pointless to fight Willa on this. Although, having off-duty FBI on my back made seeing Elise impossible if we weren't going to tell her colleagues. I waited for her to jump in and suggest a private security team, but she stayed silent and still.

"Please do. We can work out a billing system, right?" Willa stood and handed George one of her business cards. Letting her pay for nearly everything had been the hardest part about getting used to having an obnoxiously rich friend. "Age, can I use your phone? I've got to check in with the Virginians or they'll all be on a plane tomorrow." I nodded and heard George mention that he was going out in the hallway to arrange for a security detail on his cell phone. Willa grasped my arm lightly before she left. "You're really all right? Or at least as much as you can be?"

"Yes, thank you for everything, Will." I felt better that she seemed to drop the initial anger, or fear rather, by making herself useful.

When she disappeared through the kitchen doorway to use the phone in the guest bedroom, I turned back to Elise. At least she was looking at me now, but her eyes stayed unreadable.

"Elise?" I moved to get up but the pain in my swollen ankle never allowed for complete liftoff.

An eternity passed before she spoke in a hoarse voice, "You're still in love with her."

My head snapped into a double-take, not digesting her statement before words flew out of my mouth. "What? Willa?"

"Yes, Willa, of course, Willa." Elise shifted her weight, finally breaking her impression of a statue. "I knew there was a chance, but I didn't think it was fully developed."

"Elise, no."

"Don't," she ordered in a pained voice, lifting up a palm for emphasis. "You're going to tell me what? That you're not? You're obviously very comfortable with her being here. You couldn't stop touching her, and I've become familiar with what makes you blush. I realize you've known her for years, that you touch easily, and that you're often embarrassed. But you're letting her take care of you. One thing I know for certain, you don't give up control to just anyone."

If there'd been jealousy in her tone, I'd be more prepared. Quiet resolve, though, I didn't know how to refute.

"She's my best friend, Elise. Even when she wasn't a millionaire, she took care of things. It's how she shows affection. We all had to learn to accept it." I tried to stay calm, fighting my rising wave of panic.

Running a hand roughly through her hair, she looked away but not before I caught the start of tears in her eyes. "I thought if we…if you were willing, and the last few weeks, that I might have been mistaken. God, I'm so foolish. I can't believe I've fallen for someone who's already given away her heart."

She just said "fallen," as in past tense. Like she's already in love with me. Did I hear that correctly? My heart beat wildly in hope and erratically in fear. "You—you're—did you just…" I didn't trust my ears anymore.

"I don't do this, Austy. A five year break from even dating, and I go after the worst kind of unavailable. I'm always so careful, but I thought you were worth the risk."

"Elise, this is crazy. You're reading something here that doesn't exist," I pleaded, my mouth going dry.

"I don't blame you, Austy. I'm the one that made a mistake." She looked over at the sound of Willa coming back through the kitchen. In a quiet and sincere voice, she informed me, "I hope loving her gives you enough, because you deserve all the best."

Suddenly Joe's theory of having sustained a head injury didn't sound too far off. This couldn't really be happening. Too many responses and protests jumped into my head, making it hurt terribly. I barely noticed George walk back into the loft and exchange words with Elise and Willa. It felt like my thoughts were processing at a dial-up rate when everyone else worked at broadband speed. Did she just break off our relationship? Over an unverified guess?

Whatever they were talking about, I didn't comprehend a word. When I saw Elise moving out the door, I sprang off the couch and my ankle buckled, sending a sharp pain all the way up to my knee.

"Elise!" I called, but Willa's surprised yelp drowned me out. She rushed to assist my hobble. "I'm okay. Is Elise leaving?" I looked at George who nodded. With excruciating difficulty, I started toward the door.

"Age, you shouldn't be walking on that. What if it's broken?" Willa slipped an arm around my waist hoisting some of my weight against her.

"It's just a sprain. I have to talk to Elise."

George stopped my progress. "She's headed back to the office to file this report; then I guess she's leaving town for the weekend. She told me to tell you that she'd check in the next time she's at the courthouse."

"But she—we're supposed—that's—" I finished with a frustrated growl. I prayed that this was just an emotional meltdown on both our parts and common sense would patch things up. Right now, I could hardly move from the pain and tension of the evening.

"We're getting you to a doctor, Age. That ankle looks bad, and my sister's only so good at first aid." Willa didn't allow for my protest about emergency rooms. "Nykos is dating a doctor right now. When I talked to him, he asked her if she would see you tonight. She's expecting us at her office in a half hour."

All the fight had left me anyway. I'd come very close to experiencing the worst event of my life again, got thrown out of a moving van, had my privacy invaded, and severely distressed my girlfriend all in one night. Thankfully, I didn't have a dog to lose otherwise I'd be living a country western song.

Chapter 18

The worst thing about having overbearing friends is that they're, you know, overbearing. They don't know the concept of privacy or alone time. For instance, they can make chasing after a gorgeous woman to beg forgiveness pretty much impossible. They'd insist on knowing about the whole misunderstanding which centered around one of the overbearing friends. Back to Seattle lesbian suckage. Oh, and crutches suck, too.

Monday morning my entourage included Lauren, Willa, Quinn, and one of the four rotating off duty FBI agents whose name I kept forgetting. We'd worked out a system of revolving Virginia friends to stay with me at my loft and off duty FBI agents to shuttle me safely to and from work or any other activity. When I say "we" worked out a system, I meant that Willa and the rest of the clan imposed and enforced the system. My slight concussion and ligament tear apparently meant that I couldn't think for myself. I'd forgotten how I used to let them roll all over me in Virginia.

The entourage would stay with me for the arraignment of Evenzolo. Afterward, Willa would go back to work, Lauren and Quinn would do some sightseeing, and hopefully the bodyguard would realize that the U.S. Attorney's office inside the federal courthouse with all its metal detectors was all the protection I'd need.

"How're you doing, Aust?" Mary asked as I took everyone to the front desk for visitor badges. She examined my bruised face, cut lip, bandaged hands, ankle brace and crutches before even glancing at the four people standing behind me. Quinn carried my briefcase, Lauren my umbrella, and Willa my overcoat. Off duty Kevin Costner carried an imposing presence. "Got to say, girl, I've seen you look better."

My laughter died in a cough of pain, reminding me of my still tender ribcage. "These are my friends Lauren, Quinn, and Willa. Get used to seeing them because I don't think they're ever leaving. This guy," I pointed at Larry, that was his name, "I hope won't have to be around that long."

"Whatever." She was the very picture of nonchalance, although there was a lingering glance at Lauren and back to me as if trying to figure out if I was using "friend" as a euphemism. I knew we'd be discussing it the next time we had lunch together. Just what I needed, another overbearing friend to add to my gaggle. "Word is the Chief is sitting in on your arraignment this morning. I don't need to ask if you're ready, do I?" She winked and handed the badges to my friends.

Swinging down the hallway on crutches with my merry band of friends, it was like I'd become the most popular woman in the office. Roger must have held his own version of show and tell before I arrived. I steeled myself for a long day with the only bright spot hinging on whether or not Elise would come to the hearing. Both my office and the FBI thought Louie Evenzolo was big. Surely, the investigating agents would want to show up when we charged him and decided on bail.

"Comparison point number 413: you'd have a much bigger office if you joined my, excuse me, *our* law practice, Age," Lauren indicated as we entered my cramped workspace. Since deplaning on Saturday, she'd been coming up with reasons why I needed to move back to Virginia. Evidently, she had over 400 items on her list.

"It wouldn't have this view, though, would it, Lanky?" I retorted with the same exasperating airiness I'd used all weekend. I loved Lauren, but as my closest and longest standing friend, she could be the most overbearing. Almost none of my defenses worked on her.

"Will's rich enough; she can build this view for you back in Charlottesville, right, Will?"

"L," Quinn warned calmly, her role all weekend. She always sensed when people had just about enough.

I stuffed the case file and legal pad with my case notes into my briefcase. Arraignments weren't that much work, but the added pressure of the big boss being there made me double check that I had every contingency covered.

Roger showed up at my door and looked momentarily startled by the five people stuffed in my office. "Hey, you're Quinn Lysander, aren't you?"

"Yes," Quinn acknowledged with a modest smile.

"This is great. My daughter and I used to watch you play for the Storm. She's a junior, now, pretty good player herself. Hoping to get a scholarship."

"Subtle, Rog," I informed him sarcastically. Quinn suffered these beseeching hints all the time, one of the hazards of her job. "Roger, these are my friends, Quinn obviously, that's Willa and this is Lauren, and you know Larry, don't you?"

"Hello everyone. Quite an ensemble, Austy." He gave me a meaningful look like he knew Quinn was gay and probably heard that Willa was her partner during all the publicity surrounding her company's IPO last year, which made me a lesbian by association. Roger's shortsighted assumptions tended to be obstacles in our cases together; he just happened to be right this time. What I really liked was that he made the association, digested it, and moved on. "How are you doing, anyway?"

"Fine, Rog. How are you?"

"Good, as long as you're ready?"

"*Pronto. Andiamo, amici!*" I find that Italian exclamations are the only way to get my friends to blindly follow my lead. I charged out of the office, knowing that Quinn would grab my briefcase.

Reporters swarmed outside the courtroom, hankering for a gallery badge from the bailiff. Roger opened the door for all of us, and I crutched down the center aisle, parking my crew in the second row on my side. Quinn followed and set my briefcase beside me before returning to sit next to Willa. The courtroom was partially filled, and I glanced about hoping to find Elise.

"How's everyone working out, Austy?" George came up along the first row of seats.

"Great, thanks, George. I'm feeling a little ridiculous about the whole thing."

George ran his eyes from my braced ankle up to my bruised face. "It's not ridiculous."

Trying for offhand, I asked, "Is Elise here?"

"She's been temporarily reassigned to a new taskforce. She'll be available for this trial when it goes, but the FBI's exploiting her other talents right now. Your office doesn't need to worry, though, we've got a couple other agents that work computer forensics all lined up."

"I see." But, not really.

George turned back to the seats, passing Roger as he took second chair at our table. I clanked my crutches onto the floor and unpacked my briefcase before setting it under the table. Coffee breath on my ear made me look up as I was taking a seat.

"What happened, beautiful?" Gregory Stokes asked in a husky voice.

"Some guy wouldn't stop hitting on me, and let's just say, I'm in better shape than he is," I said, complete with batting eyelashes.

"Meeoow!" Gregory mewled and chose to ignore my eye roll. "Stick with me, baby, I'll treat you right."

"What are you doing here?"

"Defending my client."

"You're representing Evenzolo?"

"Only the best, babycakes."

"Okay, that's gonna stop."

He backed up a step. "Just wishing you luck. Roger, good to see you."

Roger grunted hello from beside me. A flurry of voices came at us from the entrance. We both turned to watch the big boss, the U.S. Attorney himself, walk into the courtroom.

"His Highness has arrived," Greg mumbled and sidled over to his table with four or five other expensively suited lawyers from his firm.

"Austine, Roger," Reginald Barclay, the U.S. Attorney, greeted us from beside our table.

"Reginald." Roger rocketed out of his chair.

"Sir." I took a little longer to rise and shake his hand.

"How are you, Austine?"

He was asking about my injuries, but I guessed he really wanted to know about the case. "Ready to go, sir." After only six months in the office, I didn't feel as comfortable as Roger in addressing Reginald by his first name.

"Good to hear. I'll be right here if you need me." He stepped back to the front row and sat beside Short Stack and two other chief prosecutors. *Well, well, the gang's all here.*

A clerk sounded out, "Oye, Oye, court is now in session for the U.S. District Court for the Western District of Washington. All rise for the Honorable Gail Cosin."

I tucked a grin against my chest as I rose out of my chair, resting my ankle brace on the ground to keep my balance. Judge Cosin was my favorite; fair, no nonsense, and a quick draw with rulings. Freaked out some of the lawyers, but I loved it.

A gavel sounded and Judge Cosin spoke, "Please be seated. A little crowded in here today, Sally," she addressed her courtroom deputy. "If you're throwing me a party, I think the surprise is ruined." Ripples of polite laughter rolled through the room. "What's on the docket?"

Down a level and to the left of the judge, Sally stood from her post. "The United States of America v. Louie Evenzolo."

Greg and I rose together like we'd been part of a synchronized swim team for several years. "Austine Nunziata for the Prosecution, Your Honor."

"Gregory Stokes for the Defense, Your Honor."

Her eyes did a quick flicker from me to Greg and right back to me. I really didn't think I looked all that bad, but maybe bruised women make everyone nervous.

"Ms. Nunziata, is standing a difficulty for you?"

"No, Your Honor, but thank you for asking." I could have sworn I heard a snort coming from the defense table. Louie Evenzolo must have snuck in while we were kissing our boss's ass. He slouched confidently in the chair closest to Greg and looked smug enough to snort in a federal courtroom.

"Does your client want to add something to these proceedings, Mr. Stokes?" Judge Cosin must have heard it, too.

"No, Your Honor."

"Fine. Mr. Evenzolo, you're being charged with Money Laundering, Extortion, and Fraud under the Racketeer Influenced and Corrupt Organization statutes. How do you plead?"

Gregory crooked a hand under Evenzolo's armpit and forced him out of the chair to respond. "This is all just a little mix-up, ma'am."

If I weren't being watched by my boss, my boss's boss, several reporters, and a judge that I highly respected, I would have laughed loudly at his response. No one was that uninformed about courtroom procedure; he must be trying for disrespectful. I cocked my head to take in his fine wool suit, flashy diamond and gold watch, and equally pricey pinky ring. The kind of ring that could cause blindness if the sun slanted against it at the wrong angle.

Judge Cosin looked up from the briefs on her dais and,

without turning her head, flicked her eyes at the defendant. "This is an arraignment in my courtroom, Mr. Evenzolo. You'll enter an official plea, and you'll address me appropriately."

Gregory whispered frantically to his client, but Louie brushed him off. "I'm innocent, Judge."

"Here's your one free, remedial courtroom lesson, Mr. Evenzolo," Judge Cosin began in a tone that would sound stern to the untrained ear. More accustomed to it, I immediately picked up on the intended caustic wit. "After this you'll have to pay your counsel five hundred dollars an hour to learn how to behave properly in this courtroom. You're here to enter a plea on the counts of Money Laundering, Extortion, and Fraud. There are two possible answers: guilty or not guilty. Your alleged innocence has no relevance in these proceedings."

I was starting to develop a little crush on Judge Cosin. She was breaking out all kinds of sass this morning. If I even looked in her deputy's direction, I knew we'd both start giggling if Evenzolo didn't wise up soon. Sally and I spent many lunch breaks rehashing courtroom antics. She had a million great stories, but this one would rate pretty high.

"Not guilty." Nothing like progress.

"So entered. How long will the U.S. need for a trial?"

"About two weeks to present all evidence and testimony, Your Honor," I replied.

"And the Defense?"

"About a week."

"Sally, first available date for a three week trial?"

"September second, Judge."

"Any objections to a speedy trial date?"

"None," Greg and I both said, perfecting that synchronization thing.

"Very good. I assume you have a recommendation for bail, Ms. Nunziata?"

"I do, Your Honor. The Prosecution believes that Mr. Evenzolo has a nearly unlimited asset base and poses a credible flight risk. I offer affidavits prepared by the investigating officers identifying Mr. Evenzolo's financial accounts to verify our concern for his flight risk. If I may enter these documents?" She nodded her head in reply, and I waited for the clerk to collect and carry them up to the dais. "We are asking that no bail be granted in this matter."

"Your Honor, that's—"

Judge Cosin put up a hand to stop Greg from continuing. She thumbed through the documents I'd provided. The figures impressed her enough to raise her eyebrows and look expectantly at Greg, dropping her hand.

"This is not a violent crimes case, Your Honor. There is no statutory reason to deny bail. My client has many ties to the Seattle area. He even vacations in Washington State. There is no evidence to suggest that he is a flight risk."

"He certainly has the means, Mr. Stokes." The judge flipped through the last affidavit.

"As you're aware, Judge, means and evidence are two separate difficulties and only one is pertinent to this hearing."

"Perhaps you and your client can study courtroom decorum together, counselor. Maybe give him a discount on your billing rate while you discover that it's never a good idea to tell a judge what's pertinent to a trial. What do you say?"

Crushing pretty hard, right now. Probably on the good side of her sixties, Judge Cosin no longer seemed too old for me. She was definitely on fire today, and I fought the desire to smile at her scolding.

Humbled, Greg continued, "You're right, Judge. I didn't mean to imply that you weren't up on procedural content. I will state, however, that a defendant should not be penalized or treated unfairly due to his economic status. We're seeking reasonable bail on this matter."

Judge Cosin glanced at me to see if I'd chime in again. Other than her tongue lashing and hope that she'd consider his ability to jump bail at any time, I didn't expect her to deny bail. She seemed to be asking me to give her some reason, but case law didn't provide one.

"While I agree that his means are vast, to deny bail in a RICO case without murder charges would be unprecedented. Bail is set at two million dollars."

So not fair. Two hundred grand would feel like pennies in the coin jar to this guy. Defendants who have enough for the cash bail shouldn't be allowed the ten percent surety bail option.

"Thank you, Your Honor," I spoke up, knowing it was the best result we could get.

"Yes, thank you, Judge," Greg thought to add after he heard my polite reply to her ruling.

"We'll see you back here on August eighteenth for any pretrial motions." She cracked her gavel to signify the end of our arraignment. "Let's break for fifteen minutes to clear the courtroom for the next arraignment." She gave another concerned glance at my condition, nodded, then swept from the room.

"Well done, Austine," the chief said loudly from the front row.

"Thank you, sir."

He took full advantage of a judgeless courtroom and regaled the press who'd pushed in toward him. My friends got boxed in, and I was tempted to bolt through Judge's chambers to enjoy a moment alone. Roger stepped up beside Reginald to feed him any details about the case. Gregory took up his own post near the defense table with the rest of the reporters. I wondered how bad a tongue lashing they'd get if Judge Cosin returned from break and these two were still acting as ring masters in their own fabricated circuses.

Knowing it would take a while for the aisle to clear enough for my crutches to glide through, I took my time stuffing the case file back into my briefcase. I leaned down to grab the crutches off the floor. Just as I propped one under my left arm, I heard a deep voice at my ear.

"I bet you used to be a pretty little thing. Too bad you ran into somp'um hard." Louie Evenzolo stood about as close as another human can get without touching. The menace in his voice triggered my adrenaline, and I felt the tremble start with the throb in my ankle and pulse through my whole body. If I said or did anything, he'd see my fear, but the alternative seemed even worse. "Or maybe you fell outta somp'um? Cases like this can be hazardous to your health."

"Exit's that way, Mr. Evenzolo." An equally intimidating voice spoke from the other side of him. The tone I didn't recognize, but the voice belonged to Elise. Just realizing she'd made it to the hearing brought about a sense of relief; knowing she wouldn't leave me alone with Evenzolo expunged my fear.

"Just having a friendly little chat," Louie practically sang in smugness.

"There's a sign over the door marking your way in case you get lost." Elise was all business.

"What? It's a free country, little lady. I can talk to whoever I want."

"Actually, you can't." My voice returned without a tremor I'm proud to say. "It's called ex-parte when you talk to me without your attorney, and it's 'whomever.'"

"It's sad seeing a pretty girl all beaten up like this." Louie gave us the kind of look that only comes from a man who's used to saying and doing whatever he wanted.

Elise moved to stand closely beside me and said forcefully, "This one's protected. You understand, Louie? If you touch her again, I'll make sure your prison time is unpleasant. Made guys don't like wannabes, and I can get you transferred to a facility where you'll be surrounded by a whole lot of the real deal. Am I making myself clear?"

"Now, now, baby, you're too gorgeous to waste your life on empty threats. Come home with Big Louie; I've got more than you could ask for."

Elise stepped forward, her five-six slim frame half a foot shorter than Louie's ominous form, but an intimidating power rolled off her in almost visible waves. "Listen up, Louie. You shouldn't be worried about what I can do to you if you come after Ms. Nunziata again. You should be worried about whether or not I'll enjoy doing it. Leave here before I feel the need to brandish my weapon and make everyone nervous."

He flippantly raised two palms in defeat, but the glint in his eyes told me that he wasn't intimidated. What must it be like to have an ego that large? He backed up and swung around to join his lawyer and the frenzy of reporters.

"Thank you," I said before I could summon one of the rehearsed if-I-see-Elise lines.

"No need," Elise replied gruffly, glaring over at my supposed bodyguard who was busy chatting with George.

"I'm so happy you're here, Elise." I spoke in the soft tone I didn't know I possessed until meeting her. "Can we please talk?"

Elise snapped her stern look back to me. Only her eyes softened as she dropped her gaze to take in my ankle brace and back up to gage the progress of my bruises and cuts. "Are you all right? Your ankle?"

"Partial ligament tear. I'm off the crutches in a week, the brace a few more."

"But otherwise?"

"Yes, I'm fine, thank you."

"Good." Elise's voice revealed her concern. "George put together a solid detail for you. Follow their instructions, and you'll stay safe."

"Elise, please, I don't want to talk about that. The other night, I wasn't entirely myself. I couldn't even fathom what you were saying. I didn't—"

"Really? Couldn't fathom it, huh?" she cut me off and made a show of turning to pick out Willa through the crowd of reporters still hounding my boss. "There's nothing else to say, Austy. It looks like you have everything you need." She took a step toward the gallery.

"Elise, wait," I pleaded, grabbing her arm.

She looked down at the placement of my hand on her arm.

The one I used to hold occasionally when we walked together because I couldn't keep myself from touching her when I was around her. "Please respect my boundaries. We've got to continue working together, and I'd like to keep that uncomplicated." Her voice and message carried the same finality of tone as on Friday night.

This was me being dumped by my first Seattle girlfriend. I let go of her arm and my hope fell with the drop of my hand.

"All right. I'll do whatever you want." I knew my voice gave away my anguish, but she no longer seemed to care.

Chapter 19

Days drifted into weeks of the same routine with different Virginia houseguests. Had they not all planned to come visit me over the summer anyway, I would have put an end to their protectiveness. At least I'd progressed past the crutches to a walking boot, which I'd get to ditch at the end of the week.

The personal security detail functioned more as a chauffer service than protection. Not one incident had occurred since being stuffed into a van nearly three weeks ago. No one following us, either. I'd broached the subject of dropping the security crew, but they were convinced no one had attacked me because they were around. As much as I hated to admit it, their logic made sense.

Working a high profile case allowed me to turf most of my other cases to different litigators in the office. One more day left on the kidnapping trial then I'd be able to devote more of my time to Willa's case. Hers started next week, and after that, the case against Evenzolo in three weeks. Both were shaping up nicely, which meant all was well on the work front.

For fun, my Virginia friends forced me out to a bar once a week. The singles, Lauren and Jessie, had ulterior motives in wanting to go, but even the couples loved the change of pace from their favorite club back in Charlottesville. My friend Cyrah enjoyed having me around more often and really liked the Virginians. I sat at a pub table daydreaming about Elise while they danced, laughed, and drank. They had a grand ol' time, and I, not so much. Hopeless, I know.

As for Elise, she'd been absent from our offices for weeks while she worked her taskforce. Even Scott wasn't around, having taken some of his summer vacation to visit his mom. With him gone, it eliminated the off chance of running into Elise outside of Joe's shop checking on him as she'd done so often while we were together. Actually, having Scott out of town wasn't such a bad thing. The last time we ran into each other outside Joe's, he could barely look me in the eye. As much as he seemed to like me, he knew that something had happened to end my relationship with his cousin, and he didn't know how to handle it. Well, take a number, 'cause neither did I.

"Austy?" Short Stack stood in the doorway, his fingers drummed against another case file. If I gave in to Lauren's demands to join her law firm back in Virginia, I'd at least eliminate this repetitive scene from my life. "You're going to love this one."

"I'd love it even more if it landed on someone else's desk."

"Ha-ha. Insider trading. Small brokerage boutique in town whose owners are related to the owner of a tech IPO. They forced their associates to purchase hot issues in personal accounts with money loaned by the owners of the brokerage firm."

"And I'm enamored of this how?" Sarcasm: the cynic's attempt at humanity.

"One of the associates kept computer records of all purchases, gains, and transfers. Very neat and tidy, and she went to the NASD to get the investigation started. All that's missing is a pretty bow to go with the gift wrapping."

"Fine, but I'm taking a week off after Evenzolo closes. After that, I'll calendar this one and all the others you'll give me between now and then."

"Get a guilty verdict on Evenzolo, and you'll deserve it." He tossed the file folder onto my desk and disappeared down the hall.

"What if I don't win?" I muttered out loud. The invasion of the Virginia clan limited the opportunities to talk to myself.

I gathered up my case file on the kidnapping trial and clomped down the hallway to the elevator for the start of the afternoon session. People were still being overly kind to me, holding doors open, tossing greetings like we were old friends even after the bruises and cuts had cleared up. Once the ankle boot came off, I guessed their impulsive courtesy would fade.

As I walked toward the courtroom, I dodged my way through a stream of people leaving the courtroom up and to the left. A shock of dark brown hair caught my eye, as it always did over the past few weeks. Partaking in my new favorite pastime of torturing myself with hope, I twisted my head to verify that this brunette wasn't Elise. After a perfunctory glance, I went back to concentrating on keeping people away from my ankle boot while wading through the crowd. Like a film suddenly coming into focus, the glance I'd taken registered. I came to a standstill in the middle of the corridor. It was Elise, gorgeous as ever, even more so since I'd been denied the vision for weeks.

Someone bumped into me from behind at my abrupt stop, and the collision caused Elise to look in my direction. Her gait hitched, but her companion didn't adjust her stride and found herself a step ahead. They'd been chatting quietly with smiles and walking closely together. Jealousy kicked into high gear, and I'm not a jealous person.

Over these past weeks I'd done some soul searching, missing Elise, dealing with my fears, and examining my choices. All of which led me to the current realization that I was in love with her. Yes, I'm slow; I get it. At least I'm admitting it now. This was real love, not the stuff of fantasies I'd been living for so long with Willa. Admitting it and dealing with losing it pretty much took over every spare moment of thought I had.

If I wanted help dealing with it, all I had to do was pick up the phone and call Lauren for one of those talks that she'd been dying to have since we first became friends. She liked details, always had. Too bad for her she had a best friend who didn't share many details; just enough to keep her satisfied that she was my only confidant. I'd yet to make the phone call because I knew I'd have to tell her about Willa. Jessie's lecture had been embarrassing enough, but Lauren's concerned reaction would be tainted with disappointment and pity. She'd also be upset that I never mentioned my crush, not at any time while she continued to ask me why I rejected date offers, put off her set-ups, and deflected personal questions. I didn't want to hurt her like that, not just so I could get some sympathy that I didn't deserve. She wouldn't know what to do any more than I. Lauren might be thrilled that I'd called and shared with her, but I'd feel like crap after the call, and things would still suck as a lesbian in Seattle.

When she was two steps away, Elise's companion figured out they were out of sync and slowed to realign their steps. Because I was the only statue in the busy hallway, she glanced at me then stared outright.

"Your name's Austy, isn't it?" she asked.

Dragging my eyes from Elise, I focused on the black-haired woman who'd come to a stop in front of me. "Yes," I replied, and because I love punishment, I offered, "Hi, Elise."

"Hello," she said quietly.

Her friend talked over her, "You guys know each other? Oh, that's right. Jake left you with a couple of his cases, didn't he? I'm sorry I can't remember your last name?"

"Nunziata," I supplied and studied her anew. Somehow she knew me, and I wracked my brain to place her. Short, bone thin, Asian, pretty…nope, still not recognizing her. "I hate to sound rude, but do we know each other?"

"I've seen you around the courthouse, but we met at

Girl4Girl a few months back. Cheryl Akino." She reached for my hand.

Flushing at the mention of G4G while in a professional setting, I hurried my apology. "Sorry, I was a little out of my element that night."

"I do remember a deer-in-the-headlights look about you." She chuckled and elbowed Elise lightly. "First timers are never prepared. I've been wanting her to go with me for years whenever she's in town, but she prefers the quiet life. Trying to get her out to any of the bars is like trying to give a cat a bath for the first time." Cheryl slipped an arm around Elise for a quick squeeze, and I wanted to test the heftiness of my ankle boot somewhere on her person to disconnect them.

"Cheryl." Elise shook her head, telling her friend or colleague or, please no, girlfriend to drop the subject.

"It'll be good for you, Lis." She turned back to me when she couldn't get the appropriate rise out of Elise. "You broke my friend's heart, you know?"

"Pardon?" Stunned didn't begin to describe the feeling pressing into me. I shot a glance at Elise, but her eyes were as wide as mine.

"Well, Kami is a bit of a drama queen. One date and she couldn't stop talking about you for a month."

Come on! Seattle is ten times the size of Charlottesville. How do all these lesbians know each other? Way to keep a low profile, moron.

"Of course, that's how she hooked up with Ruth," she continued unaware that I'd only begun to internally berate myself. I'd now have to plan some time this afternoon to continue the self-flagellation because I've got houseguests and it would be rude to carry on in front of them. I tuned back in to hear her say, "…time trying to find out stuff about you that Ruth took every opportunity to convince her that she was a better match."

There were so many things wrong with that statement I didn't even bother to start. "Oh." I really should come up with other universal conversation fillers.

Cheryl pushed out a wheezing laugh. “You seem really broken up about it.”

I shrugged and said in what I hoped was a courteous tone, “Honestly, it was one date, and it was months ago. I’ve had other concerns since then.”

“I heard a little about that.” She looked down at my ankle boot. “George is happy with his moonlighting gig. Need any other bodies?”

“Actually, I’m thinking of dropping the effort. There doesn’t seem to be a need, and it’s interfering with a real life.”

“You’re not serious?” Elise looked genuinely concerned.

My eyes went back to hers and tried to convey just how much I missed and loved her, but she wasn’t reading my mind anymore. Nonverbal signals suck. “There haven’t been any other threats, no tails, nothing. It’s useless and a burden.”

“The trial starts in a few weeks. You can’t hold out till then?” Gentle pleading entered her voice, and I yielded at the sound.

“Well, it has been nice not having to ride the bus with my ankle. I’ll reevaluate when this comes off at the end of the week.”

“I wish you wouldn’t.” Elise spoke from a place that I’d gotten to know fairly well while we were together.

“I’ll think about it.”

Cheryl sensed the tension around this topic and changed the subject. “We’ve just come from the grand jury hearings on our chat room pedophile investigation. Busted the guy last week, and now he’s going to trial. Elise trapped his handle and cell site. He’s going away for a long time thanks to her genius.”

“Congratulations.” I looked at Elise, hoping it meant she’d be shifted back to computer forensics.

“Thanks,” she replied automatically.

“It was a huge bust. We’re headed to a celebratory lunch. Want to join us?” Cheryl asked.

Elise started forward as if wanting to physically take back the offer before it reached me. Then she realized she couldn't say anything.

I let her off the hook. "Thank you for the invitation, but I'm headed in to finish up another case. It was nice meeting you again, Cheryl. Pleasure to see you, Elise." Master of casual, that's me.

"You, too," Cheryl responded and gripped Elise's elbow to get them started down the hall. Elise gazed at me until she'd passed by.

"Oh, and I'm in love with you," I whispered to the now distant departing figure. So there's no way she heard me, but something in that final gaze gave me hope that she hadn't moved on yet.

Chapter 20

The aroma of musky wood oil accosted my nose as I entered the empty courtroom. I'd grown to love that smell, but other scents overpower it when people file inside. Often before big trials, the fragrance calmed my nerves, and I made every effort to arrive early for a whiff.

Under other circumstances, I wouldn't consider this a big trial. The defendant faced five to ten in prison and moderate fines but nothing as grand as in my last four trials. What made this one big was the fact that it involved my best friend. I wanted to do well for Willa and prove to everyone that my move here was a good thing.

Yesterday, we concluded our opening statements and got through direct on Nykos's testimony. I put him up first to establish motive, having been the one to fire Dean Raymond. Surprisingly, the goofball that I'd come to know didn't show up in court at all yesterday. Nykos showed himself to be authoritative, adept, and exacting, surpassing my greatest expectation during the trial prep. His testimony wouldn't be enough to win the case, but the jury believed and liked him. Defense counsel had her hands full this morning for cross examination.

"I just saw Willa with everyone heading in the main

doors," Lauren stated when she got back from examining the rest of the courthouse. Lauren was here in an official capacity as Willa's corporate attorney. She'd been at my place for over a week and provided a great deal of help in preparing for this trial. Every day she was here, she made it more difficult to refuse her offer of becoming her law partner back in Charlottesville. She continued to be my only unrelenting regret about moving to Seattle.

Today, I faced the toughest day of the trial, emotionally that is. After cross and redirect of Nykos, I'd bring Elise to the stand as the investigating agent and expert witness. Other than a quick prep over the phone, I hadn't spoken to or seen her since my impression of a statute in the hallway last week. That's just what I'd need, freezing and stammering once she took the stand. Not exactly the stuff of courtroom legends.

My mantra for the day: I'm a professional. Of course, I'd need to remember not to say it out loud while she was testifying.

Lauren came to a stop in front of me, her beautifully freckled face displaying concern. "Are you doing all right, Young'un?"

"Sure," I responded automatically.

"You've been quieter than usual. I know having people staying at your place puts you off, but I don't think that's all it is this time." She reached out and cupped my face with one hand.

"I love having you here, you know that. I just want to do well on this trial." Half-truths were how I conversed these days.

"You don't always have to be so strong, Austine. It's okay to let me help you, even if all I do is listen, you know?" Her hand pressed more firmly against my jaw and cheek.

I blinked against the surfacing emotions and responded quietly, "You always help me, *Amica.* You are often my only source of strength."

Her turquoise eyes grew shiny as she enveloped me in a

hug. "God, I miss having you around."

"*Anch'io. Nessuno può prendere il tuo sosituirti. Sei l'amica migliore che io abbai avuto.*" I knew she'd probably only pick up every fourth word, but the important ones like "same here", "can't be replaced" and "best friend" would jump out. She often asked me to speak Italian for her, and I'm convinced she now knows enough to be dangerous in Italy. Fills me with pride to think about it.

"I think I got all that. You said you miss me so much that you're coming back to Virginia to share my law practice, right?" She pulled back from the hug with a face splitting grin that did its usual job of pulling me out of any gloomy mood.

The doors opened and Willa flowed through with Quinn, Helen, Joe, her friend Zoë, and our friends Jessie, Caroline, and Sam. They were here to show Willa their support but also to check on me. Over the past month, I'd seen them more often than I usually did during an entire year in Virginia.

"Morning, A.J. Same places today?" Willa asked when she reached me.

"Good morning, everybody," I replied, assuming my courtroom demeanor. "Please, take the first row. Lauren, right behind me in case I need to verify anything in the testimony. Where's Nykos?"

"I called him twice to make sure he got up in time," Willa said.

"I called him, too," Quinn chimed in.

Willa grabbed up her cell phone and pressed a button. "Kos? Where you at, man?"

"…ants on and hold your horses, woman," Nykos said into the phone as he walked through the courtroom doors. "You're bossy in the morning. No wonder I don't get to work until the sun sets."

"Shut up." Willa snapped her phone shut.

"Grouchy, too. Howdy, all." Nykos grandly waved to everyone. "Are we all set, A.J.? Do I look the part?" He gestured to his suit, the second one I'd ever seen him wear.

"Very nice," I commented, concentrating more on the testimony I'd be presenting.

"Give me hot at least?" Nykos implored.

"Give her a break," Willa instructed him. "She's trying to win our case. Let her get her game face on."

"Then someone else needs to tell me I'm looking hot. Throw Daddy some love."

"You look hot," Jessie deadpanned to the delight of the group.

The doors opened and in walked the defendant, Dean Raymond, and his team of lawyers. Cathy Kallen dressed like the high-powered defense attorney she was. High end designer wear and shoes that probably equaled a day's pay, but unlike some other schmoozey attorneys, she'd been courteous and straightforward in her opening statement.

I nodded hello and sat at the prosecutor's table, waiting for the judge to call court into session. This judge set off my nerves. I knew almost nothing about him other than the fact that he either didn't believe in interrupting attorneys or didn't pay attention in court. I don't know which worried me more.

His clerk opened court and Nykos headed back to the witness stand. Cathy tossed a few soft pitch inquiries at first to set the tone with the jury. She then led him through a lot of yesterday's information, obviously hoping to trip him up with contradictory responses. Sharp Nykos didn't fall for it, but the whole process took nearly an hour.

"Will you characterize what type of employee Dean Raymond was for your company, Mr. Ander?" Cathy asked the first of our anticipated questions.

"He was determined, detail oriented, and like most people really good at their jobs, condescending and difficult to handle at times."

"Would you classify him as a programming expert?"

"Yes," Nykos followed my instructions completely, never giving more information than asked.

"I'm confused then. You're saying he was an expert at his

job and, yet, you fired him?" Normally I'd object as to relevance, but on cross, it's always wise to pick your objections carefully.

"Yes."

"Was he fired for cause?"

"No."

"No? That's unusual, isn't it?" Cathy spun toward the jury, her blond hair tossing perfectly over her shoulder. She was going for sexy-girl-next-door, and the guys in the jury watched every strand fall into place.

"Not really," Nykos began. "This is an At Will state. Employees can be hired and fired at will." Zing! Nice one, Nykos.

Cathy turned her head back but left her body or ample breasts, rather, squarely facing the jury. She wore a scoop neck shell designed for maximum cleavage exposure without inciting a contempt of court charge. "I'm aware of what At Will means, Mr. Ander. Even though Washington is an At Will state, it doesn't mean a company can fire its employees without any wrongdoing otherwise they'd face discrimination claims."

"Objection, Your Honor!" I called out from my table. "Is there a question in this lecture?"

Judge Sandburg's head snapped up like he'd fallen asleep without supporting it. His eyes looked first at Cathy then figured the objection had to come from the person not conducting cross. He focused on me to sustain the objection before turning to Cathy. "Please refrain from adding commentary during your cross, Ms. Kallen."

"Thank you, Judge. Mr. Ander, was Mr. Raymond's tenure with your firm rife with misconduct to the point where he needed to be released?"

"He wasn't perfect," Nykos responded.

"That wasn't my question, Mr. Ander." Cathy laced her tone with smugness.

Unfazed Nykos replied, "Rife? No, but he wasn't outstanding. He made some costly mistakes."

The unrehearsed drop of Cathy's hand to the jury box showed her dismay at his reply. She took a long time to recover. "You said he wasn't fired for cause, though, didn't you?" She waited for Nykos to reply in the affirmative. "Then why was he fired?"

Mistake number one. Never ask an opened ended question to which the answer may come as a surprise.

Nykos looked to me before he responded. He guessed that wasn't the right question to ask, but we'd prepared an answer just in case. "Mr. Raymond violated one of the employee conduct policies outlined in our personnel manual."

"Are you telling me that no employee violated conduct policies before Mr. Raymond? Don't you have a warning system in place?"

"We do on most policies; however it depends on how egregiously the policy was violated. In Mr. Raymond's case, the policy was abused to the utmost degree."

"You're saying that Mr. Raymond said or did something so destructive that he was fired for violating a personnel policy without any warning?"

"That is not what I said." As much as I enjoyed his snarky reply, I raised my right index and middle fingers off the table to indicate that he needed to rein in the superiority a bit. As an attorney, you never want to shake your head at one of your own witnesses, so it's best to set up a signal system to communicate simple instructions.

"So, he didn't violate a policy egregiously?"

"He did, but he was warned twice before I fired him."

Cathy wasn't prepared for that one. Even her chest failed her and turned away from the jury to point at Nykos. She tried to collect herself, but she'd already opened the door to allow why he was fired to be entered into evidence. "Which policy did he violate?"

"Mr. Raymond showed excessive prejudice toward a member of the firm and voiced derogatory terms in front of the entire office." Nykos paused for effect. "Three times."

Cathy had two choices now. Either she raise the particular prejudice and hope that there were some homophobes on the jury or move on to avoid dwelling on her client's transgression. Respectfully, Cathy chose the latter, but Nykos performed as splendidly for the remainder of cross.

A spur of the moment decision had me asking only one question during redirect. "Mr. Ander, as Mr. Raymond's executive producer and someone who reviewed his work, in your opinion, does the game entitled *Dirge of Darius* copy your game called *Xerxes' Lament*?"

"Objection! This witness is not recognized as an expert."

"This witness owns a software game company and operates as the executive producer on all of its games. We can go through the process of establishing his expertise; however, I asked for his opinion as Mr. Raymond's supervisor."

"I'll allow it." The judge looked bothered by the sudden expectation that he work while sitting on the bench. Little good that will do, since Cathy got her distraction.

"Yes, I believe it's a copy of our game."

"Thank you, Mr. Ander." I turned to the judge and surprised him and Cathy by saying, "Nothing further for this witness, Your Honor."

The judge leaned forward in his chair before issuing his orders, "You are excused Mr. Ander. We'll take a fifteen minute recess before you call your next witness, Miss Noonsetia."

An influx of nerves suppressed my annoyance at his choice of title and mispronunciation of my name. Somewhere outside the courtroom door, my perfect mate waited to testify. At least, I hope she did. Usually I take this time in every trial to dash madly into the hallway to check that my witness is on the premises. I felt like stalling this time around to gather my wits, but I knew I couldn't postpone this any longer.

Many unrecognizable faces mobbed the hallway as I came through the door. Must be a full day at the courthouse today. While scanning the corridor, I caught a flash of a fit leg out of the corner of my eye. *Oh, come on! She's wearing a skirt again. This is so unfair. I'm a professional. I'm a professional. I'm a professional!*

"Hello, Elise. I hope you haven't been waiting too long?" I channeled my best professional manner.

She expelled a quick mirthful breath with the start of a smile. Just as suddenly, she interrupted its progress and looked away. "Hi. No, not too long."

I desperately wanted to know what she'd found humorous and try to get her to smile for me again, but work and reality beckoned. "Nykos just wrapped, which means you're up after the recess."

"I'm ready." She uncrossed her legs, unknowingly tormenting me further.

"Good to hear. We've got about ten minutes," I began then noted the apprehensive look on her face, like she didn't trust me to stick to my promise of not crossing her boundaries. Only, not exactly, more like she didn't trust herself. Of course, that could just be me projecting. "Can I get you anything? Coffee or water? You may be on the stand for a while."

Her expression softened with relief as she responded, "No, thank you."

I nodded, tightening my lips to keep from declaring my need for her. "Okay, well, I'm going in to review my notes then. The bailiff will be out to get you in a few minutes." Waving casually, I turned to flee before I threw myself at her.

"Call your next witness," the judge instructed after the recess.

I stood from my table and said, "The Prosecution calls Special Agent Elise Bridie."

The bailiff vanished through the door and reappeared with Elise in his wake. I held open the gate and waited for her to swiftly make her way down the aisle. She wore a midnight blue suit with a burgundy blouse, her brown hair swept off her face and kept in place by a barrette. If it's the barrette I bought her at the street fair we went to after our first night together, I was going to lose it. That warm vibration I felt on my skin whenever she came near began to hum intensely as she brushed past me through the gate. A glutton for agony, my eyes moved up to examine the barrette. Not the one I gave her. Okay, all emotions still manageable.

As much as possible, I avoided looking at her while I established who she was, why she was here, and her level of expertise. I let her take us through the process of investigating the case and discovering that it wasn't simply a copyright violation but also corporate espionage. She had the ability to sound both cerebral and comprehensible which kept her from alienating the jury when she sounded like a techie geek.

Once she'd been perceived as an expert and explained the intricacies of the case, I began the process of proving that the defendant had duplicated the code for the international company. "You examined the code for both games, Agent Bridie?"

"Yes."

"For those of us who aren't computer programmers, perhaps you can explain what you mean by code?" In Seattle, this question shouldn't be necessary, but it's better to be safe.

"Sure, code refers to lines of symbols, words, and punctuation that together directs the program to execute a command. For instance, when you want to save something on a computer, the code instructs the program to save the words that you've typed by indicating that a mouse click or menu selection will collect those words into a document deposited on your hard drive."

Some of the members of the jury looked enlightened, while others nodded their head in agreement. I guess it's true what they say about Seattleites: either they know how to make good coffee, or they know how to program software.

"Thank you for that explanation. What makes a program's code one of a kind?"

"In order for a program to be copyrighted, it must have either different functionalities or a different look. Either difference means that the code will have unique commands."

"And what did you find when you examined the code for both *Xerxes' Lament* and *Dirge of Darius*?" I stood alongside the jury box to let her look in their direction without actually looking at them. Direct eye contact with juries often unnerved them.

"The code was virtually identical in both games."

"By virtually, do you mean there are enough changes to warrant a new copyright?"

"No, I mean that other than the two extra levels or what some might call, scenes, within *Dirge*, there is no difference between the programming codes."

"Wouldn't the addition of more parts to a game be enough of a difference?"

"No. In fact, not even for Jucundus Interactive. If they'd produced this game, they'd have to call it a new version of *Xerxes' Lament*. They couldn't obtain a copyright on it under a new title."

"So, in your expert opinion, *Dirge* is a rip-off of *Xerxes'*?"

"Objection!" Cathy bolted out of her seat as I knew she would when I used the trigger word "rip-off."

"Sustained." The judge ruled appropriately but not before I'd planted the seed of malice aforethought.

Elise gave me a mouth twitch, knowing exactly what I'd done. For a moment, I was transported back to the first trial where her slight lip curl kindled my romantic awareness of her. Turning back to the jury, I asked the next question, "Let me rephrase, Agent Bridie, would you say that *Dirge* is a replica of *Xerxes*?"

"Yes. Even the title isn't significantly different." Elise was doing my work for me again. "Dirge and lament are synonymous, and Darius was Xerxes' father."

Loving her! This time for being a superb witness, but, you know, also in general. Time to push on to tying the theft of the code to the defendant. "We heard from Mr. Ander that the defendant was the lead engineer on *Xerxes'* while with

Jucundus and that he left the company involuntarily. Is there any evidence that directly links the defendant with *Dirge*?"

"Several links, actually."

I looked from the jury over to Cathy's chest. Just as I thought, Elise was winning out. Ultra hot and armed trumps ample cleavage. "Please list them for us, Agent Bridie."

"The defendant applied for and received a visa to work in Hong Kong, the country where *Dirge of Darius* was produced. He was in Hong Kong for the six months prior to publication of *Dirge*. While the company would not release his employment records, several of their employees confirmed his contract position. I believe you'll call them later in the trial." She paused to allow me to nod in confirmation. "The defendant's bank account showed deposits during this six month period that were twenty times larger than the salary of those other engineers that we questioned. All told, the deposits amounted to one million dollars."

Several members of the jury hissed audibly. Even Cathy Kallen didn't hold her composure, twisting to stare at her client, probably thinking about upping her hourly rate.

"Any other links, Eli—" I cut myself off before I called her by her first name. I'd let the jury's reaction throw me. *I'm a professional. I'm a professional.* "Agent Bridie."

"Yes. Some programmers use notes that identify them as the author."

"And is that what Mr. Raymond did here?"

"He did. For the three games he worked on at Jucundus and also on *Dirge*, Mr. Raymond inserted the same notes after each of the last twenty lines of code."

"And the notes are exclusive to Mr. Raymond?"

"Yes. The last letter of every line note spelled out, 'Deano ruled the Rat Pack.'" Elise smirked along with the jury.

Dean Raymond blanched at Elise's discovery. Willa'd told me that some programmers have an all-mighty complex that leads them to believe they are more clever than nearly everyone.

One more line of questioning to close the door on his guilt. "Wouldn't someone who worked with Dean Raymond know that he added this," I paused, turned to the jury, and smiled like I wanted to use air quotes around my next word, "message?"

"It's possible."

"What's to say that one of the other programmers at Jucundus Interactive didn't create the game *Dirge of Darius* and try to pin it on Mr. Raymond?"

All eyes of the jury widened at my question. Clearly they hadn't thought of that, but I needed to make sure that they considered me the attorney who thought of every possibility.

"You mean other than the fact that all of the programmers who worked on *Xerxes' Lament* are still happily employed by Jucundus Interactive?"

I love this woman! "Yes, other than the unlikely scenario of a current Jucundus employee stealing and working on that programming code for a company in another country."

"Well, when I arrested him on suspicion of corporate espionage and copyright violation at SEA-TAC airport deplaning a flight from Hong Kong, the defendant had on his person two CD Read-Write disks. One contained the programming code for *Dirge of Darius* and the other had the original code for *Xerxes' Lament*."

The jury reared back in their seats, knowing they'd just heard the tech equivalent of finding a smoking gun on the defendant. I had a few more questions planned, but I thought about ditching them and letting Elise's statement hang in the air for a while.

Defense counsel made my decision for me. She stood and gravely asked, "Your Honor, I'd like to request a recess at this time."

I checked the wall clock to the left of the judge's head and saw that we were still about an hour shy of lunch. Not surprisingly, while Elise was on the stand, the judge stayed alert. He checked his watch to see if he should call a lunch break but knew this recess meant a potential end to the case. I wanted to jump up and down in victory but managed to contain my joy.

"Fifteen minute recess. You're excused for the moment, Miss, um, Agent Bridie." He stood after the men and women of the jury and exited at the same time.

Elise walked toward me with a smile. Elegant, gorgeous, sensuous Elise. I'd be content to stand here all day for a glimpse of that smile.

Before she reached me, Cathy Kallen was at my side. "Which room can I find you in?"

Swallowing my smile, I told her where we'd be if she wanted to accept a deal. While I couldn't believe that she didn't at least want to cross-examine Elise, I could understand how much worse her client might end up looking.

I turned to find Elise being congratulated by everyone in the group. Willa nearly hugged her, which for someone so averse to touching would have been unprecedented.

Days like this were why I'd become an attorney.

Chapter 21

Our break would be spent in my "lucky" attorney consultation room. It had served me well in the past, and after Elise's testimony, it surely wouldn't fail me now. Interrupting the group's glee, I led them out of the courtroom and down the hallway. Willa herded Elise along with us, not allowing her likely escape.

We all crowded into the room, taking up the available chairs around the solid table. Nykos took up my usual post of waiting at the door until everyone passed through first, so I made a beeline for the coffee station to begin doling out beverages to the crowd.

"This is a good thing, right, Age?" Willa asked.

All heads turned to me, but Lauren, who'd always had a knack for teaching, answered, "Really good." She went on to break down some of the tactics used in the court for the nonlawyers in the room.

I set cups of coffee prepared how they like it in front of Caroline and Sam, Helen and Joe, and Quinn and Willa. While I was working on tea for Jessie and Lauren, I lifted a cup in the air to Nykos and Zoë to ask how they liked their coffee. Zoë waved it off, but Nykos mouthed "black."

Adding just the right amount of skim milk to another

coffee, I set the cup in front of Elise. She turned her head in surprise as I was still leaning over her shoulder. Her face, about an inch from mine, exhibited a flicker of yearning. My body reacted to the revelation contrary to my desire. Rather than lean in to kiss her, despite the amount of razzing I'd receive, I stood up in astonishment. *She still wants me. I don't think I'm imagining that.*

Elise whipped her head around to face the rest of the room, focusing on Lauren who was now holding a veritable class on what transpired in court this morning. Politeness forced me to continue with my task when all I wanted to do was drag Elise from the room and beg her to give me a second chance. I finished Lauren and Jessie's tea and brought Nykos his coffee. Unfortunately, the only chair open was on the other side of the long table from Elise.

"You're kicking ass, A.J." Nykos exclaimed after Lauren finished the recap.

"That was all Elise," I admitted proudly.

"You sure you don't want a job, Elise? I can promise you a better salary than what you're making now. Hell, after that testimony, you can name your salary," Nykos boasted.

"Thanks, but I like my job," Elise declined with finality.

"That's some kind of will power," Sam announced, disbelief enlivening her dinner plate shaped face. "He does mean any salary. You know they're small country economy rich, right?"

Elise looked at me before responding, "I've heard."

"Nykos, Willa?" I wanted to change the subject. "You need to decide if you're all right with a plea bargain."

"Absolutely," Willa said enthusiastically. She'd never wanted this to go to trial in the first place. Nykos waited a little longer before he nodded. Something told me he took Dean's betrayal personally.

"If you wrap this up before noon, A.J., you and I can be on a red-eye back to Dulles. We've got to start working on all those cases I've been ignoring," Lauren said definitively, and all eyes turned to me. She'd been saying something similar all week long despite my protests.

"You're moving back?" Caroline practically screamed and leaned over to wrap her long arms around me. "I knew Laur could convince you. Now you'll be safe, and I'm throwing in free bagels for life at my café."

"That's great, Age," Jessie put in. "It's nice here, but I'm glad you'll be back home."

When this crew got started, it's hard to stop them. I looked from person to person, each feeling that she had the right to decide my life for me, before my gaze hit Elise. Her eyes conveyed acceptance.

"You've decided?" Willa asked, pulling my stare from Elise.

"Yes," I said, but before I could finish, the Virginia crew broke into spontaneous applause and whoops of hooray. I waited them out to clarify my answer, but there was a knock at the door that interrupted us. I ordered, "Come in."

To my surprise Gregory Stokes walked in. Slick, coiffed, studly Gregory Stokes stepped inside with a confident strut, taking in everyone in the room before seeking me out.

"I heard you were here this morning, Austy. Thought I'd check your favorite hideout. Hello, everyone, Gregory Stokes." He waved regally as I introduced him to each of my friends. "When I heard you were on another trial today, I wanted to find you to make two offers."

"Should we go outside?" I asked, thinking he might be talking about the Evenzolo case.

"Seeing as these are your friends, we can discuss it here. I wanted to see if we should move the motion hearing to a later date if that's more convenient."

Not sure where that offer was coming from, I balked. "No, thank you. I've got permission from Judge Sandburg for that morning off if we're still going by then."

"Just thought I'd suggest it." Greg spread his palms out in compromise. "Which brings me to my second offer, the true purpose for sniffing you out today."

Wanting him to leave soon, I simply nodded to encourage he get on with it.

"You've been brushing off my advances since our first trial together. I'm here to pin you down and tell you how great a time you'll have with me on a date." Greg oozed confidence, so much so that he didn't notice the giggles from the rest of the crowd.

"Please don't," I implored seriously, mortified that he was doing this in front of anyone, much less my friends.

"I'm not leaving until you say yes. One date with me and you'll never be the same again. Not many guys can say that." He hit me with a full-toothed, pride-filled grin.

"Greg, I'm flattered, but not interested. Thank you anyway." I could feel the heat burning my face and knew everyone could see the blush.

"Aw, give me a chance, Austy. You're hot, know enough not to be boring on a date, and most importantly, you'll look good on my arm."

His statement was so egotistical I coughed out a laugh in amazement. "That's how you convince someone to go out with you? Tell her she'll look good on your arm? Unbelievable. I said I'm not interested."

A small fissure in his confidence tightened his grin. "What are you…gay?"

Typical egomaniacal male reaction. A woman doesn't want to go out with him; she must be gay. My point would be so much more influential if I weren't. "Yes." I replied simply.

"What? You're a—" he stopped himself from using what would probably be a disparaging term. "You just haven't had the right man, baby. I know how to use my equipment. I'll show you right."

Anger rose through me like someone had wrenched the side bolt on a fire hydrant letting the substance splash up and out onto a scorching hot afternoon for all the kids to wade through. I was getting sick of being told how I felt and what I should do. The murmurs from the rest of the crowd didn't have a chance to make it to full volume before I let go.

"Do you have any idea how insulting and crass that remark is, Greg? By your blank expression, I gather that's a no. Since my polite attempts to decline your invitations didn't seem to set in, maybe all you understand is insulting and crass. So, let me speak on your level. I don't need a Masters and Johnson study to verify that, most of the time, men cannot satisfy a woman with that equipment you seem so proud of. I won't tell you how unlikely the possibility is; I'll leave that disappointment for you to look up on your own. But even if I weren't a lesbian or uninterested in you specifically, I'm involved. The kind of involved where you don't even notice other humans, involved. I'm done for, that kind of involved. I'm guessing you don't even know what I mean by that, which makes me sad for you. So once again, I'm not interested in dating you. Please leave."

"Dyke!" Greg snorted and slammed the door on his way out.

Everyone began talking at once. "Snap!"

"Vicious awesome!"

"Damn, A.J.!"

Nykos joked loudly, "Did you say all men or just some?"

A wave of guilt replaced the erupting anger as people laughed at his joke. I hate confrontation, avoided it as much as I could. Yet I'd let my irritation get the better of me. By day's end I'd be known around the courthouse as the Man-Hating Dyke Bitch. *Great career move, moron.*

"Comparison point number 441: that kinda stuff won't happen when you're back in Virginia, Age. Everyone at the courthouse already knows you're a lesbian," Lauren declared proudly.

Since it had been so effective before, I decided to let my ire run free again. In a calm but strained voice, I began, "Stop it, please. When I said 'yes' before, I meant that I've made a decision about this being my home. I'm not moving back. I made a choice for my career and to move forward in my life. I love and miss you all, but please, stop asking me or telling me that I need to move back. I can't take much more of it before I'll want to stop seeing you all entirely." All eyes widened at my unyielding tone. "I've appreciated your company over the last few weeks, but no matter how many of you try, I'm not going to relent. This is my new home, and this person you see here," I gestured to myself, "longer and now brown hair, who doesn't try to accommodate whatever her friends want and says what she thinks for the most part, this is me. Oh, and I changed my mind, Willa; I do want to be called Austy, because that's who I am now."

A variety of reactions reeled through the room. A few gasps, a few nervous laughs, and a few beginning defensive protests. Willa's voice rose higher than the rest of the din and stated with finality, "Good for you, Austy." When surprise flew her way, she sliced a hand through the air, silencing them. "Austy's turned the corner, guys. We all need to support her decision now."

Her statement made it easy to remember why I'd been so convinced I was in love with her. She appeared to give unconditional acceptance and love to the people she cared about, but nobody can do that. Now that I'd experienced real love, I'd take that over my unrealistic fantasy any day.

After the shock wore off, most of them tested out my name a few times. Nodding heads and smiles told me they could handle my requests. Lauren snapped her head up and fixated her intense near turquoise stare on me. "Hold on a second, sister; how come I don't know about this woman of yours? Or were you making it up to ditch that guy?

"No, that had to be real. Did you hear her?" Caroline leaned forward intently. "She's done for. I've never heard anyone put it like that. Spill, Age, I mean, Austy."

Similar comments sprang from nearly all of the Virginia crew. Even Nykos seemed interested in my answer. Beside him, Elise's strained look told me she didn't want me to tell anyone about us. Not that there was an "us" anymore.

"She doesn't have to say," Jessie warned gently, staring me down. I realized she thought I was talking about Willa and might acknowledge it.

"Excuse me." Elise stood from her seat and began to walk toward the door. "I need to check in with my office. Page me if you don't get a plea acceptance before I'm needed back in court." She spoke to my forehead, purposefully not looking into my eyes. Did she think I meant Willa, too?

"Elise." I started to get up to stop her exit, but she opened the door to Cathy Kallen.

"Oh, you startled me. I was just about to knock." She moved to the side to let Elise walk past before finding me in a half crouch. "Austine? Can we discuss the case for a minute?"

Letting go of all things social, I stood and indicated the room across the hall. Once we'd cleared the doorway, Cathy came right out with it. "We'll consider two years, one suspended and a million dollar fine."

Brash, I'll give her that. "I've given the jury direct evidence to go along with all that circumstantial evidence, Cathy. They'll come back with guilty, and you know it. The only question is how harsh is this judge? Max puts your client away for ten years, out in eight or so, and the fines will be the profits of the game and his payment for stealing and handing over the code. One year and one million isn't good enough."

"What's your offer?" Cathy asked tentatively.

"Five with parole and three million in fines."

"What? Profits weren't that much, and my client certainly doesn't have it." Cathy's composure was starting to crack. Just where I wanted her.

"They will make that kind of money if they keep publishing the game. In two years time, we'll have their company shut down by international law after they spend double losing this case in court. Get your client to have them agree to stop publishing this game voluntarily, turn over the master code, and we'll have no reason to pursue a case against them in international court. We'll take Mr. Raymond's payment of a million and hold a judgment for another two million against him. If he wants to convince them to cough up the other two million, fine, but otherwise, he'll have wages attached for years after he gets out of prison."

"He can't do five," she indicated sheepishly.

"He's going to do ten if the judge goes max."

"Suspend two years, three with parole? He's not a hardened criminal. He won't last five in prison."

"We're talking minimum security, Cathy, no hardened criminals to worry about. He stole from his former company and caused them harm. One thing I didn't tell you is that Willa Lacey happens to be a good friend of mine. There's no way I'm agreeing to suspend anything. Five years with parole means he's out in three and change."

Her eyes blinked in consideration. "I'll sell it to him. It might take a while before he can convince the company in Hong Kong to drop the game voluntarily. Shall we ask for a break through lunch to finish this?"

"Fine. I'll meet you inside." Reaching back, I opened the door for her and then walked across the hall to my group.

"We've worked out a plea," I informed them after stepping through the door.

Everyone turned to Willa to wait for her response. "Good," she breathed out in relief and Quinn wrapped a supportive arm around her.

Even Nykos seemed happy after I relayed the details of the plea. "You mean we wouldn't have to go through another trial against the company in Hong Kong?"

"Not if Dean can convince them to drop it. You wouldn't need to pursue international charges, and the company would stop publication. I doubt they'll agree to sign a document that admits conspiracy to stealing your code, but they will sign an agreement that says they unknowingly purchased stolen code and agreed to stop publication once they found out."

"I can accept that. Nykos?" Willa looked at her business partner.

He considered it for a while. "As long as we don't have to

spend more time in court over this, and they stop putting out their knock off."

"Lauren, what's your opinion?" Willa asked.

"International copyright infringements and corporate espionage are nearly impossible to prove and will take years. You make great software games; focus on that and let Austine finish this for you."

"Go to it, Austy," Willa encouraged with a smile.

With my assuring nod, they all stood to follow me from the room. As we spilled out into the hallway, Nykos called ahead to the only other guy in the group, "She didn't really say all men, did she, Joe?" Everyone broke into controlled hysterics again.

Jessie and Lauren sidled up next to me on our way back to the courtroom. "So, Elise, huh?" Jessie beamed and brought an arm around my shoulders to squeeze me against her.

Stunned by her guess, I spoke before thinking. "Jessa, this whole intuition thing is starting to freak me out."

"Intuition? Jessie? Who are you talking about?" Lauren put her arm around my waist, sandwiching me between these tall, gorgeous women. "Joe told us. Said y'all had a fine little love affair going. You will give us details over lunch, Young'un."

"Even the old me liked keeping my private life to myself, and that hasn't changed."

"Whatever, but she bolted pretty quickly, shug. You must have done something to piss her off." Jessie stopped any possible retort with a raised palm. "No, I don't want to hear a word. She seems great, and she's certainly fine enough for your striking self. No excuses. Fix it."

"It's not that simple," I stated weakly.

Jessie turned when we got to the courtroom door. She smiled confidently and informed me, "It is when you're you. So, fix it."

With that, she and Lauren left me in their wake, joining the others inside. Blessed doesn't begin to cover what these friends are to me.

Chapter 22

When George pulled up to my curb, people spilled out of Mod Fare carrying plastic tumblers and napkins with scrumptious looking edible concoctions. An impromptu Jucundus party it seemed, not surprising since Nykos once threw a party at his office because it happened to be a day that ended in "y."

"Lot o' people," George declared.

"Looks like my friends Willa and Nykos are throwing a celebratory party."

"You joining them or heading upstairs?"

"I better duck in and say hello. Knowing them, you'd be more than welcome to join the party, no pressure." I reached for the door handle.

"I'm here until you're locked safely inside your place. Are you sure your friends won't mind?"

"I know they won't, but there are people everywhere. I'll be completely safe. You can head home if you don't want to get your party on."

"You're worse than my five year old, Austy." He issued a parental look. "We've had this discussion before. I only agreed to drop the overnight security if we get you inside and you stay there. So, if you're partying, I'm partying."

"Austine!" Lauren exclaimed when she spotted us getting out of the car. "Finally, you're here!"

"Hey, Lauren, what's going on? Weren't you thinking of heading back tonight? And wasn't Nykos going to hibernate while Will, Quinn, Caroline, and Sam headed out on that cruise?"

"Change of plans. They're using the excuse of being done with this trial to throw a launch party for their newest game. The whole company's here, even some of the folks from Charlottesville." She circled an arm around my shoulders and looked over my head. "How're you, George?"

"Good, Lauren. You?"

"Fine, now that my workaholic friend is back from the office. You're going to love this party."

She led us into the crowded restaurant. I easily spotted all of my friends and several of the people from the Virginia office, including Kevin, Willa's second in command. Kevin spent many nights hanging out with us at our favorite club in Charlottesville. Several of the Jucundus employees from the Redmond office nodded hello as we walked through.

"How much do you love me?" Jessie asked when she came toward us. She grabbed my face in both hands and brought hers down to stare directly into my eyes.

Flocks of lesbians in Virginia would kill to be in my spot right now. They'd hurl fire stopping jealousy my way if they saw that I had Jessie's undivided attention in a room full of people, asking me to consider my feelings for her.

"What's up, Jessa?" I guessed she had a reason for her question.

"You are so going to love me. Well, Willa and Nykos, too, but I'm the one who—" she interrupted herself, noticing George for the first time. "Hey, George. There's a lot of great food over there. L and I need a private moment with your charge. Do you mind?"

"Sure thing, but don't leave the restaurant without me, all

right?" He waited for my agreement before leaving.

The crowd swallowed him up almost instantly, and I turned my attention back to Jessie. Suspicion crept into my tone. "What did you do?"

"You will love me for the rest of your life."

"Me, too," Lauren leaned into our conspiratorial circle.

"*Dimmi*," I commanded, asking them to tell me what they were talking about. I couldn't help but share in their excitement. Today had been a good day; I embraced excitement today.

"We asked Willa and Nykos to issue an invitation to the party tonight. They had to make several phone calls, but finally, success," Jessie reported.

"What?" I felt myself being spun in the direction of the kitchen. Hoarders grazed along the food tables on either side of the kitchen door. "What am I looking at?"

"Wait for it," Lauren informed me.

"What's with the cryptic?" I continued to glance about but hardly recognized anyone. As I turned back to glare at Jessie, I caught sight of a familiar figure inside the kitchen. She carried an empty platter from one side of the open doorway to something past the other side. "Elise?" I breathed in wonder.

"You're loving me right now, aren't you?" Jessie reached down and patted my rear end playfully.

"Jessa!" I jumped forward in surprise. "How'd you get her here? I gave up trying to get her on the phone a while ago."

"Willa told her that they'd postpone the party indefinitely until Elise could make it. Nykos said they'd call her every day until she agreed to come," Lauren said with a sinister smile.

"Show us some love," Jessie ordered. I wrapped an arm around each of them for a squeeze, delighting in my disbelief. Nerves kept me attached to them, but Jessie smacked my butt again and said loud enough for people around us to hear, "Get in there and fix it."

They shoved me toward the open door of the kitchen. Helen called out the moment my face hit the doorway. "Hey,

Aust. I was hoping you wouldn't avoid the party. Congrats on the case. Will's so relieved she's actually having fun tonight."

"She looked it." I summoned my bravery. "Hi, Elise. Great job today."

"Thank you," she responded in a clipped manner. She kept her eyes glued to the platter of crab puffs she'd been helping to arrange and said, "I've got an early morning tomorrow, but I wanted to drop by for Willa's sake. It was nice seeing you again, Helen."

"Stay for a minute, please?" I tried to catch her eye, but she seemed intent on staring a hole through the platter before her.

"Yeah, don't go yet. Will and Nykos are drinking, so I can guarantee you hilarious speeches later on." Helen picked up on Elise's avoidance posture and raised her eyebrows at my despair. She was aware that we'd stopped seeing each other but hadn't asked why, thankfully. Without a word from me, she put together my need to be alone with Elise. "I'd better get these out there before riots erupt. Thanks for your help, Elise." She scooped up the platter taking away Elise's focus and glided through the door.

"Elise," I started but stopped when she turned toward me, eyes blazing.

"Austy, I'm here because your friends are persistent. At some point, I'd like to do that whole 'friends now' thing with you, but I'm not ready for that yet. So, I'm going to leave."

"Please don't leave. I really want to talk to you."

"I heard all I could stand to hear this morning." Elise stepped toward me trying to make her exit.

"No, you obviously didn't." If I didn't love her so much, I'd be getting angry at her complete lack of regard for what I needed to say.

Her eyes burned into mine. "You're in love with another woman. You announced it to that jerk this morning in front of all your friends. I really don't need to hear any more on this subject."

When she finished talking, she brushed past me out the

door not giving me a chance to start a protest. Willa, Nykos, and Helen impeded her exit, but I knew if I tried to join them she wouldn't be any more open to listening to me right now.

Resolve steeled me and propelled me into action. I couldn't let her leave without telling her how I felt, but I needed to get her alone. I wound my way through the kitchen and out the back exit, figuring my friends wouldn't keep her for long. At this point, I didn't care if I seemed like a stalker. This might be my only chance to clear up her confusion and try to get her back.

The night sky was darkening rapidly over another splendid summer evening in Seattle. As I passed behind Joe's shop, I heard him rolling the kayak cart into his shop. Now that all the kayakers were done for the evening, the party would really start hopping.

The restaurant's parking lot was empty of people and no sign of Elise's car. Only a few places remained to park without a permit, so I headed toward the overflow parking lot farther away. I almost started skipping when I spotted her Infinity in the last row, closest to the exit. No way she could leave without hearing me out now.

Because it was the quickest route to her car, I squished between two SUVs parked so closely together neither driver would be able to get into them later. Once I'd cleared the bumpers of the monstrosities, a crushing pain flashed along my arm followed by an unpleasant twinge in my shoulder when someone grabbed and yanked me to the left.

They didn't bother with hoods this time, which was the first thing I noticed. After that, I became aware of the smarting in my back after they slammed me up against the rear of the enormous SUV. Without hoods, they were less scary; yet I knew the opposite should be true. By not wearing hoods, they were telling me they didn't care about me identifying them. Dead people can't make identifications.

"Here, kitty, kitty, kitty," that creepy, deep voice sounded off to my right. Louie Evenzolo himself surfaced through the darkness. "Ooh, I was right about you being a pretty little thing. What a waste. If you woulda just listened, we wouldn't be here needing to tear through your face now, would we? An Italian face, too, that's just a shame."

Standing here, pressed against the back of a truck, staring at four imposing men, knowing any one of them could easily break me in two, I was surprised to find that futility smothered what should have been my reactive emotion. I couldn't move past how stupid I'd been to walk out here alone in the dark. Everything that George drilled into me over the last few weeks I'd disregarded, and now I'd pay for it. Fear would come soon enough, of that I was sure.

"We're gonna have some fun with her first, aren't we, bosco?" the raspy voiced one asked. His face matched his voice about as well as Mike Tyson's did.

"HELP! FIRE!" I managed to yell loudly before the guy with the hand who'd hit me last time clamped my mouth shut. His other fist landed a blow to my stomach, and I doubled over, gasping for breath. Having never been punched before, I didn't realize how much my stomach would burn or how every organ inside of me seemed to swell to the point of overcapacity. They pulled me upright and took great pleasure mocking the tears that stung my eyes.

"You're a dumb bitch, ain'tcha? Ditching your security detail at night, whatcho paying 'em for? Did you think we'd forget about you?" The last of the trio suffered from short man's complex and crowded me while he spoke so that he could feel taller.

I kneed him in the groin. Even if they were going to kill me, I couldn't stand another moment of the shame of not fighting when I had the chance. Short Stuff dropped to the ground, swearing profusely. I took the opportunity to yell out again, but Raspy took over, clamping his hand over my mouth and shoved my head against the SUV's back window. A branching bolt of agony shot through the back of my head, over my scalp and down to my sinuses.

Short Stuff whimpered on the ground, clearly unable to handle pain. Louie, ever the sympathetic one, kicked him out of the way to get up in my face. His hands pressed down on my thighs to limit my ability to inflict damage. Fingers slid between them and brushed against my crotch. My right leg reacted on its own, jerking up, but he moved his hands lower to keep them pinned in place. At least they weren't molesting me anymore.

"Now that wasn't nice. He's gonna be pissed when he stops crying like a girl. We won't let him have you until last, or he might kill you before we have our fun," Louie promised.

With a head nod from Louie, Raspy started dragging me along the aisle. I kicked out, jerked away, planted my leg to trip him, but nothing worked. Raspy carried close on three bucks. Self-defense classes could only help so much when someone's three times your size. Desperation swallowed me whole, and I felt the now too familiar numbing acceptance take hold.

Louie walked beside me and used one of his hands to move up my thigh and around to maul my ass. "You're gonna enjoy being my slut tonight."

"FBI! Let her go, Louie!" Elise's voice sounded through the dark. My head swiveled in search of her, and I felt something like an explosion inside my chest at the sound of her voice.

Louie pulled me roughly against him, using me as a human shield with a trapping arm around my sternum. A cold, hard object jammed against my neck just below my jaw, and I didn't need to see it to know he had a gun. His three goons all produced identical handguns and pointed them in the general direction of her voice.

Elise still hadn't appeared in the darkness, but I clung to the hopeful looking shadow near the hood of a car several spaces down. "You're not listening, Louie. Let her go, now."

"You see me with a gun to her head, bitch?" Louie called out in front of us. He whipped his head around frantically and barked to Short Stuff and Backhand, "Find her." They started walking in opposite directions, moving hesitantly guided only by the dim moonlight.

"I'd be more worried about your own head, if I were you," Elise called out from a different part of the parking lot. "I won't miss; I can promise you that. Your only chance of leaving this parking lot alive is to let her go."

"I ain't gonna miss either, you stupid bitch. My gun's right against your little girlfriend's head, and you're talking to me about making a shot from a distance? You wanna risk never having this hot piece of ass in your bed again?"

"I let you take her, and she's dead anyway. Isn't that right, Louie? Isn't that what I heard you say when I walked out here?"

"Where the hell is she?" Louie yelled out to his two thugs.

"She ain't here, boss."

"Not here, either, bosco." Both voices yelled from the far corners of the overflow lot.

"I'm here." Elise moved out from between two cars a few spots away. Both hands gripped a pistol, held straight out from her shoulders. She advanced swiftly.

Louie pulled us backward and readjusted me against him. His heavy arm squeezed me to him, and his hand gripped painfully. "Don't take another step or your whore gets it." He'd begun to sweat so profusely that the smell distracted me from some of the fear that had finally started twisting my organs into balloon animal shapes.

Elise stopped ten feet away. "What are you thinking, Louie? You kill the prosecutor, your case gets dropped? How ignorant are you?" She kept her gun and stare trained on Louie, but flicked her eyes briefly over to Raspy when he started moving toward her. He tilted his pistol to the side like in a gangsta rap video. "You keep moving; I'm shooting your boss."

"I got a gat on you, and Louie's gonna take care of your dyke shorty. You're outmanned in every way." He rasped a laugh at his own pun. Not only did he carry his gun like he was in a rap video, he talked like he was in a rap video. I wondered if he knew that fat, Italian men were never in rap videos. The ridiculous thoughts fear can introduce: an essay by Austine Nunziata.

"One more time, Louie, I will not miss," Elise promised. "If you pull that trigger, you're dead, and my colleague's going to take out your thug."

I should be reassured that she was less than ten feet away, armed, and good at her job, but she was gambling with my life. She didn't sound like she was making up the fact that George was with her somewhere, but so far he hadn't appeared.

"You're bluffing. You're all alone with two guns, soon to be four, against your one. No more talking. I'm taking your slut home with me," Louie hissed at her. The stench of his body odor magnified when he took a step back, yanking me with him.

Elise moved with us, her eyes locked on Louie. She hadn't looked at me once. "You're moving closer to death, Louie. Let her go, or I will shoot you. I haven't fired my weapon at a person in a long time. I'm getting anxious."

"Bite me, bitch. You won't risk her life. Now, shut the hell up and go back inside."

Elise almost smiled. Just before she spoke again, her eyes moved to mine and flicked down. "George?" she called out.

"Got the shot." George's voice surprised us from behind.

Louie whipped his head around at the sound, and I felt the gun barrel move off my neck. My self defense teachings kicked in, and I stomped hard on Louie's instep then elbowed his ribcage to break free of his grip. Three shots rang out, and I heard Louie scream then slump to the ground behind me. Without a sound, Raspy folded to the pavement when his leg buckled under him.

Both Elise and George rushed up, weapons still aimed purposefully. They kicked away the abandoned guns from their downed targets. One of the other goons came running into the aisle two cars away. He was winded with his gun down at his side, thinking his boss had the upper hand on the situation.

"Drop it," George shouted before the guy could move his weapon into firing position. The one who liked to hit dropped the gun and raised his arms without being asked. "Get over here. Plant your face down next to your friend."

Elise pulled out some plastic loops from her jacket and cuffed Louie's hands behind his back, keeping his face down on the ground. "There's one more out there," she told George. "Northwest corner last time he checked in. They were doing a sweep for me."

George nodded and cautiously began a crouch walk through the rows of cars, checking undercarriages before moving on to another row. Efficiently, Elise secured the hands of the two in front of her. Blood seeped through Raspy's pant leg, and he moaned when she tightened the plastic around his wrists. She stood up from the knee she'd planted on his back, kept her gun at her side as she pulled her cell phone out to call for an ambulance.

"Are you okay?" she asked me in a concerned tone after making the call.

My ears rang from the gunshots, but her voice sounded like a symphony after years of being denied any music. I didn't care that my head throbbed brutally or my back ached from being thrown against something hard or my stomach felt like someone had pitched an inning against it. All that mattered was that I was alive and able to look at Elise who'd miraculously not been shot.

"Yes, thank you. Are you?"

"Yes, but I need you to move over here against the back of this SUV." Elise pointed at the truck nearest her. Collecting the guns from the men, she placed them on the bumper beside me.

She moved over to Louie and pulled him to his feet. A string of obscenities flew from his mouth while she walked him over to join his friends. Elise pushed him to the ground and tended to his bleeding arm by tearing his sleeve and wrapping it around his wound. Raspy got the same treatment next, but he was much quieter having passed out from the pain.

A siren sounded in the distance, probably no more than a minute away. I felt the ebb of adrenaline fade away which brought about the now familiar shaking fear. Shock could be a wonderful drug, dampening the pain in the moment and numbing the fear afterward.

"Found him!" George called out and emerged from a dark spot in the aisle. He had Short Stuff shuffling in front of him, hands clasped in back. The thug's head hung in shame, and it reminded me how stupid criminals were.

"I'll flag the bus," Elise announced and jogged toward the street.

"You all right there, Austy?" George set the last goon next to bleeding Louie.

"You saved my ass, George. Thank you." My voice only quavered once.

"If you were my five year old, I'd be lecturing you about disobeying me." He was only half joking. A new kind of shame planted a seed in my abdomen. I'd been such an idiot for leaving the party without security.

The ambulance careened up the aisle toward us and halted. Two medics jumped out and went to work on Raspy and Louie. A police cruiser followed the ambulance in and the officers sprang to action. They muscled the two uninjured men into the back of their car.

"I'll be with these two in the bus," Elise indicated from behind me. "George, can you process the others?"

George nodded and spoke with the police officers, probably explaining the FBI's jurisdiction. They didn't seem thrilled, but they helped load the injured into the ambulance anyway.

Elise walked over to me. "I need to go. George will walk you inside. Please have one of your friends go up to your place with you. You could be in shock; you're shaking pretty badly."

I studied her eyes for a moment, bewildered that I couldn't

read her tone or expression. She was probably right. I felt sluggish both physically and mentally. Technically, these charges would be added to the racketeering case. I should want to make sure they're booked properly and start writing up charges, but all I wanted was to step into Elise's arms.

"Austy?" she asked softly, trying to get me to focus. "Will you ask Lauren to go up to your place with you?"

"Okay," I agreed because it didn't take any thought. Plus, she sounded like the woman I remembered, and I wanted to please her. "Will you come back?" I asked because it made sense that she'd come back to be with me tonight. It never crossed my mind that she wasn't my girlfriend anymore or that I had no right to ask her.

Elise tilted her head in concern. "I need to get these guys processed and write up the report."

"Oh," I said, completely bewildered because she didn't answer my question. At least I don't think she did. My head felt heavy and empty all at once. Maybe shock wasn't so great. Almost as an afterthought, I offered, "Thank you for saving my life, Elise."

She studied me in silence until the medics yelled at her. "You're welcome," she responded seriously with that softness that I missed desperately. Then she walked over to the ambulance and hopped into the back just before it rocketed toward the hospital.

The police cruiser moved off the lot behind the ambulance. George turned us back toward my building. I knew he'd get me to my loft and run down to collect Lauren or Jessie or someone who wasn't the woman that I wanted to be with tonight. But right now, I'd be grateful to have someone with me who could think clearly.

Chapter 23

The alarm clock blasted a song directly into my inner ear, and my torso catapulted off the bed on its own. The sound ignited a little drummer who took pleasure in practicing incessantly on the soft tissue of my brain. Raging headache, check. Sore abdomen, check. Back stiff, check. What the hell happened last night?

"You awake, Aust?" Jessie knocked on my bedroom door.

Ah yes, now I remember. "Yeah," I called out.

Jessie opened the door and walked over to sit on the bed. "How are you feeling?"

"Fine, thanks, Jessa. Guess you stayed over last night?" My honed detective skills recognized the same outfit she'd had on at the restaurant last night. "God, I don't remember that. What are you doing up so early? Lauren's here, isn't she?"

"I'm always up this early, especially when I sleep on a couch. Lauren's still in her room, probably sleeping. Are you sure you're okay? You were pretty out of it last night." She reached out and ran her hand over the back of my head. "At least the goose egg went down."

My hand flew up to check the shape of my head and found a raised bump which would account for the pesky guy with the drumsticks inside my head. I didn't want to check my stomach and back, afraid that I'd find an artist had used her supply of black and blue in some sort of fun pattern.

"Your office called. Some guy named Kyle said the arraignment is at eleven. If you felt up to it, he'd like you there. He didn't know how badly you were hurt this time."

I scoffed mechanically. Short Stack hadn't given me one iota of sympathy when I crutched into the office after the first attack. Since this one involved Even Louie personally, I guess he's suddenly all compassion. "Did you tell him?"

"Give me some credit, shug." Jessie grabbed my hand, too afraid of causing more pain if she touched anything else. "I told him you'd call if you couldn't make it to the arraignment."

"Thanks, Jessa." I checked the alarm clock which I'd set for my regular wake time. "He called this early?"

"He called last night after you crashed. I think George filled him in." Jessie watched me wince when I turned my head back too quickly. "Worse than a hangover headache?"

More than a decade since my last hangover, I couldn't imagine that it ever felt this sharp, dull, swollen, throbbing, and piercing all at the same time. "I'm fine."

"No, you're not, but you'll take two more Advil, another ice pack, and soak in a tub for a while. Shock wreaks havoc on your muscle flexibility. Stay in there a while. You fought me last night and only took a shower, which is why you're still sore. I'll have breakfast ready by the time you're done."

Jessie worked as a fitness trainer and probably knew more ways to manage injuries and sore muscles than doctors. My head and body hurt too much to protest her care giving. "Thank you," I said and slipped tentatively out of bed. Legs worked just fine, but I found that my back hurt less if I stooped forward a bit.

Jessie dashed into the bathroom and started the water in the tub. She resurfaced with two tablets and a glass of water. "Elise called last night, too."

I choked on the water that had helped down the pills. Now my head felt really super. "Is she all right?"

"She was calling to check on you, sugar." Jessie enjoyed her role as know-it-all a little too much this morning. "She seemed very concerned."

"She thought I'd gone into shock in the parking lot."

"You did, and she called to make sure you were doing better. That's a good thing, right?" Jessie's eyebrows shot up in concerned inquiry.

"She didn't give me a chance to talk in the restaurant. Then I go and put her life in danger, force her to shoot somebody, and all I can say is a lame thanks when she saves my life."

"Don't be so hard on yourself. You didn't put her life in jeopardy; that creep did. She is in law enforcement, you know. She certainly didn't seem upset."

"Well, I'm glad she's okay," I muttered. Frustration added to my dull aches and the change in water sounds beckoned me to a nearly full bath.

"I'll drop it for now, but only because you look like you're in pain and your morning hair is scaring me a little."

I laughed mostly in gratitude and retired to soak in the tub. I didn't feel the need to rush to work if Short Stack only wanted me to make it to the arraignment. Too bad it takes getting attacked to enjoy a flexible start time.

***

By the time I got to the courtroom, only the front two rows had spaces available for seating. The reporters had multiplied and took up most of the gallery. Much of my office felt it necessary to attend as well. Short Stack and I had argued over who would conduct the hearing given that I was a victim in these charges. Our boss ended the argument, stating that this was an arraignment not an evidentiary hearing.

Short Stack sat front row, one seat to the right of the aisle, literally placing himself as the U.S. Attorney's right hand man. I directed Jessie and Lauren to the second row because they wouldn't leave my side until Louie Evenzolo was in jail. Thankfully, Willa, Quinn, Caroline, and Sam agreed to stay away after much pleading. George moved from the first row to drop his coat next to Lauren in the second row. He preferred my friends to the pompous asses of my office, and I didn't blame him.

"Morning, Aust. Doing all right?" George joined me in the aisle.

"Much better, thanks. I don't know how you found me out there, but you honestly saved me. I'll never be able to thank you enough."

George's posture straightened in pride at my gratitude. "Hey, I'd love to take all the credit, but I'm ashamed to admit that I didn't even know you'd left the restaurant. You were supposed to tell me before you tried to leave, remember?"

"Uncle!" I exclaimed sheepishly. The man had saved my life; I should be bowing to his greatness right now. "How'd you find me then?"

"Elise. Apparently she was on her way to her car when she spotted you. She used her cell to tell me she'd try to draw the other two away and wait for me to get into position. I don't think I've run faster in my life."

"Thank God for cell phones, huh?" I shivered, now realizing just how close I'd come to dreadful harm.

"Amen to that." George looked relieved himself. "Not that I want to talk myself out of extra income, but these four are the extent of Even Louie's mob. If you keep them from getting bail, you're out of danger."

"Now, I'm extra motivated," I admitted and took my post at the prosecutor's table.

Roger joined me just before the U.S. Attorney and a flock of first assistants and chief litigators entered the courtroom. We'd already strategized back in the office so he was free to suck up to the boss until the arraignment started.

Jessie's prescription worked like a charm. My back had lost its stiffness, the head drummer stopped hammering, and my stomach stayed tender but bruise free. The only fear that remained involved Elise not showing for the hearing. As hazy as some of the details from last night still were, I remembered that I'd been headed to Elise's car to plead my case. I still wanted that chance.

Gregory Stokes slinked up to me before heading to his table. "Austy," he said by way of greeting. "I'm sorry about your ordeal."

Because it was the first time he hadn't hit on me and seemed genuine, I turned to look him in the eyes. "Thank you, Greg. Listen, we're going to come across each other in court often enough, I'd like us to be amiable. Why don't we both forgot what we said yesterday and continue trying to whip each other in court. What do you say?"

Greg smirked half-heartedly. "Works for me. Hey, nothing personal about my client list, right? If I'd known he'd hurt you, I wouldn't have taken him on." He moved off to his table.

Two bailiffs walked through the newly opened side door which led to the holding cells. Behind them the four defendants followed, cuffed and sour looking. My heart started a slow thud and my back stiffened in alarm. In the light of day, these guys represented my brush with death. It sounded unbelievably dramatic to admit that, but I had to believe if they'd managed to take me with them I'd be severely injured at a minimum.

My panic breathing exercises kicked into high gear, but they failed to ease my anxiety. A swarm of dizziness affected my vision, and for the first time, I doubted if I could do my job. I turned to find Roger still busy with our boss and took a step closer to get his attention. In the same line of vision, I spotted Elise sitting next to George in the second row, eyes full of concern as if she knew I was losing it. Strength flowed from her through me with her gaze, but I didn't have time to acknowledge it before the door to the judge's chambers opened.

Roger and I faced forward as the clerk brought everyone to their feet with an "all rise." Judge Cosin looked up briefly and took her seat, allowing us all to do the same. Sally called our case, and Greg and I did our standard introductions.

"Mr. Evenzolo, back with friends, I see." Judge Cosin frowned down at the complaint papers. "You've been busy, Assault, Attempted Kidnapping, and Attempted Murder to add to your other charges. Mr. Stokes, are you representing all four defendants?"

"Yes, Your Honor."

"All right. How do each of you plead?"

All four muttered, "Not guilty, Your Honor," in succession.

"Surprise, surprise," the judge said to herself, forgetting her microphone would pick that up. "So entered," she said in a louder, more professional voice. "Ms. Nunziata, I'm sure you've prepared something on the question of bail; although, I don't think I'll need much convincing."

"Thank you, Your Honor, I have." I stood to deliver my argument. "The Prosecution would like to request that Your Honor deny bail based on the severity of these charges and the incidents occurring while out on bail from earlier charges."

"Mr. Stokes? I'm having a hard time not immediately agreeing with Ms. Nunziata, at least in regard to Mr. Evenzolo. Do you have a credible basis for why I shouldn't remand Mr. Evenzolo into custody right now?"

Greg stood to begin his argument. "Your Honor, these charges should be considered separately from my client's earlier case. I'd like to bring to your attention—"

"Wait a minute, Mr. Stokes." Judge Cosin held up a stopping hand, her head bent over the complaint pleadings. "Am I reading this correctly?" She dropped her reading glasses to hang on their chain around her neck and stared up at me. "Ms. Nunziata? They came after you?"

"This is highly prejudicial, Your Honor," Greg sulked loudly from his table.

The judge's eyes blazed first at him then moved to include all four of the defendants. "Your clients are charged with, among other things, Attempted Murder of an Assistant U.S. Attorney. The very same prosecutor who is assigned to the RICO case that involves one of those clients. I don't believe in coincidences, Mr. Stokes. What would be prejudicial is if I asked Ms. Nunziata how she's doing in open court, but I won't do that. Instead, I'll just deny bail for each of the defendants. I'm also going to suggest that you get together with the Prosecution and try to work out some kind of plea. If Ms. Nunziata is as prepared as she usually is, then I'm afraid your clients will be facing a certain guilty verdict."

"Your Honor! I must protest," Greg declared emphatically.

"Protest all you want, Mr. Stokes, but I take the endangerment of any officer of the court as a serious offense. I permitted bail for your client, essentially paving the way for him to harm Ms. Nunziata. I don't like making mistakes, and I won't make another in regard to your client. Bail is denied for all four defendants. Mr. Evenzolo's case starts in a week. Ms. Nunziata, do you need extra time to prepare on these additional charges?"

A little shocked by her sudden fury, I said, "No, Your Honor. The Prosecution is ready to go."

"Fine, these charges will be added to Mr. Evenzolo's current RICO charges and tried starting next week."

"I'll need more time to prepare a defense, Your Honor." Greg's tone adopted a whine.

"Denied. Your client should have thought of that before committing another crime, especially one against the prosecutor working his case." Her stern stare would have beaten anyone into submission. "Sally, can I have the first available date for a two day trial on the remaining three defendants?" Sally named a date next month. "Calendar that, Counselors. I'll see you both next week for the start of Mr. Evenzolo's trial, unless you come to an agreement before that time."

"Thank you, Your Honor." I wanted to run up and hug her. Seattle judges rule!

She didn't let Greg thank her, not that he looked like he would. "Bailiff, take the defendants into custody. We'll take a fifteen minute break before the next hearing. And if Ms.

Nunziata happened to mention the status of her general health somewhere in the vicinity of my deputy, ex parte wouldn't apply." She winked at me before leaving the dais.

I watched the defendants being herded through the other door to the detention pens with a freeing relief. No more need for a security detail, and the judge stood clearly on my side. Life as an AUSA was good.

Over at the other table, Greg deflated before my eyes. I wanted to feel badly for him, but the sentiment never hit me. Up at the clerk's dais, Sally lingered longer than usual, and I realized that the judge hadn't been kidding about making sure I was all right. Stepping through the counselors' tables, I approached and let her know that I was shaken but not seriously injured. She gave me a thumbs up and retreated after her boss.

"Are you really okay?" That sultry voice that I'd come to love spoke from behind me. I turned to find Elise standing a few steps away. Suddenly, all other courtroom activity blurred with only Elise's beautiful and caring face in pristine focus.

"I'm humiliated at my own stupidity, mortified that I put your life in danger, angry that I made you discharge your weapon at somebody, but I'm alive thanks to you."

She pressed her lips together, considering me. "What were you doing out there alone? George told me you'd been following procedure carefully up to last night."

"I was—I went—I wanted to talk to you. You didn't give me a chance in the restaurant. I figured if I stood in front of your car, you'd have to hear me out."

Her mouth dropped open, shocked by my revelation. She looked like she wanted to say something, but I cut her off.

"I know I'm making you uncomfortable right now. We're at work, and you seem to think everything is resolved. But I'm going to keep trying until I've had my say. Please, Elise. If you don't ever want to speak to me outside of work after that, I'll respect your wishes."

"Austy?" Roger interrupted from the first row of the

gallery. "We're headed up. You ready?"

I waved a dismissive hand to let him know that they should leave without me and implored one last time, "Please, Elise?"

"After work." She probably relented because she'd learned that my friends had been right about me being stubborn. "I'd stop by your place on my way home, but you've got houseguests. My house?"

"Thank you." I took my leave before she could change her mind and before she could see the giddy grin taking over my expression. I had a whole afternoon to obsess over what I would say, wear, and do when I saw her, but for now, I was the happiest lesbian in Seattle.

Chapter 24

Unsolicited advice in hand, I gunned the MINI north on I-5 in the evening sunshine. Jessie and Lauren, who were supposed to be making return trip reservations, spent their afternoon rummaging through my closet. Unfortunately, neither agreed on what I should wear tonight. Lauren chose professional dressy, and Jessie went for "ho" chic, something I didn't even know I owned. I took Jessie's top and Lauren's slacks, let them agree on my earrings, and ignored their instructions on how to beg a woman properly. One more reason the move to Seattle was so right: getting away from the busy bodies.

Traffic seemed interminable today, but it was probably just the usual late rush hour crawl. The commute only added to my nerves. I hadn't worked out what I was going to say, but I'd stay until I got through it all. Usually, I never had trouble coming up with a closing argument in one day. I hoped my aptitude wouldn't fail me now that it really mattered.

When I parked in front of Elise's house, I slowly pried my fingers from the steering wheel, unaware that I'd been gripping it so firmly. They ached when I flexed them to get the blood moving, and I used the excuse to stay parked in the security of my car. No more excuses. I wanted this chance, I asked for this chance, I needed this chance.

Stepping out of the car, I clutched my stomach, rubbing the tangle of tension that had been snarling inside since Elise granted me an invitation. On my way to her front door, it was hard not to remember the last time I was here. I glanced at the fence that closed off the backyard from the front of the house. What she'd done to me in that backyard after the barbeque. I'd never done anything that risqué before, but that didn't stop me from welcoming her roaming hands and practiced lips. Zero to orgasm in under five minutes. Erotic, I know.

Elise answered the door after a brief delay. She'd changed into jeans and a cotton cap sleeve shirt left untucked. Even trying to look laid-back, she was dazzling.

"Hello," she greeted in a reserved manner. No sexy smile. No soft tone mixing joy and relief. No matter. She agreed to let me talk, and that was all I could hope for right now.

"Hi. Thanks for seeing me, Elise." I attempted carefree, reserving my right to beg later.

"You were right. I haven't been fair. You deserve closure, too." She stepped back and waved me inside. "Especially if it keeps you from doing something dangerous again. Would you like some ice tea?" She gestured to the couch on her way into the kitchen, intent on getting the ice tea whether I wanted it or not.

"Thank you." I accepted the proffered glass when she returned and took a sip out of politeness. I glanced up to watch her vacillate between sitting and standing.

"Listen, Austy," Elise began with a tone that sounded preventative, but at least she decided to sit. "I meant what I said. I'm not angry with you, and I'm getting over being angry with myself for rushing into the relationship we had. I do want us to be friends, and maybe we can start on that tonight."

Talk about stubborn. I wasn't sure I could even make the JV squad of her stubborn team. I blew a short breath through my nose and started carefully, "The problem with being so damn good at your job, Elise, is that you have a hard time accepting when your best guess might be wrong." I waited until she locked eyes with me before I continued. "And you're wrong about me. I'm not in love with Willa. I might have kidded myself into a crush for a while, but nothing about it was real."

Her eyes contested my statement before her mouth did. "I know what I saw, Austy."

"I know what you think you saw. Willa and Lauren are my best friends. Lauren because, well, if anyone was born to be a friend, it's Lauren. There's no one better at it. Willa and I are a lot alike, which makes us close by default. Also she doesn't pry which makes her the least aggravating of the Virginia clan. I can relax around her because I don't have to worry about her asking some personal question designed to embarrass me. But, unlike Lauren, there's not much that I actually know about Willa. Like I don't know what she'd want to do if she had a whole day to herself. Or even what her perfect day includes. That's something that most best friends know about each other. And it's definitely something that you know about the person you love.

"Willa makes a wonderful friend for me, but when it comes to what I want and need in a relationship, she's not it. I think I convinced myself otherwise for a while because I couldn't maintain a relationship to save my life. I wanted to blame my lack of success on something, like maybe I was hung up on somebody already. It was easy and stupid."

Elise stayed quiet, her eyes looking off to the left. Other than blinking, she didn't move. She showed no sign of processing what I was telling her. Desperation made me want to resort to shaking her just to grab her attention.

"I can see that you're either not hearing me or not believing me. Even if I told you that, whenever you have a day to yourself, you'd head down to the waterfront, grab a coffee, listen to some jazz, and watch the boats and people until the sun sets. Or that your ideal day puts you on a deserted ski slope with nothing but turns to slow you down. Every once in a while you'd stop in an isolated spot to hear the snowflakes crinkling as they fall on your parka because I know that's your favorite sound. You'd finish the evening out on the deck of a lodge, drinking hot chocolate, content to watch the snow mist or count the stars."

Her chest rose and fell a little more rapidly, but otherwise she didn't react.

Crap! That was it, my best argument. If she didn't accept that, if she couldn't see how much it was killing me not to touch her, not to hold her, she would never change her mind about me. How could I have blown this? She wasn't just my first Seattle girlfriend or even my first girlfriend in years. She was it, the one, the best thing that's ever happened to me, and all those other sappy clichés. And I blew it.

Biting down on my infuriating frustration, I barely managed to keep from bursting into tears. "Since it looks like I may never get the chance to say this again, I need you to hear me." I reached out and gently pulled at her chin with my fingertips to make her look at me. Her eyes looked fearful that I'd say the wrong thing, only I no longer knew what the wrong thing was where she was concerned. I just knew that I had to tell her. "I'm crazy in love with you, Elise. I've lived in my head for so long, wasting my heart by imaging a fantasy life. But you made me realize that it's not better than the real thing. You got me to acknowledge to myself that I'm done for. I'll never find anyone as perfect as you are for me."

Those inscrutable eyes filled with tears, making the green shimmer. She stared in disbelief, not ready to abandon her deductive skills and the protective shield she'd put in place for the past few weeks. "But…Willa?" she asked with almost no fight left in her.

"You were right about one thing. I am comfortable with my Virginia friends being in my house. Like I'm comfortable with you there, but it was a year before I invited any of them into my home. With you, it only took a month, and I've certainly never told them why I don't let people come over. You made that easy for me." I reached for her hand because the need to touch her was stronger than any craving I'd ever had. Those talented fingers grasped mine without hesitation.

"You love *me*?" Her emphasis on "me" told me she wasn't quite there yet.

"I love only you, Elise." Our hands began that familiar exploration again. I'd loved it the first time she tried it with me and ached for it in all the time that we were separated.

"But you let me leave that night?"

I shook my head vigorously. "No, I tried to run after you, but my ankle wouldn't cooperate. I've tried to tell you every time I've seen you since, but they call me stubborn!" I let a little tease filter into my tone. "I love you, Elise. I love that you came out of dating hibernation for me. I love that you spent your first morning-after with me. I love that you understand me better than anyone ever has and that I don't need to tell you what I want because you already know." I inched closer to her and spoke softly. "I love *you*, Elise."

"Oh God!" Elise exclaimed joyfully. She completed the lean and kissed me with those incredible lips. Her tongue joined in, and she gasped before she pressed her torso against me. I felt her heart pounding against mine and her right knee slid in between my legs to slant fully against me. She broke the kiss, breathless, eyes staring in amazement. "I can't believe this. I've waited so long to hear the woman I love tell me she loves me. Thank you."

My smile threatened to peel back part of the skin on my face. "Now, who's the polite one?"

"I love you, Austy. I was so sure I'd never get to say it, but I think I knew from that moment in your office when you denied anyone could be enchanted with you. I already was, and the fact that you couldn't even imagine it told me you weren't like so many women I'd known. I stopped dating because I didn't think I'd ever find someone like you."

"So, if I ever tell you I need to talk to you again, you'll let me talk next time?" I couldn't manage a serious tone. Looking up at my favorite smile, I reveled in the feel of her body covering mine.

"Only if you start with 'I love you' before you say anything else." She kissed me again, lips pulling on mine, tongue coaxing me into her mouth. Her hands started to slide down my sides, heading toward my rear. She stopped their progress and pushed off me. My shock sparked a look of wicked delight on her face. "You better call Lauren and Jessie and tell them you're not coming home tonight."

"Are you kidding?" I laughed, heart still thundering from what her mouth and hands had started. "They wouldn't let me in if I did come back. They were pretty intent on me working things out with you. Plan B involved luring you to the loft, locking us in, and I think I heard something about a trained crocodile. I learned long ago not to ask."

She laughed with me. "So, you're all mine?"

"Completely." I pulled her to me for another kiss. I flattened my hands and moved down her strong back. I'd planned to flip her over on the couch, but her hands grasped my wrists and pinned them to my sides.

"You just said you're all mine. I'm going to take advantage of that right now on this couch." Elise smiled then dipped her head to kiss my neck while her fingers unbuttoned my shirt. The sensations her gifted mouth created drew a soft moan from me. I felt her shiver against me. She liked making me moan, a quality I so admired about her.

Warm breath dusted my skin, just slightly cooler than the scorching blaze I felt spreading along every cell of my body. Needing to feel her skin on me, I began to undress her. Our hands bumped against each other as we tried to shed our clothes, needing that last barrier gone. Elise giggled at our efforts and sat up, straddling my lap. She finished taking off her shirt for me while I slipped mine off my shoulders. She brought my hands up to her bra, and I didn't need any prompting to unhook the lace and reveal her pert breasts, nipples straining for my touch.

"Austine?" she breathed, watching me look at her again. Her eyes searched mine with only a hint of a question.

"I love you," I spoke the words I'd been dying to say since she walked out weeks before. I tilted up and kissed her, feeling her breasts crush against mine. "I love you, Elise."

"I love you, too," Elise whispered. She stood up and pulled me with her to finish the task that had been so difficult while we were prone. "I've missed you so much. Everything about you and how you make me feel when I'm with you." Fingers skimmed over my shoulders and down the length of my arms. "I really missed being able to touch you."

Bending my head, I snaked my tongue out and lightly dragged it over the centered mole on her sternum. She clutched my arms and tilted her head back, exhaling audibly. "I've missed this mole, and the three others that I'll get to in a moment. Your soft skin, your skilled hands, your sexy smile." I widened my fingers and ran them down, brushing against her breasts, before spreading out around her torso. "These," I stroked the scars on her ribcage and dropped my right hand lower to trace the line of her mangled hip joint, "and this," I looked up into her eyes that harbored a touch of worry, "made you into the Elise that I love."

Those eyes, no longer burdened with worry, blinked back moisture, and she said in that joy-relief tone, "Thank you, Austy."

"That," I nodded and looked at her mouth, "I've missed hearing how you say my name."

Because I couldn't control myself any longer, I covered her mouth with mine, pressing my body against hers. She moaned against my lips and my left hand slid down her back to hook under her leg to pull it up against my hip. I felt her weight shift slightly, melting into me. My right hand moved across her hip seeking her hot, wet center. Her responding moan was loud and long into my open mouth.

"I'm supposed to be taking advantage of you," she spoke between deep panting breaths.

"Don't ask me to stop. I don't want to stop touching you. Ever."

My fingers slid through her plump lips, tantalizing the slippery crevices. Her hips rocked against my hand, nearly knocking us over. Pressing back against her to brace our stance, I kissed down her supple neck, directly on that mole, and down to her breast. My tongue laved her areola before my lips kissed, then sucked the nipple into my mouth.

"God, Austy! I love your mouth." Her breath licked at my ear, words creating a vibration inside my head. "Come inside me. I need you inside me."

Angling two fingers, I slowly penetrated her tight entrance, filling her need. Her tunnel massaged my fingers as I began to pump into her, our hips getting into the rhythm of each thrust. I felt her hands grip my shoulders and back more firmly to stay upright.

"You feel so good inside me. Don't stop," she commanded in a near growl.

I smiled against her breast, licked her nipple then nipped along the swell. I tickled the back of the knee that I kept gripped against my waist as I rocked into her. My fingers coated in her juices started to fly in long, sure strokes.

"I'm so close. Please make me come." This time her command was part moan, part whisper.

The dewy sheen under her knee spread from the pores covering her body. She hadn't needed to tell me how close she was, but her words aroused me even more. I pressed the fingertips inside of her toward me and continued pumping. Sliding my thumb into place, I massaged her hardened clit and lightly bit down on her nipple.

"God, yes!" she cried out, her body started to convulse as she climaxed. Her trimmed nails dug into my shoulder blades, and the leg I still held hooked around the back of mine. My invading fingers felt the squeeze of her inner walls pulsing against their thrusts. "Yes, so, so good," she drew out on each exhale of breath.

The leg holding her weight started to buckle and I shifted

my leg between hers. The hand that had been hooked under her knee moved around her waist to hold her up through the unending pulsations of her orgasm. Her forehead dropped into the bend of my neck and shoulder, breathy moans still emanating from her lips as her shuddering turned to shaking then to trembling. When her throbbing contractions stopped, I eased my fingers from her and brought my hand to her hip to steady us both. Her leg finally dropped to the ground, making my task a little easier.

"I definitely missed that," I confessed, kissing my way up to her neck, barely reaching it before she tilted her head to capture my mouth.

"Amazing…you're so amazing." She looked into my eyes and, like every one of her compliments since we started our love, I accepted it with a smile.

"You're the amazing one, *cara mia*," my heart spoke for me, and I watched her face light up at my term of endearment.

"I love you, Austy." Her eyes flared as her hands slid to my shoulders and pushed me onto couch. "Taking advantage now."

When her body covered mine, I knew I'd found home. Her nipples scraped against me as she dragged her body first up to kiss my mouth, then my neck, and along my sternum. I moaned at both the feel of her mouth and the slickness coating my thighs.

She kissed her way to a breast and sucked the nipple into her mouth, suctioning her lips to the tip and letting her tongue flick across my rigid nub. When her teeth joined in, I arched off the couch, pressing my pelvis into her flat stomach.

"Ooh, you like that, don't you?" Elise asked, already knowing the answer. "Tell me, Austy."

I breathed out audibly. This was a new request. I wasn't the talker in this relationship. I felt her mouth pull off me and looked down to see her staring at me full of love.

"I love you. Trust me. I've been asking you to let go since our first time. I'm going to make love to you, and I want to hear how much you like it. For instance, when I do this," her lips slid over to my breast and her tongue flicked back and forth against my nipple, "I want you to tell me how much you like it."

"I'll try," I breathed, suddenly nervous.

Her tongue darted out and licked the underside of my breast. She smoothed her hands down my sides and along my thighs. Her knee slipped in between my legs and pressed against my now throbbing crotch.

"Mmm, you're so wet, sexy," she whispered, her mouth working over to my other breast.

I moved against her knee and gasped when her teeth scraped my nipple. My body flushed hot when her hands found their way around to my inner thighs. I clenched up, unable to control my need to grind against her.

Her mouth finally started moving down my stomach. She stopped at my belly button and tilted her head so that her chin rested on me. "Tell me what you want."

The tension in my body increased with need. She looked so amazing lying on my stomach. I felt her fingers dancing lightly under my knees. I wanted those fingers on me and in me, to possess me.

"I don't want you to hold anything back with me. I need all of you, Austy. Trust me. Let go with me."

Not that I needed more proof that she was perfect for me, but her request made me understand just how well she knew me. Knowing she would be there to catch me, I let go like she asked. "Please, Elise, touch me, kiss me, take me, just please, I need you so badly!"

"That's the woman I know and love." She gave me a sinful smile before tilting her head and lowering her mouth to lick my dripping lips. "I missed your taste," she moaned, sending her tongue through my folds. Her licks were long and attentive, torturing me by not touching my most sensitive tip. Her fingers moved up to slide beneath my ass and settle between my cheeks. Her other hand massaged its way up to my breast and relentlessly tweaked my nipple.

"Yes, just like that," I moaned, grasping her hand with one of my own and coaching it along my nipple. I reached down to cup her head as it worked methodically on me.

Finally, her tongue reached my clit, licking up and down, then side to side. Her lips joined in, pulling on my hood, making me writhe against the sofa. The hand under my ass dragged slowly down, and I felt the fingers probe my lips before one of them slammed up inside of me.

"Yes! Elise, please," I groaned loudly.

Elise gave a muffled moan, not wanting to take her mouth off me. She added a second finger and moved them in and out, brushing up against my G-spot with each thrust.

"Elise!" I yelled when her skilled motions brought me to the edge. My crashing orgasm gripped her fingers and bucked her head up trying to stay attached to my spasming body.

She continued to lick but extracted her fingers as another wave of shuddering thundered through me. The climax wouldn't stop, and I experienced the buildup and crashing over and over. She resisted my hands trying to pull her off her mission.

"Stop, stop! I love you, but you have to stop!" I pleaded, feeling deliciously helpless.

Her tongue followed my command and allowed me to slowly pulsate through my recovery. She brought her mouth off of me and glanced up at my sated, strung out body. Crawling up over me, she kissed my neck, face, and mouth until I stopped breathing so hard.

She flashed my favorite of her smiles, slow and sexy. "Oh yes, I like when you're all mine."

Okay, being a lesbian in Seattle doesn't suck at all anymore.

Printed in the United States
77564LV00002B/84

9 781598 009590